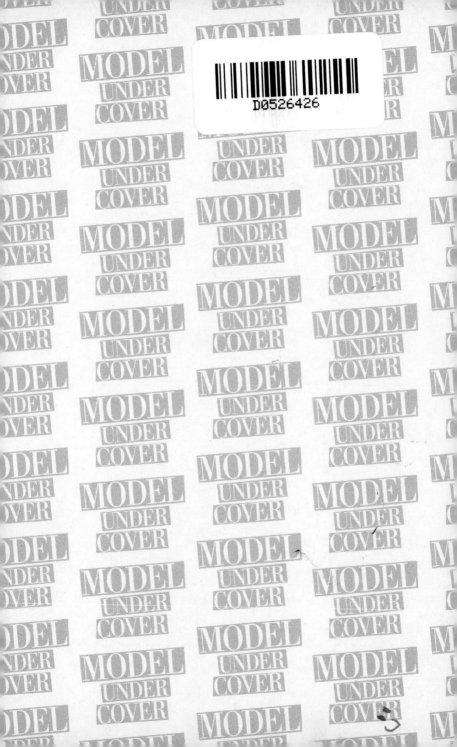

MODEL
UNDER
COVER

"The police were just here, at my home," Ugo said. "And that's why I'm calling you, Axelle. You see," he continued, "I'm in a bit of a...*situazione difficile*. Do you understand? It concerns the death of Elisabetta Rinconi..." He went quiet.

"Yes?" I said.

"The thing is, the police seem to think that she may have been poisoned...they've even gone so far as to suggest that she might have eaten something here, in my house, last night, that made her ill. *Per favore*, Axelle, I need your help..."

To Kelly and Priscilla

First published in the UK in 2016 by Usborne Publishing Ltd., Usborne House, 83-85 Saffron Hill, London EC1N 8RT, England. www.usborne.com

Copyright © 2016 by Carina Axelsson

Cover illustration by Yusuf Doğanay

Author photo by Anne-Marie Mulot

The right of Carina Axelsson to be identified as the author of this work has been asserted by her in accordance with the Copyright, Designs and Patents Act, 1988.

The name Usborne and the devices ♀ ⊕ are Trade Marks of Usborne Publishing Ltd.

This is a work of fiction. The characters, incidents, and dialogues are products of the author's imagination and are not to be construed as real. Any resemblance to actual events or persons, living or dead, is entirely coincidental.

A CIP catalogue record for this book is available from the British Library.

ISBN 9781474906913 JFMA JJASOND/16 03954/1

Printed in the UK.

MODEL UNDER COVER

Dressed to Kill

CARINA AXELSSON

USBORNE

TUESDAY MORNING

An Editor's Exit

Surprisingly, since landing in Milan, Italy, I've had nothing but fun.

If you're wondering why I say *surprisingly*…well, that's because I'm here working as a fashion model…and modelling is something I definitely *do not* consider fun. In fact, as far as I'm concerned, the words *fun* and *fashion* are about as mismatched as Kate Moss and the Queen's wardrobe.

And yet here I am in this sophisticated, bustling fashion capital, with a day of Italian *Vogue* behind me, and a week of castings, go-sees and bookings ahead of me and, remarkably, that relentless, gnawing frustration I normally feel when I wish I had a case to solve (which is basically always) isn't eating away at me…at least not too much.

"I told you that at some point you'd start loving fashion and forget all about being the next Sherlock Holmes," my modelling BFF, Ellie B,

teased as we prepared to step out of our model flat. Our modelling agency, Calypso Model Management, had organized it for us for the duration of our stay in Milan.

"Yeah, right," I said as I rolled my eyes and quickly looked through my black quilted leather Mulberry rucksack, making sure I had the supplies I'd need for a day of modelling in the studio:

- My modelling book (or portfolio). A model never leaves home without it!
- Zed cards – or comp cards – in the pocket of the book.
- Seamless skin-tone coloured underwear, just in case the white stuff I was wearing showed through the clothes I'd be modelling later.
- A small cosmetics bag filled with make-up remover, cotton discs, moisturizer and a hairbrush – so I could leave the studio without looking as made up as an ancient Egyptian queen.
- My phone. For research…after all, a case could come up at any moment…

Speaking of which…

"Frankly, Ellie," I said after I closed my rucksack and quickly bent to tie the laces on my Converse, "I think my having fun here has less to do with a sudden passion for fashion than it does with the fact that I've just finished solving a case… I haven't even had chance to think about a new mystery yet…

"Anyway," I continued, as we shut our flat door behind us and clattered down the cool, stone stairwell of the building, "maybe even detectives need holidays…" I thought of all the sights Sebastian and I planned on seeing within the next few days – and after failing to show him any in London last week, I was really looking forward to catching up now.

I met Sebastian, my case-cracking partner (and, yes, the guy I've been "seeing" over the last few months) in Paris, where he lives. To begin with we mostly only saw each other on Skype, but last week he finally came to visit me in London.

Unfortunately, I ended up being totally sidetracked by a tricky case involving a mysterious memory stick full of fashion images. I spent the week in a race with the past, digging for clues in order to solve the case before someone got hurt. In the end I cracked it, but not before I'd also ruined all the plans Sebastian had so carefully made. A pang of guilt shot through me as I thought about it. *This week*, I told myself, *things will be different…*

"If only your parents could hear you," Ellie laughed as she skipped down the stairs beside me. "Detectives need holidays too…not thinking about a new case…no mystery to solve… I'm not sure I believe you, but it sounds good!"

"Ha ha." I gently yanked her braid.

But Ellie had a point – I wasn't sure I believed myself – and I was sure my mum wouldn't if she heard. In fact, on our way to the airport on Sunday, Mum's conversation (I use the term loosely) had basically been one long, stern warning against getting involved in any more dangerous mysteries.

"Life isn't a game of Cluedo, you know, Axelle," she'd said. "It'll be better for all of us if you concentrate on your modelling this summer."

Grrr!

I pushed my glasses up the bridge of my nose and brought my mind back to Ellie. "Yeah, well," I said as we reached the bottom of the stairs, "my parents won't have anything to worry about this time. The agency here has filled every time slot in my schedule, plus Sebastian and I have so much sightseeing to do that I'm not sure how I'll be able to fit it all in between the modelling assignments. Besides," I whispered, "with you-know-who standing guard over us…" I nodded towards the courtyard, where a short, round figure stood watering the plants in the morning sun, "I'll be lucky if I'm allowed to breathe – let alone chase after suspects."

"You have a point," Ellie said as she stopped to apply some lip balm to her full, pouty lips and glanced at Signora Buonanotte.

Ellie and I were staying on our own in the model flat –

something my mum had never allowed before. At first I thought she'd relented because Ellie is a couple of years older than I am and, as a newly minted supermodel, knows the ins and outs of working abroad. Besides, even a mum can go with the flow sometimes, right?

Wrong.

Upon landing in Milan on Sunday evening, Ellie and I had been picked up at Linate Airport by the car service the agency had arranged. From there we'd been driven straight to the model flat near Porta Romana, and within five minutes of stepping out of the car I'd understood the reason why my mum had been so cool with the idea…

Signora Buonanotte was the building's caretaker but apparently she'd been assigned to look after me too – or, more specifically, to make sure that I didn't stay out late. If I wasn't back at the flat by 10 p.m. sharp every night, she'd call my agency.

"But why is she only looking out for me? What about you?" I'd asked Ellie on Sunday night as Mrs B glared at us.

Ellie whispered. "I'm eighteen. You're only sixteen. Agencies can get into trouble if they're not seen to be looking after underage models."

This much was true: Calypso had had a file of papers about working hours ready for me to sign, and I'd had to have a doctor's appointment to check my health – all because I was sixteen.

As we left the courtyard Ellie turned to me. "Well,

sightseeing plans and modelling aside," she said, "just remember that fashion never sleeps. You might be dragged into a case before you know it."

A while later we were walking towards the wide open piazza in front of Milan's towering cathedral, the Duomo. The cathedral dwarfed the square. I tilted my head back and gawked at the great structure, open-mouthed. I'd arrived on Sunday night, and worked all day Monday (yesterday), and then had to do food shopping with Ellie after my booking had ended, so I hadn't had time to see anything of Milan yet, which was why Ellie had promised to quickly show me the Duomo this morning before work. And while I instantly recognized the famous cathedral from Instagram (every model who goes to the Milan fashion shows takes a selfie at the Duomo) just looking at it left me speechless. Its steep, pitched roof is crowded with Gothic spires of varying heights, each one topped with a statue reaching for the sky.

Ellie pointed and said, "Can you see the Golden Madonna?" I followed her fingertip and, at the top of the tallest spire in the middle of the cathedral's roof, I spotted a tiny golden statue (well, she looked tiny from this far below) serenely glinting in the early morning sun. "They say that no building in Milan should be higher than she is," Ellie told me.

The square in front of the Duomo was already crowded and busy. Ellie and I slowly moved through the brightly clad tourists and chicly dressed locals. The early morning heat gave an unrushed, holiday feel to everything, along with the sounds of laughter, cooing pigeons, and the animated snippets of Italian that punctuated the warm summer air. All was friendly and relaxed; it was hard to imagine anyone ever being in a bad mood here, let alone committing a crime.

I turned to Ellie. "You might be right about fashion never sleeping," I said, "but, seriously, I bet nothing sinister ever happens in a place as sunny as this…" I cut myself short, however, as another thought suddenly occurred to me.

Ellie had stopped to check her reflection in one of the windows of the covered arcade but now caught my eye in the glass, her eyebrows raised in curiosity. "Or?"

"Or maybe this is just the calm before the storm," I laughed.

Ellie and I parted ways at the Duomo. From there I took the subway to Megastudio, the large complex of modern studios where I'd be shooting a day of editorial for the Italian magazine, *Amare*. Once there, I signed in at reception and was directed to Studio Three on the first floor.

The studio looked much like every studio I'd worked in so far: clean and airy, with white-painted walls, high ceilings, polished cement floors and ample space for a large set, hair and make-up area, as well as a separate dressing room. Sunlight streamed through the glass roof that covered the entire space, infusing the studio with good spirits. Taylor Swift was playing, while the air conditioning whirred in the background.

The photographer and his two studio assistants were busy getting the set ready for the first shot, while a digi-tech guy was at the computer. Hair and make-up, meanwhile, were laying their equipment out on the clean tables that stood against one of the windowless walls. Each table was placed directly underneath one very large and long mirror that had tubes of especially bright lights running all around its edges – not that we'd need the extra light this morning, the sun was so strong. In fact, the make-up artist, with the help of a studio assistant, was busy adjusting the roof blinds directly over the make-up area; if the light was too bright it would be hard to see how the make-up would look later on, under the softer light on set.

I said good morning to the whole team before loading up a plate with a couple of Italian-style croissants, a muffin and some fresh fruit salad from the breakfast buffet laid out at a small table near the entrance of the studio. With the plate in one hand and a cup of peppermint tea in the other, I walked to the hair and make-up area and sat down.

The photographer, Craig McLeod, was someone I'd met on a go-see when I'd been in New York City a few months earlier, and although I'd never worked with Giulia, the make-up artist, I knew of her by name. The fashion editor still hadn't arrived, but through the open curtain that divided the dressing area from the rest of the studio, I could see her assistant steaming the wrinkles out of the colourful dresses I'd be wearing later. They hung on a clothing rack, a pretty jumble of sorbet-coloured shades, embroidered flowers, pastel tulle and even a canary-yellow fur jacket (fake, I hoped).

As for the hairstylist, Benoit, I'd met him a few months earlier in Paris; I'd been there for my first ever Fashion Week – and my first ever fashion case!

Benoit was happy to see me and while he started working on my hair, and I munched on my breakfast, we chatted about what we'd been doing since Paris – although I didn't go into *everything*. After all, discretion is paramount if you want to be a good detective, and the last thing I needed was for the fashionistas to know that my real interest lay in solving fashion mysteries – or I'd be frozen out faster than you can say Dolce & Gabbana.

There was a sudden buzz of excitement at the studio's entrance; Elisabetta Rinconi, the *Amare* fashion editor, rising international fashion star, and the woman in charge for the day, had just walked in. She was tipped to become the editor-in-chief of *Amare* one day. Today, however, was an accessories story and she'd be styling the shoot herself – as she always did.

Through the reflection of the mirror, I watched as she waved and said *"Ciao!"* to everyone before going straight to Craig. They exchanged a few ideas and discussed details of the day's shoot, most of which I could hear from where I was sitting: colour and black-and-white shots, candy-coloured jewels, pretty frocks, some gloves, and a couple of handbags. As for the day's hair, make-up and styling, the inspirational starting point was the 1960 Italian movie, *La Dolce Vita* – so, glam, but updated for *Amare*'s edgy younger readers, with messy hair, little make-up and dewy skin.

A minute later Elisabetta came up behind Benoit and me. *"Buongiorno*, Axelle and Benoit. Sorry I'm late, but I haven't been feeling well since very early this morning." She brought her hand up to her forehead as if checking for a fever. "Headache, nausea, and a dry throat – so no kisses today, darlings," she added. I guessed that also explained the enormous sunglasses perched on her delicate nose.

"I think I celebrated a little too much last night, but I'll be fine," she said. She caught my eye in the mirror. "I've pulled some really fabulous dresses for us today, Axelle. Benoit, would you mind letting Axelle try some things on for me right now?" He nodded and she beckoned me to follow her into the dressing room as soon as I could.

Benoit pinned my hair, so that the work he'd started wouldn't be messed up as I tried the clothes, and I watched Elisabetta carefully as she teetered on her heels towards the dressing area.

For someone who wasn't feeling well she still managed to pull off an impressively stylish look. Tall and lean (I'd heard she'd modelled a bit before becoming a stylist), she appeared to be in her mid-thirties, but with a fragile air that made her seem more like an über-cool older sister than an ambitious know-it-all fashion editor.

She wore black-and-white palazzo pants (they looked vintage), with a loud pattern that clashed (on purpose, no doubt) with her long-sleeved, black-and-white silk blouse. She'd tied the neck bow on the blouse loosely, and its long ends fluttered as she walked off in her red strappy sandals. A wicker basket with bright green fabric lining stood in as a handbag, adding a whimsical touch to her otherwise sophisticated ensemble. Generously cut diamond studs twinkled in her ears and a huge blue butterfly ring decorated her right hand. A thin diamond ring in the shape of a vine with thorns adorned her left hand. Her hair was nearly as long as her legs and hung, straight and clean, but slightly roughed up.

She looked amazing. I watched her out of the corner of my eye until she disappeared behind the curtain of the dressing area.

When I joined Elisabetta a few minutes later, I could see that beneath the glamour she was wilting quickly. Nevertheless, she put on a good show. While her assistant, Marzia, continued steaming dresses on the other side of the dressing area, Elisabetta turned to me. "It's so nice to work with you, Axelle," she said in her breathy, heavily accented English. "I've been following you since you started and I'm glad things are going so well for you."

I thanked her and told her that modelling had turned out to be a lot more interesting than I'd thought it would be.

"Yes, too many people think fashion's pure fluff."

"I agree," I answered lightly – the fashion crimes that came my way were anything but "fluff".

Apart from this initial chit-chat, though, Elisabetta didn't say much else and I wasn't sure if that was just her way – aloof, fashionista-style – or whether she wasn't feeling well enough to talk. After a minute Marzia turned to Elisabetta and spoke in rapid-fire Italian. From what I could make out Elisabetta declined Marzia's offer of tea, but told Marzia to get something for herself and for me.

Elisabetta finally asked me to try on a dress and gloves – "No hats today," she said to herself through pursed lips, looking ruefully at the colourful headgear laid out on the styling table, and handed me the gloves. "Craig does not like to shoot hats…"

I zipped myself up into a Dolce & Gabbana embroidered brocade dress and put on the gloves. I stood while Elisabetta eyed me, her long thin hands gently resting on her slim hips. Then she abruptly turned to the styling table and picked up a pair of large crystal chandelier earrings. She held these up to my ears, her head on one side as she assessed the look.

We were alone now in the dressing room; the curtain that separated us from the rest of the space was shut, dulling the noise of the studio.

As my eyes followed Elisabetta I couldn't help but notice that she was moving more and more slowly, until she became noticeably clumsy. And she was drinking a lot of water. I watched as she reached yet again for a large bottle on a tray with glasses at one end of the styling table.

"My throat is so dry," she said by way of explanation, "I shouldn't have stayed up so late last night, even if it was to celebrate. I'm paying the price now. Ugh. The pain and the nausea…" She took a deep breath and emptied her water glass. I heard her mumble out loud as she turned and reached for her basket. "I should probably take something for my stomach – it still feels odd. I have to start feeling better by tonight. What I have to do is so important…"

I watched as she set her basket-bag down on the edge of the accessories table and attempted to look through its contents. I wanted to suggest that it might help if she removed her sunglasses, but the basket promptly fell off the table and half its contents spilled out. "*Grazie*, Axelle," Elisabetta said as I rushed to help her pick up the various things. Then I poured her another glass of water and watched as she swallowed some pills for her stomach pain.

"I feel terrible," she said. "I'm so sorry about this – and it's your first *Amare* shoot, too. I hope you are not superstitious?"

"No," I smiled.

"Good, me neither." She tried to smile back. "Anyway, don't worry – you and I will definitely work together again – hopefully at some wonderful location to make up for today."

Why fashionistas partied so much was beyond me. What was the point? Unless I had suspects to chase down, I found fashion parties so dull. Of course, Elisabetta had won a major award last night, so I suppose some celebrating was in order…but still…she really must have partied hard, judging by the way her skin had just gone from ghostly white to puke green right before my eyes.

By the time she asked me to try on a second outfit, she was slumped in a chrome and leather armchair near the far wall, between a small sofa and the edge of the long accessories table. Her basket lay at her feet. As per her instructions (she'd lifted her arm a bit and twirled her hand in the air) I moved a few steps back from her and turned in a circle so she could have a good look at my outfit.

I stood watching her, waiting for her to say something, but she didn't. From behind her huge sunglasses she was inscrutable. I could imagine her sitting in the front row at the fashion shows with the exact same expression on her face. How often had I walked down the runway as various editors sat watching, sunglasses on, mouths glued shut, showing no visible signs of life?

I continued to wait for Elisabetta to make her final pronouncement. Did she like the ensemble she'd put together or did it need tweaking before I wore it on set later? The large-faced clock on the wall behind us ticked loudly in the silence.

Great, I thought, *the day has only just begun and already it's ticking by slowly. I won't be able to buzz out of here for hours yet...* At least I had my sightseeing with Sebastian to look forward to later. He was going to pick me up (on his rented Vespa scooter) at the studio this afternoon before we zoomed off to see Leonardo Da Vinci's famous fresco, *The Last Supper*.

I was just about to ask Elisabetta what she thought about the outfit when I heard her cough. Okay, maybe "cough" wasn't an accurate enough description. It was more like a gurgle that started from deep within her, then rose to the back of her throat. By the time it reached her lips it sounded less like a symptom of late-night excess and more like the noise you make stepping on a large bug with soft-soled shoes: painful and squelchy.

"Elisabetta?" I asked.

As I waited for her to answer I caught sight of my phone – it was lying on the table next to me, lit up with a message from Sebastian:

What time shall I pick you up? Can't wait! Sxxx

I still hadn't had a chance to ask what time we'd be finished today – and this clearly wasn't the moment to ask Elisabetta anything. Sebastian would have to wait.

Elisabetta had gone very quiet and still, but she sat as front-row ready as ever: long legs tucked under her chair, arms crossed in front of her and with her pretty basket on the floor by her side. From behind her Jackie O shades she gave nothing away. Was she asleep? I wondered.

"Elisabetta?" I asked.

No answer.

"Elisabetta?" I walked up to her and gently tapped her shoulder with a finger, but got no reaction. She didn't move at all. Hmm…she must be asleep. Well, like it or not, I thought, I had to wake her – an entire team was waiting for her to get the ball rolling. Slowly I leaned forward, intending to tap her arm and talk directly into her ear. But as I moved towards her and my hand settled on her shoulder, I got a bad feeling. Even if she was sleeping, there was something odd about the way she was sitting. I pulled back suddenly as an icy creepiness stole over me.

It couldn't be anything more than a deep sleep, could it? Besides, she hadn't been feeling well; she'd just taken some pills, so wasn't it likely that she'd fall into a deeper sleep than usual?

Well, there was only one way to put my mind at ease, I told myself with a feigned cheerfulness before lowering myself to her eye level. Gently I shook her shoulder.

No response.

I shook her again, more forcefully this time, but still nothing.

Carefully, I lifted the sunglasses from the fine-boned bridge of Elisabetta's tiny nose and peered at her eyes... That's when a cold, clammy fear grasped at my throat and I recoiled in horror.

The glassy stare of her open eyes burned into my mind as I staggered backwards, struggling to find my voice. The glasses slid back down her nose and above their rim her blank gaze followed me. Her eyes were flat and glazed; they looked as lifeless as two wet marbles.

Now I understood why she sat so still.

Elisabetta wasn't asleep.

She was dead.

Thoughts swirled full-speed through my mind senselessly. The overriding emotion, though, was shock; after all, I'd never seen a dead body – let alone had someone die right in front of me.

I had to get help.

My voice was blocked by fear; I didn't trust myself to call out. I staggered over to the heavy linen curtain and pulled it open. For a moment I stood looking out at the others milling around the set on the far side of the studio – everything seemed so normal. The music played loudly and the sound of laughter floated across the vast space beyond me. Everyone else was busy, happily consumed by their work.

I desperately wanted someone – anyone – to come and see Elisabetta and explain to me what had happened.

My legs still shaking, I finally managed to call out, but no one responded. Even to my own ears my voice had sounded barely more than a whisper. I called again and waved my arm and from across the studio one of the photographer's assistants saw me. He must have thought I was motioning for Marzia because she turned to me, holding up two fingers to signal that she'd be with me in a couple of minutes. For me, right now, that was enough; someone was coming, help was on its way.

Then a thought occurred to me: what if she wasn't really dead? I forced myself to take as deep a breath as possible. I straightened my back and moved towards Elisabetta. It had all happened so quickly, I had to check. I kneeled by Elisabetta's side and steeled myself before taking her wrist. I felt for her pulse but there was none. I tried her other wrist but it was the same. Then I stood up and leaned in close to her face, straining my ears to listen, but I couldn't hear a thing. There wasn't the faintest movement or sound of breath.

She must have had some kind of heart attack, I thought as I pulled back, still in shock. I'd heard of things like that striking even when people were in the prime of their lives. I could hardly bear to look at her frail form, dressed in such lively clothes. She was sitting there so elegantly, her pretty basket at her feet and not a hair out of place. Except for the sickly hue of her skin, she looked as startlingly pretty in death as she had in life.

I felt panic begin to overtake me again. Where was Marzia, what was taking so long? I called her name from where I stood, my voice louder this time, more frantic. Then I turned away from Elisabetta, closed my eyes and tried to slow my breathing. When I opened my eyes again, time seemed to stand still for a moment as I stared across the room.

My gaze fell on Elisabetta's basket. Without really thinking, I bent over it and reached in, searching for the medication she'd swallowed earlier. I'd have to make the emergency services aware of what she'd taken. It felt strange rifling through her belongings – I could see the corner of her wallet poking out from under a spray can of facial mist, a notebook of some kind, a newspaper, a make-up bag, and a clear plastic bag with a pair of white Nike trainers inside. All completely normal – and yet weird. They'd never be used again; their owner was dead.

At last I found the tablets and took them out of the basket, then turned back to the curtain. What was keeping Marzia? Looking out, I saw she was halfway across the studio, heading towards me.

Thank goodness. I'd been alone with Elisabetta for long enough. The shock and panic I'd been unable to shake was starting to subside into the nausea of horror.

Marzia walked in, smiling, until she met my eyes. "Axelle, what's wrong?" She hastened towards me.

Without a word I turned and pointed to Elisabetta. Marzia advanced upon her boss but stopped suddenly, frozen with shock. I watched as she looked at Elisabetta. She moved her hands to cover her mouth but a second later she dropped her arms again and let out a shrill, high-pitched scream that reverberated around the studio.

The shoot was immediately cancelled. After Marzia had gone screaming out of the dressing room it had taken a few minutes for the team to understand exactly what had happened.

Craig, the photographer, was the first one to come running to the dressing area, while the others followed behind him to see what the fuss was about. One look at Elisabetta, though, was enough to make it clear that something was very wrong. "What's happened?" Craig asked, taking charge as he rushed to her side and grabbed her wrist.

"She's dead," I blurted, my voice sounding wobbly. The whole situation seemed so unreal, yet here I was saying it out loud. "There's no pulse, she was just sitting on that chair feeling unwell one moment, and then coughed and died the next – all while I was trying on my outfit."

Giulia ran out, hands over her mouth, while Benoit and the studio assistants stood frozen and silent, their eyes wide with shock.

"Call for an ambulance," Craig told one of the studio assistants. His voice was sharp and matter-of-fact. "And then call the studio management – they need to be alerted, too."

The assistant ran for help and I explained what had happened in more detail while Craig checked Elisabetta's other wrist for a pulse and put his ear to her mouth to listen for breath.

After a minute or two, the studio assistant returned. "An ambulance is on its way and the studio has called the police. A team will be here in a few minutes. They've asked us all to stay…they'll need to speak to us…"

Craig nodded as he carefully pushed Elisabetta's sunglasses back up the bridge of her nose. "We don't need to keep seeing her eyes," he said. Then he took a deep breath before turning away from her. "I don't think there's anything else we can do besides wait for the police. I just need to make a few phone calls…"

"Me too," Benoit said as he filed out behind Craig, the two studio assistants beside him. I decided to do the same – I had to call my agency – and Sebastian!

As I walked towards the set, however, I remembered that I was still wearing the dress, jewellery and gloves Elisabetta had asked me to try on! I stopped with a jolt – I was suddenly desperate to get back into my own clothes. I turned around and pulled the curtain shut behind me before changing as quickly as possible, trying to forget Elisabetta's glassy eyes staring at me from behind her large designer sunglasses.

Automatically, I reached for my phone in the back pocket of my jeans; it wasn't there. I walked out to the hair and make-up table but my phone wasn't there either. Next I had a quick look in my bag – which was still next to Benoit where I'd left it – but I didn't find it.

Then I remembered that I'd had it with me in the dressing area when I'd been with Elisabetta – Sebastian had texted me, I'd seen it light up. I was just heading back behind the curtain when the police arrived. I stopped and watched as they strode into the studio, their determined strides and easy chatter making it clear that, for them, unexpected death was a normal part of their lives. Another siren wailed outside; I stood aside as Craig led some of the officers into the dressing area. "You should come with us, too, Axelle," he said, "to explain what happened."

The studio was suddenly humming with activity. While the paramedics and a pathologist examined Elisabetta, a uniformed police officer took out his notebook and spoke to Craig. Two more officers looked around the studio and another two began photographing the dressing area and Elisabetta. While Craig spoke with the police, I started quietly searching for my phone. But after a quick sweep of the area I still couldn't find it. I must have knocked it onto the floor…

Craig and the police were still deep in discussion so I bent down and scanned the the area carefully. But nothing caught my eye. Well, almost nothing.

Under the small sofa just in front of me, next to a ball of dust and hair, there was a suspiciously neatly folded gum wrapper. A bit further under the sofa, I thought I spotted a piece of thin grey cardboard. It was easy to miss because in the shadows under the sofa it was the exact same colour as the floor. Without further thought I rapidly swept up both items with my right hand.

I'd have a look at them as soon as I had a moment to myself. I did quickly note, though, that what I'd thought was a piece of cardboard was in fact an envelope – and there seemed to be something in it. Could it have fallen out of Elisabetta's basket earlier? Possibly. We'd looked around carefully at the time but maybe this had slipped under the sofa unseen? Elisabetta's name wasn't on the front though…

I suddenly stopped myself: I was acting as if I was working on a case and looking for circumstantial evidence when, actually, it was more than likely that Elisabetta had had a heart attack…

Or was it?

The tiniest inkling of suspicion suddenly broke through the lingering shock I still felt. After all, Elisabetta was young and in seemingly good health. It couldn't have been natural for her to just die like that. I know it happens… but, still, that kind of thing is rare. I stood, quietly reflecting on the events of the morning. And somehow I couldn't help feeling that I'd just witnessed more than a straightforward natural death.

I struggled as thoughts of my mum suddenly floated through my head. "Don't start meddling in things which are none of your business, Axelle," she'd say.

But now that I was slowly getting back to normal and the police were here, I couldn't ignore the idea that maybe there was something fishy about Elisabetta's sudden death.

Think, Axelle, think.

If it turned out later that something shady had indeed happened to Elisabetta, wouldn't I kick myself for not having looked for any clues? And for not taking the gum wrapper and envelope with me when I'd had the chance? Of course, they were more than likely forgotten rubbish… but, still, why risk leaving them behind to be swept away by the studio clean-up crew? In fact, I suppose I had a duty to hand them over to the police…

It was then that Craig called me over.

As I walked towards him and the two police officers, I finally spotted my phone on the table lying amongst the accessories for the shoot, so I slipped it back into the pocket of my jeans. Then, after a quick introduction, I began to explain to the police exactly what had happened

– making sure to show them the medication Elisabetta had taken. But if I'd been expecting an exciting television crime show kind of interview session, I was sadly disappointed. It was nothing of the sort *at all*.

The police listened to everything I had to say about what I'd witnessed (it took some time – they didn't speak great English and I certainly didn't speak any Italian), asked me a few questions about my arrival in Milan, took down my contact details, agency details and passport number and we were finished. That was it. No interesting questions, no *why do you think it happened* – none of that.

Out of earshot of the police I talked to Craig about it.

"Obviously she just had a heart attack or something. So what's there to ask?" Craig shrugged his shoulders.

"But how can they be so sure?" I hissed. "For all they know I might've had a long-standing grudge against Elisabetta and wanted to do her in." It popped out before I could stop myself.

Craig looked at me oddly. "Um…Axelle, are you trying to tell me that you'd *rather* Elisabetta had been murdered? And that *you* want to be a suspect? Because that's seriously weird. Why don't you just go back to your flat and take a break – seeing Elisabetta die right in front of you can't have been easy."

"I'm fine, Craig, thanks. I just think the police are letting me go too easily."

Craig pursed his lips. "You know, Axelle, maybe you

should talk to your agency. I'm sure—"

But I didn't want to hear any more of Craig's advice, so I turned to the police while he was mid-sentence and held out my hand with the gum wrapper and dirty envelope. I tried telling them in English, slowly and carefully so they understood, that I'd found these two items under the sofa. "I thought they might be of importance to your investigation." They didn't say anything. "You know – *importante*," I said again as I tried handing them the envelope. At that moment some of the dust that still clung to the envelope flew up one of the policeman's nostrils, triggering an extremely loud bout of sneezing.

The officer's partner wasted no time in telling me that, for the moment, they didn't have anything else to ask me and that the best thing I could do to help their investigation would be to leave the dressing area. He put his hand on my shoulder and actually tried to turn me towards the curtain.

"They could be important," I insisted, although even I had to admit that under the bright lights of the studio, the folded gum wrapper and scruffy, unmarked envelope looked anything but.

As I walked out of the dressing area the curtain divider was pulled quickly shut behind me.

I wasn't about to leave the studio, though. They weren't going to get rid of me that easily... I planned on hanging around at least until that niggling feeling at the back of my mind – the one telling me that there might be more to

Elisabetta's death than met the eye – had calmed down.

I walked to a quiet corner of the studio and called my booker, Tomasso. He was shocked to hear about Elisabetta, and concerned that I'd want to fly straight home: "Of course, I understand if you want to…it means I'll have to cancel your bookings, but maybe I can reschedule them… Oh, Axelle! What a start to your Milanese week! I'll start calling off your appointments now – and to think I was so excited about you being here! And I was going to tell you, the casting director, Kristine Abrams, asked to see you today about walking in one of the men's shows this week."

I gritted my teeth. The men's fashion shows were on in Milan this week and, yes, it could be great publicity to be the only girl, or one of a small handful, to walk down the runway at a men's show, but my mind was on other things now.

One of the police officers had just stuck his head out from the behind the curtain to the dressing area and yelled out a sentence in Italian that included a word sounding suspiciously like "toxicology"…

Tomasso was still droning on as I held the phone away from my ear, concentrating on trying to hear what the police were saying – not that I understood much.

"Tomasso," I said suddenly, cutting him off mid-stream, "what does *tossicologia* mean?"

"Huh?"

I repeated the word.

"Er...it's a kind of science that, er...studies the effects made by things like..." He was struggling to answer, completely thrown by my question.

"Like what?"

"Like *veleno*." I waited while he searched for the English word. He was silent for a moment – it felt like an hour. And then finally he blurted out, "You know, like poison. But why do you ask?"

I didn't answer. My mind was whirring fast, a thousand scenarios playing themselves out and Elisabetta was at the centre of them all.

"Axelle?"

"Yes, Tomasso, I'm here – and, by the way, I'm staying. Don't bother changing a thing on my schedule."

"But what about Kristine Abrams? At what time can you see her? Surely the police need to question—"

I didn't hear the rest. I told him I'd call him back and then hung up.

Needless to say, now more than ever I was determined to stay at the studio. I was curious as to why the police wanted to run toxicology tests. It seemed even more possible that something unusual had happened to Elisabetta – and I didn't want to miss out on any developments.

I took a short breath of air and finally admitted what had been dancing around my mind since I'd lifted her sunglasses. I mean, hypothetically speaking, *what if* Elisabetta had been murdered? And *what if* someone in the studio knew more than they were letting on? I couldn't just leave now; I had to stay as long as possible and listen in on as much as I could.

I watched as one of the policemen opened the studio door and admitted an assistant carrying a tray laden with Thermos flasks of fresh coffee and tea. As I walked back towards the others, I reached into my bag and searched for the gum wrapper. The police had made it clear that they weren't interested in my finds, so I figured they belonged to me now. Without further hesitation I pulled out the gum wrapper and unfolded it, hopeful I'd find something written on it (wrappers are great places to write secret notes; nobody coming across one in your handbag or wallet would think to look twice). In the end however, I was disappointed; there was nothing there.

I walked to the nearest wastepaper bin and chucked the wrapper away, then I reached back into my bag and pulled out the envelope. I was just about to open it when I saw Benoit returning – he'd just been questioned. I made straight for him in the hope that I could glean some information. Along the way I heard the word *tossicologia* yet again. I asked Benoit about it.

"Yes, they will be running tests…although I think it's pretty standard procedure for any sudden, unexplained deaths."

"If it's not unusual then I wonder what they think they'll find?" I asked.

"Well, she was celebrating," he said with a shrug of his shoulders, as if that explained everything.

"What do you mean?" I pressed.

Benoit stopped cleaning his large black Mason Pearson hairbrush and looked at me. "Please take what I'm going to tell you as more of a warning than gossip…but in her younger days Elisabetta was known as a real party animal. She'd be up all night, hitting the dance clubs – and I mean *real* dance clubs, from the underground dance scene, not these chichi nightclubs filled with rich bankers and trust fund kids. She was dancing, but also doing drugs…nothing heavy, but, well, sometimes…"

"And you think that's why she may have died? Because she'd taken something last night?" I took my phone back out of my rucksack and carried on talking while I did a little online research. I was curious about Elisabetta's symptoms.

"It's definitely possible…but…" Benoit answered slowly.

"But you're not convinced."

"The thing is," he said, "we both stopped partying at the same time – and for the same reason – some years ago."

"What was the reason?" I asked, quickly looking down at the small screen of my phone. As far as I could see, her symptoms might be indicative of any number of things, including, it seemed, misuse of different forms of drugs. It made for scary reading…

"Our jobs – and the success that came with them. We were both working so much, and travelling all the time, that we just sort of grew out of it. It became impossible to go out every night and show up for early starts the next day with clients who were paying us a small fortune. We went cold turkey at the same time and haven't looked back since. These days we compare detox and juicing tips – or we *did*, anyway." A pained expression played across Benoit's face as he paused before continuing. "To tell you the truth, I'd be extremely surprised if Elisabetta had done more than drink a glass of champagne last night…but you never know. She did sometimes have a few drinks – but nothing like before."

"Maybe she had an allergic reaction to something?" I asked. "That might explain the need for tests."

Benoit sounded unconvinced as he put his hairdryer away. "I've never heard her mention any allergies."

"By the way," I said after a moment, "I know she was at the Moda Italia Awards last night, she won Editor of the Year. And I think I heard her say something about celebrating at an after-party somewhere. I wonder where she went…?"

"She went to Ugo Anbessa's party," Benoit said. "I was invited, too, but it was very late, very last-minute and, besides, I'd only just flown in. I opted for room service at the Four Seasons instead. I could kick myself now for not staying with her last night."

Hmm…Ugo Anbessa. Since I'd started working undercover as a model I'd learned enough to know that Ugo Anbessa was Italy's hottest young designer. Brash, savvy and talented, he was in his mid-twenties and designed for the famous Italian fashion house, Falco Ventini. And if his Instagram feed was anything to go by, he only dressed the biggest names in music, fashion and acting. He referred to them as his #Ventiniarmy.

Ugo had taken over as creative director of the Falco Ventini brand after Falco had died. He'd been an assistant designer on Falco's team and although the management had taken a risk in promoting him to the top job so young, their gamble had paid off. Ugo's sexy designs and social media savvy had driven sales to highs the company had never experienced before – even while Falco himself had been alive. Ugo was creating a new template to revive a historic fashion house and the corporate fashionistas were taking note. He was Italy's designer of the moment – and he looked like he'd stay at the top for a while.

"So she was friendly with Ugo Anbessa?"

"Yes," Benoit continued. "And Ugo won Womenswear Designer of the Year last night, you know…so after that it was inevitable that he'd invite a handful of good friends around – and yes, he and Elisabetta are – *were* – very close."

"I wonder how long she stayed? Or if she went anywhere

else after she left Ugo's," I said.

"I have no idea, but I suppose the police will question Ugo."

Benoit stopped to look at his watch. "I have to go. Now this shoot's cancelled I promised my assistant I'd help her prep for tomorrow's men's show. Lovely seeing you again, though, Axelle."

Before he turned to leave, however, I pulled out the scruffy envelope from my rucksack and quickly asked him if it was his. He shook his head. I also asked Giulia and then the two studio assistants about it, but they too said the envelope wasn't theirs. It didn't belong to Craig either. So whose was it?

After a little while I noticed that a policewoman had sat down with Giulia at the make-up table. She appeared to be questioning her. Perfect! I didn't want to miss any developments. I quickly made my way towards them and sat behind the officer, as close as I dared. I tried to listen in but the policewoman must have sensed something because she cleared her throat loudly, then spun round on her chair.

"Haven't we questioned you already?" she asked me in heavily accented English as she tapped her notebook with her pen.

"I'm just sitting here quietly – I promise," I said. "I'm still in shock, not ready to move at the moment. You'll forget I'm here."

But the policewoman wasn't having any of it. I watched as she stood up with a heavy sigh.

"I'll only stay for a while…" I made my last attempt, holding out the scruffy envelope I'd found. "Here," I said, as I thrust it under her nose. "I found this in the dressing room under the sofa. Wouldn't you like to have it? I can hold it for you until you've finished questioning Giulia."

"*Signorina,*" she said, with a tight-lipped glare as she waved the envelope away with a karate-like movement of her hand. "We have already questioned you. So, *per favore*, go home. Now. *Subito.*" She leaned in to me as she said this last word, before adding, "I've never met anyone who actually wants to *stay* under these kinds of circumstance. You are the first – and I'm not sure it's a compliment. Now go home and let us finish our work—"

"But—" I interrupted.

"Without you here," she finished, cutting me off as she placed her hand on my shoulder and pushed me in the direction of the studio exit. Then, before I could say anything, she turned round and signalled to one of her colleagues to show me to the door.

So much for my not missing out on any developments.

I stood still as the studio door shut behind me. Was that it? The end of my involvement with Elisabetta? Would I have to find out what happened to her from the newspapers? Or by extracting from Tomasso inaccurate (and probably nasty) bits of information he heard through the fashion grapevine? As I sighed with frustration, I noticed a trolley with our breakfast leftovers parked just next to me. Without thinking I reached for a clean knife. I needed a distraction – and I had the perfect one.

Nobody from the team had claimed the envelope – and the police had flatly refused to even consider it – so now I felt I could look at it with a clean conscience. Without further thought I slipped the knife blade under the sealed flap of the envelope. I mean, whether it had belonged to Elisabetta or not, I was curious about its contents.

I'd expected some kind of folded note or possibly a bit of money…but what I pulled out caught me completely by surprise. The overhead light of the corridor reflected off the metallic surfaces of three very old, very worn, but still exquisitely beautiful and intricately painted cards. A delicate sheet of protective paper lay between them – clearly they were fragile and maybe valuable, too.

I gasped as I stared at them; their extravagant and totally unexpected beauty was beguiling. Each card appeared to be painted by hand and all three were rendered in vivid, metallic paint that had worn away in places. The cards shimmered gently in the light as I tilted them in my hands.

They were rectangular in shape and, judging from the discernible weave of their surface, the thick paper they were made from looked to be hand pressed and hand cut – no surprise, I thought, considering they looked very old. I had no idea whether they were meant to be small paintings, or maybe even playing cards of some sort, but their colour palette reminded me of the medieval religious paintings we'd studied in world history at school last year.

The first card showed a bearded man who was colourfully dressed. He was sitting on a bench wearing a large hat with a wide, floppy brim and a long plume tucked into it. His hands lay on a trestle table in front of him. I peered closely at the cards. They looked like the tricks I'd seen at a Museum of Magic my parents had taken me to once. Three walnut shells were laid out in front of the magician; I guessed he would keep moving them about while the viewer had to guess which shell was hiding some little token or other. Maybe the man on this card was a magician.

I turned the card over but there was no image and no words on the back; it was painted in metallic silver and stamped with a repetitive graphic design. The backs of the other cards were all identical.

On the face of the second card was the image of a beautiful and radiant lady, her hair tucked under a large cap of shining gold. Dressed in a long and elaborately decorated dress, she rode a white horse that had a saddle and bridle as fine as her robe. I had no idea who she was and nothing on the card gave me a clue.

As for the third card, although edged with gold, the background was black, and a hollow-eyed, sickle-carrying skeleton stood in the centre. His ghoulish smile seemed to mock me as he danced in the middle of the black-and-gold card, his jawbone hanging open in a permanent cackle.

The sight of this last card reminded me of a shop my gran had once taken me to. It had been tucked away on a tiny, lively street behind Covent Garden in London. The shop specialized in the occult – and they'd had some cards there very similar to the ones I now held in my hands. The cards in the shop had been newer, with sharp edges and a flat, glossy surface, but the images had been much the same – and there'd been one just like this. I felt a surge of excitement as I finally realized what I was looking at.

Tarot cards.

What an odd thing to find! Why here? And why three of them? Where was the rest of the pack? And who did they belong to?

I stopped in my tracks and allowed these thoughts to spin through my mind. Tarot cards…hmm. They were interesting…but kind of freaky, too – the images were so spooky. But at this point I didn't see how they could possibly connect to Elisabetta…although…

A shiver ran through me again as a new thought suddenly came to me. I looked at the cards once more. Images on tarot cards are always symbolic. Nothing appears on them by chance or simply because it looks pretty. As I examined the magician on the first card I felt certain that card must refer to magic or luck. I wasn't sure about the one with the lady; mentally I put it down on my TBLI (To Be Looked Into) list.

Slowly I put the second card behind the third and studied the image of the mocking skeleton. I felt another shiver run down my spine because this image had a very clear meaning…and that was death.

I swallowed loudly as a new thought sprang to mind: *Maybe these cards do have some connection to Elisabetta after all?*

My mum's voice found its way into my thoughts, like a foghorn cutting through a stormy night: "Your imagination is running away with you, Axelle. It's just a coincidence. Do you hear me: a coincidence!"

Really?

The trouble was I didn't believe in coincidences. My grandfather had been a detective – at Scotland Yard, no less – and now some of his sleuthing wisdom came to mind: *An incident that appears to be coincidence is often some kind of plan masquerading as chance.* He'd reasoned that most people simply preferred to believe in chance than imagine there might be something suspicious going on.

Hmm…

Just then I heard a door open into the corridor behind me. Quickly I put the cards back into the envelope, stashed them in my rucksack and walked briskly forward. The cards might be valuable – and they certainly looked old. Perhaps they had an interesting history? Maybe they belonged to a collection somewhere? At the very least I should track down a tarot card collector or dealer, someone who could tell me about the cards and perhaps even help me trace their owner... And who knew, maybe my grandfather's words would be prophetic? Maybe finding the card of death in the dressing area of the studio where Elisabetta had died wasn't just a coincidence...

TUESDAY AFTERNOON

Summer Days, Deadly Ways

"What? So that was it?" I was with Sebastian and we were at a cheap and tasty pizzeria in the old city centre. I was starving now. As I looked at the menu it suddenly seemed like ages since I'd had breakfast.

Sebastian had arrived by train from Paris the previous night and was staying at a simple *Pensione* not too far from where Ellie and I were based. I'd rung him earlier to tell him what had happened and he'd been waiting for me on his rented Vespa when I left the studio building.

Because the studio management and *Amare* magazine had yet to release any kind of official announcement about Elisabetta's death, there were no journalists or nosy neighbours outside, which I was grateful for.

Sebastian and I hadn't wasted a second in zooming off and grabbing something to eat. And while I wanted to show him the tarot cards, first we rehashed my morning at the studio.

"And are you sure they were saying toxicology?" Sebastian asked as we both bit into the Margherita pizzas we'd ordered.

I nodded and pulled a string of clingy mozzarella off my chin before answering. "Yes. My booker, Tomasso, and Benoit, the hairstylist, confirmed it – although, strangely, Benoit didn't seem surprised."

"How do you mean?"

I explained what Benoit had told me about his and Elisabetta's party past. "But he said that for the most part she'd stopped that sort of thing years ago; he was sceptical that Elisabetta would have partied so hard last night…"

Sebastian watched me for a moment quietly before suddenly smiling. In the dim light of the pizzeria I could see the corners of his blue eyes crinkle. He was leaning back in his chair and ruffling his thick brown hair in that way he had. I had a good idea of what he was going to say… and yet he looked so totally cute and irresistible sitting there in his leather jacket that I was caught between two desires: one to steer him off the course I was pretty sure he was about to set out on, the other to kiss him.

As it was, neither of my desires became a reality. Sebastian moved in faster than I did.

"I think," he said, "that you feel that you're onto something… I bet you can't help but wonder if Elisabetta's death wasn't from natural causes, but something more mysterious. And that, if so, you'd like to find out what and why. Am I right, or am I right?"

Sebastian, like Ellie, thought that I was always on the lookout for a new case to solve. I pursed my lips as I considered this. Okay, so maybe, *possibly*, they had a point. But, still, I wasn't about to head off on a wild-goose chase without a good reason. After all, I was in Milan, it was sunny and warm, and I finally had some time to hang out with Sebastian. Besides, I was due to fly to Tokyo on Monday. And if for any reason I wasn't back home in London, punctually, on Saturday evening, to see my parents before flying to Japan, I'd be grounded – for life. My mum would make sure of that. Anyway, it wasn't as if anyone was calling to ask me to figure out what had happened to Elisabetta...

"You're so wrong, Watson," I finally said. "I'm *not* on the lookout for a new case. I'm simply telling you what went on today at work." I took another bite of my pizza.

Sebastian laughed. "I don't buy that for a minute, Holmes."

"Suit yourself." I shrugged my shoulders and avoided eye contact.

Sebastian went quiet for a moment. "Supposing, for the sake of argument," he continued cautiously, "that Elisabetta's death wasn't due to natural causes or some kind of overdose or allergic reaction..." He was smiling at me now and leaning across the table on his elbows. His voice was a whisper and his eyes were full of mischief. "How do you think she died?"

Ignoring how totally kissable he looked I answered as drily as I could. "It sounds to me as if you're the one craving a case to solve, Watson."

"*Au contraire*, Holmes, I'm looking forward to all of the sightseeing we have planned… But, simply out of curiosity, I'd like to know what you think…"

"Well, Watson," I said, "I'll humour you for the moment…"

"Right," he smiled, "because you haven't been asking yourself the same question."

"So," I continued, ignoring him, "based on the symptoms I witnessed Elisabetta suffer, I would hazard a guess that she was *poisoned*."

"Hmm, poisoned, you think…?"

I nodded. "The dry throat, the pain, confusion and nausea—"

Sebastian suddenly looked at me through narrowed eyes. "You've already been doing research, haven't you? You've been online and started looking stuff up…"

I blushed.

Sebastian threw his head back and laughed.

"I had time to kill while I was at the studio. And besides, it fits with the police wanting to run toxicology tests."

"Of course, Holmes, so does the idea that she may have celebrated with drugs."

"Very true, my dear Watson, although, if her good friend Benoit thinks she stuck to a glass of champagne at most…"

"You tend to believe him?"

I shrugged my shoulders. "Why not? Anyway, I doubt I'm right about poisoning. We can follow the story in the papers and I'll be sure to extract more details from my agency when they hear anything."

The image of the dancing skeleton on the tarot card suddenly flashed into my mind. *Death.* It was tempting to weave it into what had happened at the studio this morning. I hadn't shown Sebastian the cards yet, and I was curious to know what he thought.

"There is something I found…not that I'm saying it has anything to do with what happened at the studio this morning, but still…" I reached into my rucksack to pull out the tarot cards, but I suddenly felt my phone vibrate and reached for that instead.

"That's funny," I said to Sebastian as I looked at its lit-up screen. "It's a number I don't recognize – an Italian number with a Milanese city code."

"Take it," Sebastian said. "Maybe it's someone from your agency calling from a different extension."

But it wasn't. It was Ugo Anbessa, the fashion designer.

To say I was surprised to have Ugo Anbessa on the other end of my phone was an understatement. This day was turning out like some kind of twisted April Fool's. First Elisabetta's death, then the tarot cards, and now Italy's hottest fashion designer was calling me. I stepped out of the pizzeria so that I could speak more freely.

"I'm sorry to surprise you like this, Axelle, especially as we've never met, but it's important. I was given your number by Cazzie Kinlan in New York."

Ugo's accent was heavy, unmistakably Italian, and he spoke rapidly. I had to concentrate completely on what he was saying in order to understand him. "I called her just now to ask her advice and she said there was only one person she thought could help me – and that person is you. And I've heard that you are here, in Milan, *grazie a Dio*."

Cazzie Kinlan? Why had she given Ugo my number? If it had something to do with modelling then surely Ugo would have spoken with my agencies about it…

Cazzie Kinlan was the young editor-in-chief of the US edition of *Chic* magazine. A few months ago, in NYC, I'd helped her out of a tricky situation involving a stolen black diamond. Cazzie knew I solved mysteries and she knew my modelling was a cover. So if Ugo wasn't calling me about modelling, then surely it was about Elisabetta?

"I also heard through the grapevine that you were shooting for *Amare* this morning…"

"Um…yes…" I answered, intentionally vague. I wasn't about to begin explaining that I had been shooting for them until circumstances had dramatically curtailed the day's work and forced me out of the studio. In the event I didn't have to – Ugo's next comment showed me that he was totally up to date.

"To me, hearing that you were here in Milan and at this morning's *Amare* shoot was like a sign from destiny. I've heard about what happened in the studio this morning, Axelle…"

I didn't reply. *Word travels fast*, I thought.

As if he read my mind, Ugo said, "The police told me. They were just here, at my home. And that's why I'm calling you. You see," he continued, "I'm in a bit of a…*situazione difficile*. Do you understand? It concerns the death of Elisabetta Rinconi…" He went quiet.

"Yes?" I said.

"The thing is, the police seem to think that she may have been *poisoned*…they've even gone so far as to suggest that she might have eaten something here, in my house, last night, that made her ill. *Per favore*, Axelle, I need your help…"

I listened in stunned silence as Ugo briefly told me what he knew… The police had just been to his house to question him and said the pathologist's initial findings indicated poisoning. "But that is not the worst!" Ugo wailed – although Elisabetta being dead, and most likely intentionally poisoned, seemed pretty bad to me. "The thing is that I have a plant growing on my terrace and the police think that it could be the source of the poison."

"Really? What kind of plant is it?"

"It is something called monkshood. It is beautiful. In fact, the intense blue of its petals inspired one of the key colours of my last Spring/Summer Ventini collection—" He cut himself short as he stifled a cry. "But who knows how Elisabetta could have ingested it – it's not as if I put it into my ravioli and serve it to my guests!" He let out a long sigh before continuing, his voice rising in exasperation as he spoke. "The problem is that until they've figured out exactly how she died it seems I'll be labelled suspect number one. Please, Axelle, you have to help me! I promise you I have no idea how she ate the plant, but I didn't give it to her! Why would I want to kill her? We were close friends – best friends, even! Our lives have been intertwined ever since we met at fashion design school...right up until today."

I agreed to go straight to Ugo's apartment. I needed to hear everything about the party – and he was too upset to tell me calmly over the phone. Besides, there's no substitute for seeing people up close when they're being questioned. Often they can tell me more by what they don't say, than by what they do.

I walked quickly back into the restaurant, and told Sebastian that we had to get going. He raised his eyebrows in answer, a knowing smile lifting the corners of his mouth. "Is this what I think it is?"

I nodded as I pulled my rucksack over my shoulders. "I might have a new case." I was about to say that we didn't have a second to waste, when a pang of guilt suddenly shot through me. I glanced at my reflection in the mirror just next to me. My brown eyes looked back at me, excited, but a little hesitant. If I took on this case, Sebastian and I might as well forget all about our Milanese sightseeing plans. How would Sebastian react? After all, the same had happened in London last week and this trip was meant to make up for that one...

Sebastian caught my eye. "I know what you're thinking," he said.

"About our sightseeing plans?" I asked.

He looked at me and nodded quickly before turning round to reach for our helmets at the corner of the banquette.

"And?" I asked. He still had his back to me and he didn't answer straight away.

An uncomfortable thought popped into my head, a thought that had worried me before. Namely that one day Sebastian would get fed up with me changing our plans at the last minute, and leave. But what could I do? Say no when people asked me to solve a case? Besides, I wanted to solve my cases *with* him. It was more fun.

"You won't believe it, but this case has to do with Elisabetta..." I said, in a blatant attempt to interest him.

He turned back to look at me. "Why am I not surprised?"

Stepping slowly towards me, his eyes locked on mine. "So you won't be able to let it go, will you?"

His expression was unreadable, but I knew there was no way I *could* let this case go – whether he wanted me to or not. I slowly shook my head. "Not really, no."

Suddenly he bent down and brought his face centimetres away from mine. I could smell his leather jacket and the woodsy scent of his skin. His blue eyes held mine; they were dark and steely. He looked so serious. What was he thinking?

Suddenly, he broke into a dazzling smile and quickly kissed me on the lips before pulling back. "In that case, what better way is there to see a city than when we're searching for clues?" he laughed.

He'd been joking all along!

"Don't look so surprised, Holmes. I just wanted to make you sweat for a minute. I should have known something like this would happen. Our first twenty-four hours here have gone too smoothly."

Whatever guilt I'd felt immediately evaporated. I punched him in the arm as we left the pizzeria. "As if I was sweating," I answered back. "I'd solve this case with or without you, you know."

Sebastian laughed. "I know. Mysteries first, me second."

"It's not quite like that."

"Isn't it?" His words were teasing but I thought I saw a flicker of something more serious in his eyes.

I didn't answer.

He was quiet for a moment as we walked out to his Vespa. "Oh, and Holmes?" he suddenly said.

I looked at him in reply.

"I like it when you go all prickly on me. You look cute when you're being tough."

I stuck my tongue out at him and put my helmet on.

As Sebastian and I whizzed across Milan, I tried to fill him in on what Ugo had told me, yelling in his ear whenever we stopped at a light. My head whirled with thoughts of the new case and I was caught by surprise at how one phone call could change the course of my day – and probably my whole week.

I told Sebastian that, according to Ugo, the police were running with the theory that Elisabetta was poisoned. "Well spotted, Holmes, it's just as you'd suspected." The roar of his scooter as we surged forward drowned out the rest of our conversation.

Ugo Anbessa lived in the lively and beautiful Brera district in central Milan, on a very chic and relatively quiet street called Via Lovanio. I hopped off the back of Sebastian's shiny black Vespa and took my helmet off. I shook out my hair (actually, considering how frizzy and wild it is, even on a good hair day, I didn't so much shake it loose as set it free from the confines of the helmet) and then, while Sebastian parked his scooter, I looked up at the top floor of the stone and brick *belle époque* building in front of me. Verdant vegetation spilled over the elegant stone balustrade of the top floor penthouse, which (remembering how he'd described it to me) I presumed to be Ugo's.

"Are you ready?" Sebastian stood by my side. "And by the way, what's our official reason for being here? Just in case someone asks?"

"Ugo suggested we keep things simple and say that he and I are working on a project together. Because I'm here modelling anyway it shouldn't raise too much curiosity. People will assume we're working on something fashion related. Oh, and if anyone asks, you're my assistant on the project."

"Your assistant? How about your *partner*, Sherlock?"

"I'm still Holmes to you, Watson!" I yelled in his ear as a delivery van roared past us.

After walking into the elegant foyer of Ugo's building, we were buzzed through a second door by a camera intercom system. A tiny mirrored lift whisked us skyward and opened directly into the marbled entry of his penthouse apartment. As we waited in the apartment's grand hallway, I peered through the open doorways and spied lush and extravagantly coloured rooms painted in deep tones of tobacco, cognac and Chinese red. Baroque chests, lacquered Chinese screens, and large religious paintings of the Virgin Mary sat side by side with brash contemporary artwork, tables carved from petrified wood and shaggy handmade rugs. I even spotted a mirrored disco ball hanging from the living room ceiling. Opposite me French doors opened onto the wild growth of his terrace and its vibrant turquoise tiled floor.

Moments later, we heard the click clack of stiletto heels behind us. Sebastian and I turned at the same time and I reached to shake the hand of the person coming towards us. "I'm here to see Ugo," I started to say, but the words never made it past my lips.

"Hi, I'm Francesca Ventini, I'm Ugo's assistant," said the tall, curvy apparition in front of us, as she reached out for Sebastian's hand. "You must be Axel? Ugo told me you were bringing your assistant," she added unenthusiastically as her gaze swept rapidly over me.

She locked her large hazel eyes back on Sebastian, batted her long, dark lashes for a moment and then pushed up the sleeves of her crisp white jacket, revealing her perfectly tanned, honey-brown Mediterranean skin.

What really annoyed me, though, was that rather than correcting her about whose assistant was whose, Sebastian went along with it!

"It's great to meet you," he said as he reached for her outstretched hand.

To say that I was irritated was an understatement.

I nudged Sebastian sharply in the ribs, then stepped in between him and Francesca.

"Actually, Francesca," I said, "I'm *Axelle*." I made sure to emphasize the correct pronunciation, rhyming it with the verb *excel* and not the car part. "And Sebastian is *my* assistant," I continued. "If you could please let Ugo know I'm here I'd very much appreciate it."

She towered over me in her heels and looked at me as if I was no more than a splash of tomato sauce that had just landed on her white jacket. She raised her eyebrows before she answered. "Ugo will be here in a moment, he had to take a call. But I'll show you in." She turned and we followed her into the living room. "If you'd like to wait here…" She motioned to a large sectional sofa covered in black suede. "Or, Sebastian, you can follow me and we can get some drinks?"

I didn't say anything as my eyes swept the room, but Sebastian coughed uncomfortably and answered, "Thank you, but I'm here to assist, so…I think I'll just hang out and…you know…assist…"

"Suit yourself," said Francesca with a shrug of her shoulders. "But if you need anything let me know…oh!" Her eyes zeroed in on the helmets Sebastian still carried in his left hand. "I'm so sorry," she said. "I didn't notice you were still carrying those. I must have been distracted." She gave Sebastian a look that could have made even a nose-picking troll swoon.

"Don't worry," he said, smiling at her. "I don't mind hanging on to them."

Francesca shook her pretty head and batted her lashes some more. "No, no, I'll show you where to put them. Follow me." Then with another smile and a languid wave of her tanned wrist, she motioned to Sebastian – and he followed her.

"I'm sorry to leave you, Holmes," he whispered as he passed me, "but as your assistant, I might pick up some useful information for us this way."

I was just about to answer him when Ugo bounced into the room. "Axelle!" he said as he zoomed over to me, clasped my hand with both of his and gave me a double air-kiss. He was dressed in a black T-shirt with a V-neck collar, black jeans and black suede boots – he looked more like a hip-hop star than a fashion designer. A beautifully cut double-breasted black jacket with satin lapels completed his look – well, that and the large gold watch and colourful assortment of bracelets on his wrist. His hair was dark, very short and tightly curled; his skin smooth and brown.

"I'm so happy you're here – and *grazie a Dio* that the police have left, their questions were so distressing! Especially when Elisabetta's death is still so fresh – too fresh!" He was silent for a moment and I thought he might start to cry, but he pulled himself together and said, "Anyway, thank you so much for coming. Please have a seat," he said, motioning towards the sofa.

I watched as he walked to the double doors that led into his living room and shut them. "What I have to say is for our ears alone," Ugo said as he crossed the room to an antique chest standing against the wall opposite me. On top of it stood a carafe filled with some kind of drink, and glasses.

"Iced tea?" he asked. I accepted and after he'd set a tray with two glasses down on the coffee table in front of us, we started talking in earnest. He asked about the morning at Megastudio; he wanted to hear every detail of Elisabetta's last moments. I told him, and as I spoke I watched him carefully.

Ugo was an edgy mix of street style and high fashion; that combination was, in fact, a part of his rags-to-riches story. I knew a lot about him from the fashion gossip I'd heard, and had refreshed my memory with a quick check online while I was at the photo studio earlier.

Ugo grew up in a deprived area on the outskirts of Milan with his single mother, who was originally from Eritrea. When he showed a talent for style and drawing at an early age, his mother did all she could to encourage him. Ugo went on to win a place at the famous design school Istituto Marangoni, and was quickly deemed "one to watch". He graduated top of his class and one of the most trendsetting Milan boutiques bought his entire first collection.

After graduation, he became accessories designer at the prestigious Italian fashion label, Falco Ventini. Company founder Falco Ventini himself hoped that Ugo's appointment would help him to draw a younger clientele, but according to fashion rumours, by that time, the Ventini fashion house was practically bankrupt – Ugo had been brought in too late to save it.

Now in his mid-fifties, Falco couldn't adapt to styles outside of his old-fashioned couture bubble. And although he could recognize that Ugo's handbag and shoe designs were exciting and trend-worthy, he personally found them too brash. So, despite plummeting profits, Ugo and Falco agreed to part company. Then, just as Ugo was about to jump ship, Falco died unexpectedly and the Ventini brand was snapped up by a large French fashion conglomerate.

The new shareholders asked Ugo to stay on as overall fashion director of the Ventini brand – an offer he couldn't refuse. With Falco gone, Ugo and the House of Ventini were a perfect match. Ugo's rocker chic jackets, tight leather trousers and gladiator stilettos became global hits and the biggest names in music and film flocked to his shows. Furthermore, his savvy use of social media ensured that the Ventini brand was discovered by a whole new generation of fashion lovers.

And now not only was he having to come to terms with the death of his good friend and fellow fashionista, Elisabetta Rinconi, he was number one suspect in her murder. No wonder he looked so stressed. The last thing Ugo needed was for the story to hit the papers – the Ventini shareholders would not be pleased. I'd have to move quickly to make sure it didn't happen…

"We came here straight after the Moda Italia Awards last night," Ugo was saying, "to celebrate our wins. We were so excited! Anyway, it seemed natural for all of us to come here for an after-party."

"Who was 'all of us'?" I asked as I pulled my notebook out of my rucksack. Before I started writing, though, I also quickly switched on the recorder on my phone – there was no way I could afford to miss a word of this.

"Friends. Close ones. We all came back here together, straight from the awards, for a bite to eat."

"Can I have their names?"

"Of course. For starters there was me and Francesca – you met her when you came in."

I sure did, I thought to myself as I nodded. "She told us she is your assistant."

"*Esatto*. But she is also more than that, in a sense."

"What do you mean?"

"She is Falco Ventini's niece. She was working for Falco as a junior design assistant when I took over as creative director. She's only twenty and had already been there a year – when I stepped in to take charge I decided to keep her on, but as my personal assistant instead."

"But if Francesca was involved with the business – designing for it even – why wasn't she asked to have a more prominent role after her uncle died?"

Ugo's dark eyes quickly darted to the closed doors of the

room before he answered. Leaning forward he whispered, "Francesca is a great girl, don't get me wrong. If she wasn't I wouldn't have asked her to stay on, but, honestly, she couldn't design her way out of a plastic bag." He lowered his voice even further before continuing. "And even as my PA she tends to think that, as a Ventini, she should have some say – quite a bit, in fact – in the business. If I'd kept her in the design department I'd be arguing with her constantly. Of course, she wasn't too pleased about becoming my assistant, but it was better than leaving the company altogether. She forgets that today the Ventini brand belongs to a different company and likes to drop in her connection to Falco whenever she can. But, honestly, as far as the business is concerned, the only meaningful link to Falco that still exists – besides the name – is the one I make."

I wasn't sure what Ugo meant by this last comment. I looked at him questioningly.

"What I mean is that for me Falco's spirit is still very much alive in the archive we have at the company headquarters. I'm very inspired by Ventini's past and all that Falco created. I'd like to think that I bring his spirit alive, but for a new generation."

The Ventini history was interesting, but I needed to stick to the basic facts for now. "So who else was here last night?" I asked.

"Well…actually," Ugo said, as he suddenly sprang up from the sofa and walked across to a high desk by the wall behind me, "I think this might be helpful." He pulled a sheet of paper from a drawer and handed it to me. It was a list of the people who'd been at the party the previous night, with a brief description of each of them.

"I asked Francesca to help me write it when the police were here. I was so upset by Elisabetta's death that when they suddenly appeared at my door I found I couldn't remember a thing. Anyway, this is a photocopy of the list I gave them – but you can have it. It might help."

"Thank you," I said, taking the sheet and running my eyes up and down the eleven names written on it.

Ugo Anbessa – creative director at Falco Ventini.
Francesca Ventini – Ugo Anbessa's personal assistant and Falco Ventini's niece.
Elisabetta Rinconi – fashion editor at Amare *magazine.*
Kristine Abrams – New York City-based casting director.
Alessandro Matteo – male model. Walked for Ventini under Falco and walks for Ugo now, too.
Ginevra Mucci – editor-in-chief of Amare *magazine.*
*Countessa Lavinia Sommerino D'Alda – worked for many years as Ventini's in-house head of PR and handled Falco's haute couture clients.
*Coco Sommerino D'Alda – Lavinia's sixteen-year-old daughter. Coco is a new Ventini brand ambassador.
*Rafaela Cruz – New York City-based supermodel.

*5Zentz – *famous rapper and Rafaela's boyfriend.*
Maria Fiscella – Ugo Anbessa's housekeeper.

With the exception of Alessandro Matteo, Maria Fiscella, Lavinia Sommerino D'Alda and her daughter Coco, I was familiar with all the names on the list, and I even knew some of Ugo's friends personally. The one I knew best was Rafaela Cruz, the supermodel. I'd met her in New York City. We'd modelled together and she'd been involved in the case I'd been asked to investigate there.

I also knew Kristine Abrams, of course, from New York City. As casting director, she'd booked me for a couple of the shows I'd done there. She was very quiet and gentle (surprising, considering she held so much sway with the major fashion players). It was difficult to imagine her raising her voice let alone poisoning anyone... But I had to remind myself of my favourite phrase: *Given the right circumstances anyone is capable of anything.*

So, nice or not, Kristine was not off the hook – yet.

Coco Sommerino D'Alda I'd never met properly – although I'd seen her backstage at the Chanel and Lanvin fashion shows in Paris; she'd been followed by a small pack of paparazzi everywhere she went. I'd never met her mother at all, though.

As for Ginevra Mucci, I wouldn't be surprised if the agency already had a go-see arranged for me to meet her

– but, if not, I'd have to see if I could finagle one.

I remembered my phone conversation with Tomasso. He'd also said something about seeing Kristine Abrams. I'd brushed him off earlier, but obviously it was time to tell him I was ready to meet her. Maybe I could see her after I'd finished questioning Ugo. If she was casting for the fashion shows then she'd probably be casting until late into the evening…and what better place to "bump" into Alessandro than at a casting for the men's shows? He was bound to be going to all of them…

Rafaela I'd call tonight, and hopefully Sebastian was already asking Francesca about Ugo's after-party. I'd need to meet the others, too, but how? I took a deep breath and told myself I'd find a way. I'd start by calling Tomasso for an appointment with Kristine. As for the others, maybe Ellie could help me.

"And what do the asterisks mean?" I asked Ugo.

"They are the friends who left early, which is important because timing is a strong factor in any kind of poisoning, apparently." He stopped and let out a long breath. "Of course, we have to wait for the test results, but the police seemed fairly convinced by the idea that Elisabetta had been poisoned by my monkshood plant."

"How do they think she ingested the poison?"

"The police talked about three scenarios, the first one being that the poison must have been in the food I served." A look of disbelief crossed Ugo's face as he spoke – and who could blame him. "Which is why they've asked me not to leave town. *Naturalmente*, this request to stay put makes me look guilty without even trying."

"Not necessarily," I said as lightly as possible before moving him forward. "And what's the second scenario?"

"That she ate it accidentally – don't ask me how." Ugo shook his head and looked down at his lap.

"What do you think about that?"

"I say no way! She knew that the plant was poisonous. In fact, nearly everyone on the list knew about the plant. I always mention it to my guests because I think it's interesting how something so beautiful can be so deadly – and I didn't want any accidents happening, either…" He shook his head in disbelief. "Anyway, monkshood tastes very bitter apparently. It's not the kind of plant that you could eat much of, even if you wanted to. So accidental deaths are nearly unheard of where monkshood is concerned…"

"So what's the third scenario?"

"That she ate it on purpose."

"To kill herself?" I felt my eyes widen.

Ugo nodded. "I don't believe it for a second – and nor would anyone who knew her. Look, Elisabetta had a bit of a chaotic life, yes. She didn't come from a happy childhood and she had some money trouble lately, too, but I mean, who doesn't? She was never depressed. She loved her life and was especially thrilled about being a fashion editor at *Amare*…and she'd just won an award!"

The idea that she'd killed herself also surely went against what she'd mumbled in the studio earlier that morning, while she was swallowing her tablets. She'd said she had something important she had to do tonight. I'd have to ask Ugo about that later.

"So when do the police think the poisoning happened?" I asked.

"Of course, they can only guess at this point, but if it's the monkshood then it must have been late – midnight maybe. Certainly not much after that. They say if she'd been poisoned at, say, 4 p.m. she would have started suffering during the awards show. As it was, it seemed she slept through the night and the symptoms only really started to kick in before she left for work."

I nodded, remembering what she'd said at the studio that morning. "She told us she'd woken up early feeling unwell."

"That's what the police said, too. Of course, her time of death also depends on how much poison she actually ingested but the tests results will confirm that."

"So what time did you eat last night?"

"About midnight – precisely when they suspect she must have been poisoned. We were back here at about ten-thirty but we didn't start on the canapés until later. The guests with the asterisks had already left by then."

"Meaning that they couldn't have tampered with the food?"

"*Esatto.*"

"Unless they'd gone into the kitchen while the food was being prepared?"

"That's unlikely. Maria, my housekeeper – you'll find her name at the bottom of the list I gave you – was the only one in the kitchen. And she didn't leave any food unattended until she brought it all out of the kitchen and laid it on the dining room table. In theory the guests could have gone into the kitchen, distracted Maria, and tampered with the food, but in reality, they would have needed one of Harry Potter's Invisibility Cloaks to get past Maria. Even I'm not allowed to taste anything before she brings it out."

"Anyway," I said, "if those guests had left by the time the food was served, how could they have been sure that the poisoned food would reach their intended victim?"

Ugo shrugged his shoulders. "Good point."

Hmm…I was quiet for a moment as I mulled over this new scenario. What if Elisabetta was *not* the intended victim? Was she poisoned by mistake? Did Elisabetta unwittingly choose a poisoned snack from the platter *after* the killer had left Ugo's apartment? What a horrible thought! But until proven otherwise, it was a possibility I had to consider. Although it seemed like an unusually high risk for anyone to take. Unless it was a random killing just for the sake of murder? A chill ran up my spine at the thought.

"And have any of your other guests felt sick today?"

"No. Not a one. They've all called me – they're all in

shock – and I think the police have questioned most of them by now, too. Anyway, like me, they woke up feeling fine. Last night was cosy and nice – nothing wild, nothing over the top. Which makes what happened today all the more strange." Ugo looked away again and I saw his eyes fill with tears.

I had to stay focused. Going with the assumption that the police were correct, and that Elisabetta was indeed poisoned by the leaves from Ugo's plant, I quickly wrote the following in my notebook:

The people who stayed until the end had the best possibility of tampering with the food, and putting the poisoned snack directly into Elisabetta's hands.

The fact that everyone other than Elisabetta felt fine this morning seems to strongly indicate that the poison was meant for only one victim.

Of course, the poison could have been intended for one of the other guests. Even the best plans can go wrong.

Another thought occurred to me: when did the guests know they'd be invited back to Ugo's for his after-party? In other words, how much time did the killer have to plan this? There was no way it could have been premeditated… was there?

"How many of your friends knew that you'd be hosting a party here last night? Had you already invited everyone?

Or was it a last-minute plan?" I asked.

"Last-minute," he answered. "I had no idea that I would win an award last night, and, if I hadn't, I'd probably have gone to someone else's after-party. It was completely spontaneous."

Which meant, I thought to myself with a heavy feeling of dread, that the murder was spontaneous, too. The killer couldn't have known that the party was going to take place, but they'd certainly taken advantage of the situation. The thing about this theory was that to me it suggested a deep and simmering, possibly pathological hatred or jealousy. Surely only an emotion of great intensity could drive a person to seize a sudden opportunity to harm someone else – there were such high risks involved. So who hated Elisabetta so much that they were willing to kill her, spontaneously, under these risky conditions?

I grabbed the list and ran my eyes over the names again. Had the poison been intended for Elisabetta? "Did any of the guests have an enemy in the group at last night's party?" I asked Ugo.

For a fraction of a second I thought I saw Ugo hesitate before answering. But it happened so fast I couldn't be sure. "As far as I know," he said, "we are all good friends. I cannot imagine why anyone on that list could possibly want to hurt one of the others – least of all Elisabetta – *everyone* liked her! She was lively, witty and loyal." He was silent for a moment. "Anyway, why anyone would take it into their head to do it *here*, on my terrace and in the middle of a party is beyond me. It doesn't make sense!"

I cleared my throat. "Well, assuming for the moment that Elisabetta was indeed the intended victim, and that she really was poisoned here last night, then we must presume that someone on that list wanted her dead. But what motive could they possibly have?"

Ugo turned his face away from mine and looked out at his terrace. "Good question," he said. Then he turned back to me and said, "I wish I knew the answer."

But as his eyes held mine for a moment, I had the distinct feeling that Ugo was holding something back.

"There is something, isn't there, Ugo? Please tell me whatever you know. Any little thing – even if it seems unimportant – might help me…"

"Well I heard from the others that Ginevra Mucci, the editor-in-chief at *Amare*, and Elisabetta had an argument on their way here last night. It happened just outside of my building. Some of the others overheard it. They said it sounded quite nasty."

"What was it about?"

"Something to do with the award. Ginevra was bitter because Elisabetta had won. She accused Elisabetta of riding on her coat-tails – of copying her ideas for editorial stories and even the way she styles things."

"Do you think there's any truth in that?"

Ugo shook his head. "No. None at all – although it's easy

to imagine there was. Elisabetta's career has followed a very similar direction to Ginevra's, but that's not her fault. Milan is a small city in many ways and it just so happens that both women started in fashion by working as freelance stylists, then they both worked for Falco Ventini and later they both happened to move to *Amare* magazine. As editor-in-chief, Ginevra was well above Elisabetta in the *Amare* hierarchy. Of course, I've heard the rumours that Elisabetta was going after Ginevra's job, but I don't believe them for one second. Elisabetta wasn't like that. Besides, as far as I'm concerned, they both have distinct styles. I know Elisabetta best, of course, but I love to work with both of them. And, yes, perhaps on occasion I've seen Ginevra's jealousy flare up – this is fashion after all, it's hardly a new emotion in our workplace. But, still, I can't imagine Ginevra was jealous to the point of murder – I mean, that's crazy!"

"So you think it's unlikely Ginevra would have poisoned Elisabetta?"

"Yes, I do." He didn't hesitate for a moment.

I sucked the end of my pen. "And what did the canapés you served last night consist of?"

"Little snacks – home-made things. Because it was Monday night and we all had to be in the office early this morning, I wanted to keep things light, even though we hadn't eaten dinner – the awards had started so early." He stopped and sighed. "Anyway, once I'd decided to invite the friends here I called Maria, and she quickly put some nibbles together for us. Little meatballs, some Parma ham and melon, and tiny slices of bruschetta. There were fresh figs and a bowl of cherries, too."

A pained look suddenly crossed Ugo's face. "Maria is furious, of course. She screamed at the police when they were here. She took their enquiries very personally – as if they were accusing her of poisoning Elisabetta. She's never been so insulted in her life. Anyway, the police followed her into the kitchen and she showed them exactly what she'd made – what leftovers we had have been taken to the laboratory for testing. But the initial feeling is that the bruschetta is to blame. The police think someone could have ripped the monkshood leaves into tiny pieces and sprinkled them over the top – it would have blended in with the basil perfectly."

"But you said the leaves taste bitter…"

"So they say. But Maria puts a lot of garlic on her bruschetta. And from what I gathered while the police were here, it doesn't take much fresh monkshood to kill someone – the leaves are highly toxic. Just one can be fatal."

"May I see the plant?" I asked.

"Absolutely," Ugo said as he stood up and motioned for me to follow him.

We walked out onto his sunny terrace. It was large and perfectly designed for a summer party or outdoor dinner. Trimmed boxwood topiary shrubs in the form of obelisks grew in a raised brick bed that ran along the whole length of the terrace. An assortment of large flowering shrubs, like roses and jasmine were growing in the same raised bed. It was all a bit wild and reminded me of Ugo's clothes – the heavy embroidery, frayed edges and rough tears that overlaid his tailoring.

As I took everything in, Ugo led me to the middle of the terrace and stopped in front of an arbour covered with a profusion of lilac clematis blooms and pink climbing roses. He pointed to the partly shaded alcove under the arbour. A striking plant with bright green leaves and blue flowering spikes was growing there in a raised bed. Its height, and the intense blue of its lance-like blooms, caught the eye. This was the monkshood.

"It's a common garden plant, actually," Ugo said, as if defending himself. "And fatalities are rare. Slugs hate them, but bees and butterflies really love them – which is partly why I have them."

"Are they toxic to the touch?"

"Well, the gardener who looks after my terrace wears gloves if he has to work with the plant – dividing the roots or whatever else – but, day to day, if he's just watering it for instance, he just has to be careful not to touch it."

"Was anyone wearing gloves last night?" I asked.

"If they did no one noticed, and no gloves have been found."

"Maybe they used a tissue or just pulled their sleeves over their fingers to rip and tear the leaves?"

Ugo shrugged his shoulders. "Maybe…"

I took a photo of the monkshood plant and as I put my phone away I noticed the time. If I wanted to meet with Kristine Abrams today then I had to call Tomasso now; she'd probably be working late because of the men's shows, but I didn't want to miss her. I told Ugo I had to get going.

"So will you take this case on?" he asked. "*Per favore*, Axelle, you have to help me – or *us*, actually. I didn't kill her! And I know that Elisabetta did not eat the poison on purpose. Her reputation must be saved along with mine! She was one of my absolute best friends. Ever. So I owe it to her to get to the bottom of this and find out exactly what has happened."

Ironically, the circumstantial evidence pointed to Ugo… The party had been held at his house, a highly poisonous plant grew on his terrace, and, perhaps most incriminating of all, Ugo had known before all of the others that the party was going to be here. No wonder the police thought he might have had a hand in the crime. But did he have a motive?

"Ugo," I said, "did you come to your house alone from the awards last night? And did you arrive before the others?"

He looked away from me and nodded slowly. "The answer is yes to both of your questions, and I know what you're thinking. It doesn't do me any favours. But of course I rushed over here to help get everything ready for my guests."

Hmm… So, he'd had time to prepare the poison. He

had arrived before the guests and could have easily pulled a couple of leaves off the plant while Maria was busy in the kitchen. That definitely didn't look good. "And who served the snacks?"

"Maria laid them out on the dining room table, but I brought them onto the terrace and passed them around. I did that for the entire time the guests were here. Of course, I could only carry one or two platters at a time, so the others stayed on the dining room table, so anyone could have tampered with them and passed them around."

Ugo could have slipped the leaves into a pocket then taken them out at an opportune moment, ripped the leaves and sprinkled them over the bruschetta in question before making sure he offered that particular one to Elisabetta. And he would have known to wash his hands afterwards. On the other hand, someone else could just as easily have done the same.

"One last thing I need to verify," I said as I pointed to the monkshood. "Earlier you said that you often tell your guests about the plant – you did last night, in fact."

Ugo nodded.

I handed him the list he'd given me earlier. "Can you tell me who, exactly, from the names on this list, knew for certain about the plant being poisonous?"

His eyes scanned the list. "With the exception of 5Zentz, everyone on this list has been here regularly. They definitely would have been aware that I had the monkshood growing on my terrace. Like I said, I often pointed it out; I thought people would be interested to know it was from a family of poisonous plants – as are potatoes and aubergines. Did you know that?"

I smiled and took back the list from Ugo. Opening my notebook, I wrote another list:

Ugo Anbessa
Francesca Ventini
Kristine Abrams
Alessandro Matteo
Ginevra Mucci
Maria Fiscella

I felt that these were the guests I should look at first. These were the people who'd stayed for the food. They all knew that Ugo had a poisonous plant growing on his terrace, but did they have a motive? I didn't know – but I'd do my best to find out.

Before heading back inside I asked Ugo again if he was aware of any long-standing grudge between Elisabetta and one of his guests from last night.

"No, only Ginevra and her professional jealousy, anyway. But I really don't believe it could be Ginevra." As he spoke his eyes drifted towards the sun and again I had the feeling he was holding something back. If he wanted me to solve this case then why didn't he just tell me?

"One last question, Ugo," I said. "Elisabetta mentioned to me this morning that there was something 'important' she had to do tonight. Do you have any idea what it was?"

He turned to look at me and answered sharply, "No I don't. Not at all."

Then he asked me again if I would take the case on.

I was slightly taken aback by his tone; I had very little circumstantial evidence to work with, and no motive...but still I was intrigued. Elisabetta had, after all, died right before my eyes. What would drive a person to carry out a murder in plain sight of half a dozen people...?

"I can't make any promises, Ugo," I said at last. "But yes...I'll take on your case."

Before leaving Ugo's apartment I asked him if I could speak with Maria.

"Maria?" Ugo said. "Of course. She's probably making dinner."

Fleetingly I thought of Sebastian and wondered what he'd been doing all this time...I hadn't seen him since he'd gone off with Francesca. But any more thoughts of Sebastian were pushed to the back of my mind as I followed Ugo back out into the marbled entry hall and down a long, well-lit corridor lined with storage cupboards. Finally we entered the kitchen. It was large, sunny – with lots of windows – and surprisingly homely considering the sophistication of the rest of Ugo's apartment.

At the far wall, in front of the stove, a scowling Maria stood guard over her dinner-time creation. I could tell from the look she shot me across the kitchen, that if I hadn't come in with Ugo she would have had sharp words for me.

"She doesn't really like visitors in the kitchen," Ugo whispered. "But she is an amazing cook. Her gnocchi is to die for." Ugo suddenly grimaced at his choice of words. "You know what I mean," he added sheepishly.

Ugo pointed to a table beyond the cooking area, where last night Maria had laid out the dishes before Ugo had taken them out to the dining room. The kitchen was clearly Maria's domain and it was indeed hard to imagine any of the guests getting a chance to tamper with the food while she was around.

Something my gran once told me came to mind. She often said it as we watched *Miss Marple* reruns on TV: "Remember, Axelle, circumstantial evidence is all fine and good, but it can't always give you the whole picture. Learn to rely on your people instincts, too. Don't forget that when you become a detective." (My gran was always convinced I would!)

With Ugo acting as my translator I asked Maria a few questions. She answered each one with a decisive and clear no. No one had tampered with the food while she'd been in the kitchen; no one had come into the kitchen, yes, well,

Ugo had, but he'd stood on the threshold of the door and he hadn't actually stepped *inside* the kitchen. And, no, she had not left the kitchen until she'd finished preparing the food. I asked her how well she knew Elisabetta (only as a guest of Ugo's and she'd never said more than *buongiorno* or *buona sera* to her), then I thanked her and told Ugo that I was finished.

With my gran's words ringing in my ears, I considered my first impression of Maria, listening to what my gut told me. She was like some kind of general in the kitchen – and I definitely felt that if she had told Ugo and the police that no one had tampered with the food before she'd taken it out, then she was telling the truth.

Before we left the kitchen, however, Maria turned to Ugo and, hands on her hips, loudly rattled off some questions of her own – and considering the way her large eyes kept staring at me there was no doubting who she was talking about.

"What was that all about?" I asked Ugo once we'd left the kitchen.

He smiled. "She didn't understand who you were and why you were asking the same questions as the police. So I explained that you are a model I know and that, although you look very young, you are very perceptive about human psychology. And that I'd asked you to help me figure out what might have happened to Elisabetta." Ugo chuckled as he said it. "You see, she knows me well enough to be able to tell when I'm lying, and after hearing your questions I couldn't just tell her that we were working together. So I gave her just enough of the truth to keep her satisfied."

Actually, the psychology part wasn't that far off base. Solving mysteries has a lot to do with psychology. "What else did she say?" I asked Ugo. "I saw her looking me up and down."

Ugo nodded. "She thinks that you must be better at human psychology than you are at modelling. She thought that despite your long legs you were quite small. But she promised that if you can figure out what happened to Elisabetta, she'll make a dinner just for you. To help you grow, as she put it." Ugo laughed. "I think she likes you, actually."

In which case, I thought, *at least being short (for a model) sometimes has its advantages.*

Before I left Ugo, there was one more thing I had to do. I asked if he had a quiet corner somewhere – I needed to make a couple of phone calls.

"Of course, no problem," he said as he led me back to his salon. Then he left, shutting the doors behind him. I called Tomasso and told him I now had time to see Kristine Abrams.

"That's fantastic, Axelle! Kristine is still casting and will be for another hour or two. She's casting for Fiore, and," Tomasso added, "Ellie will be there soon, too – she has a fitting for their ad campaign."

Perfect, I thought. I could meet Ellie there, explain the new case and ask her about any relevant fashion gossip.

"Also, Tomasso, what about *Amare*? Are they going to reshoot today's booking? Will I get to do it? Do you think I should stop by and see Ginevra Mucci?" The fact that I'd already been booked by *Amare* meant that they "knew" me, so they wouldn't usually have to see me again unless they wanted me for a different story and needed to see the clothes on me, but I was hoping that Tomasso would swallow my line and put my query down to sudden enthusiasm. I had to see Ginevra Mucci, and having my agency make the appointment would raise no suspicion at all. Fortunately Tomasso fell for it.

"Wow, wow, wow, Axelle! Now we're talking. I like this new burst of energy you have!" I rolled my eyes as I waited while Tomasso hammered on his computer keyboard, checking my schedule. "In fact I have an appointment scheduled for you with Ginevra Mucci for tomorrow morning at the *Amare* offices," he said. "But it's not about a reshoot. After this morning they've dropped that whole story, but they have another that Ginevra thinks you'd be perfect for. I'll email you the details of tomorrow's appointments. You have a few other castings and go-sees scheduled as well."

"That would be great, Tomasso, thanks." *Good*, I thought, as I took a deep breath. I was relieved about the meeting with Ginevra. Now I just had to hope that I could get her onto the subject of Elisabetta and Ugo's after-party without her wondering why I was asking.

"And just so you know," Tomasso continued, "it looks as if you might be able to squeeze in some sightseeing tomorrow between appointments."

More like chase down clues, I thought. "Great!"

"Yes, I thought you might like that, because the rest of your week is very busy. On Thursday I have you confirmed for the Cutie-Pie campaign." He went quiet for a moment and I heard him tapping on his computer keyboard before he said, "Friday looks good for another day of advertising, although Kristine Abrams already has you on option for the Lei-Lei men's show. If she books you to walk exclusively for them, then we'd rather you did that. For your career it's better you appear in a super show that everyone will see, than do a campaign for an Italian company that won't advertise outside of Italy. *Capisci?*"

"Yes, I understand, and that all sounds perfect, Tomasso, thanks."

"Anytime, *mia bella*. I love a model who's motivated!"

If only he knew just how motivated I was – *to solve this case*.

I hung up and looked at my watch. Then I messaged Ellie to say I'd be at the Kristine Abrams casting soon and ask her if she wanted to have dinner with me and Sebastian afterwards. She did, and I texted back:

Great! And, btw, you're never going to believe what happened this morning at the studio…

Ellie replied straight away:

I've just heard about Elisabetta. So sad. Everyone is talking about it. Crime certainly seems to follow you around…

A vision of Elisabetta's glassy stare came vividly to mind and I felt my insides churn. Maybe Ellie had a point!

I found Sebastian and Francesca outside on the pavement just in front of the door to Ugo's building. They were laughing and talking.

"I hope I'm not interrupting anything," I said brightly as I stepped out onto the warm street. I couldn't help a touch of annoyance tingeing my voice and I hoped neither of them picked up on it.

In the event I needn't have worried. They were so engrossed in their conversation that I could have driven up to them on a bulldozer and they probably wouldn't have noticed. I was keen to ask Francesca a few questions of my own, so I walked in between them and cleared my throat loudly. "I still can't get over Elisabetta's death," I said.

"I know – it's terrible!" she answered, after dragging her attention away from Sebastian.

"By the way, Francesca, did you happen to hear the argument last night between Ginevra and Elisabetta? Ugo told me it happened right here… How awful having an argument like that on her last night alive…"

Francesca nodded. "It was exactly where we are standing. They were practically at each other's throats."

"I thought it was just a little tiff."

"If that's what you want to call it…" she said as she rearranged the bracelets on her slim wrist.

"So what was it about?"

I watched Francesca smile at Sebastian before turning to me. "The same old. Ginevra has always claimed that Elisabetta copied her magazine editorials and advertising campaign ideas."

"And did she?"

"I don't know – I'm too busy working on my own style. The *Ventini* style."

I stopped myself from rolling my eyes. Instead I pursed my lips, then said, "It sounds like Ginevra really hated Elisabetta?"

Francesca shrugged her shoulders. "Elisabetta wanted to step into Ginevra's shoes. And the closer she got the more Ginevra freaked out. Ginevra has hated Elisabetta since *for ever*."

Francesca's version of Elisabetta's and Ginevra's

argument confirmed what Ugo had described. Hmm... I wanted to ask her about the monkshood too, but didn't want to sound too much like a detective in case she grew suspicious. Instead I asked her if she knew Alessandro.

Her smile told me she did. "He's gorgeous – lucky Elisabetta."

"Lucky Elisabetta?"

Francesca nodded. "They were dating." Ugo had neglected to mention that, I thought. I was about to ask more but a look at my phone told me I had to get going or I'd be late for my casting with Kristine – and might miss Alessandro, too.

I asked Francesca for her number. "I don't know Milan – I'd love some good advice on what to see and do." I hoped she wouldn't see through my white lie.

But she gave a tight smile and said, "Of course. Sebastian already has my number."

Sebastian looked at me with wide eyes and shrugged his shoulders. I forced myself to smile at Francesca and thank her. Why was she annoying me so much? I mean, what did I care if she and Sebastian had already exchanged numbers? After all, wasn't it useful for the case that they had?

I was about to shake her hand and say goodbye when Francesca hugged Sebastian, gave him a double air-kiss and said, "I'll call you later."

I gritted my teeth and told her I'd be in touch. Then I turned and left, with Sebastian at my side.

"You could be a little friendlier with Francesca, you know," he said as he handed me my helmet. "You seemed a bit frosty."

"Well, I'm not frosty at all."

"Good, I'm glad, because I'll be seeing more of her," he added as he swung his leg over his Vespa and revved up the engine.

"Why?" I definitely sounded frosty now.

"I'm your assistant on this case, remember? I'm here to help you solve it. As you know, Francesca is a witness... and I'd like to ask her a few more questions. The thing is we seemed to keep getting sidetracked – I didn't get to finish my line of enquiry."

I said nothing as I slipped onto the seat behind him. But as we drove out of Via Lovanio I couldn't help asking him, "So what did you find out?"

Sebastian answered me at the first red light. "She arrived with the others, she had nothing to do with the food preparation and didn't see anyone go into or out of the kitchen – apart from Maria, Ugo's cook. And yes, she knew about the plant on Ugo's terrace. She also ate some of the nibbles but has felt fine all day. And I have to say, she looked good."

I rolled my eyes.

"And when did she leave last night?"

"At the end, together with the group that stayed later – which included Elisabetta."

I nodded. So far everything tallied with what Ugo had said. So what more could Sebastian possibly need to find out from her?

"This and that," he said when I asked. "Like you, I really want to put this mystery first and make sure I cover my ground thoroughly." He turned, smiled at me and gave me a thumbs up.

Ha! I thought. *So that's what this is about. He thinks I put my mysteries first and now he wants to show me what that feels like…*

"Fine, Watson. You do what you have to do and I'll do the same."

As we wove through the traffic I could see him watching me in the scooter's rear-view mirror. Finally, as we waited for a light to change he looked over his shoulder at me and said, "You know, I was a little upset when this case came up so suddenly, changing our plans and everything…but now I think we're going to have fun and, don't worry, I'm totally into helping you out."

Yeah…helping me out with Francesca. Grrr!!!

TUESDAY EVENING

<u>Castings and Questions</u>

Sebastian made good time as we zoomed along the picturesque streets of the Brera district and went past the famous La Scala opera house. We missed the turning we needed to make, however, and ended up going past the Duomo. The sun was still out, but as the early evening light softened, the white stone walls of the Duomo were bathed in a warm glow.

We turned away from the immense cathedral and found our way to Via Broletto. Kristine Abrams was holding the Fiore show casting at their company headquarters there – it was a busy street in the middle of a maze of buildings and smaller streets between the La Scala opera house and the vast Castello Sforzesco.

Even if Tomasso hadn't given me the exact building number of the Fiore headquarters, I would have known which one it was simply by the endless stream of male models

making their way in and out of the building's large entrance arch. Most of them looked just a few years older than me. And all were slim and dressed more or less identically: jeans or chinos, T-shirt in a bright colour or with some kind of loud graphic image on the front, many with some kind of plaid shirt over the top. Sneakers were the shoes of choice, and funky hats were not unusual. All walked with long strides and most had a rucksack or man-bag, or held their portfolios in their hands. It was easy to feel like you'd walked onto the set of the next *Zoolander* movie.

Surely Alessandro would be at this casting – in fact he might even be in there now. Feeling focused, I hopped off Sebastian's scooter and walked alongside him as he eased his Vespa into the long line of scooters parked just outside the imposing, ochre-coloured building.

"I'm not sure how long this will take…" I said as I removed my helmet and shook my hair out.

"No worries," Sebastian answered as he turned off the Vespa's engine. "I'll be here. In the meantime is there something I should be looking into?"

I suddenly remembered that I still hadn't had the time to show Sebastian the tarot cards I'd found in the studio this morning. "Actually, yes there is," I said as I slipped my rucksack off my shoulders and searched for the envelope with the cards. I handed it to Sebastian.

"I found these in the studio this morning."

He looked at me, his eyebrows raised as he took the envelope from my hand.

"Open it," I said.

He pulled the cards out from the envelope and lifted his head with a start. "Wow. What are these?"

"Tarot cards, I think," I said. "And very old ones by the look of it."

"And you found these in the studio? This morning?"

I nodded. "I actually found them in the dressing area, near Elisabetta. They were on the floor, under the small sofa just behind the chair she was sitting on. The envelope caught my eye—"

"Caught your eye?" he asked with a smile on his lips.

"Yes. Caught my eye, Watson," I insisted. "And the thing is, I have no idea whose it is. It was under the sofa and I thought it might be a clue."

"Aha! So I was right – you were actively searching the scene of the crime for clues."

He really could be exasperating, I thought, as I stuck my tongue out at him. "I admit I tend to second-guess circumstances – but in this case I'm glad I did. Her death has turned out to be far more fishy than I'd imagined at first. Plus don't we all have an obligation to help out when we smell foul play? Besides, I know your dad's a police inspector, but even you, Watson, have to admit that the police aren't always particularly thorough when they're investigating a crime scene."

"I'm sure my dad would have something to say about that…"

"I bet he would…but, regardless, Watson, this envelope was on the floor. It may have slipped out of her handbag – but then again maybe not. I didn't notice it among her things…"

"You searched her bag? But she'd only just died!"

"It wasn't like that. Earlier, her bag fell over and everything spilled out so I helped her pick her stuff up off the floor. I don't remember seeing the envelope then, though."

"Maybe she had it in a pocket or something? Maybe it slipped out when she moved to sit down?"

"It's possible. Her trousers did have pockets, I noticed that. She had her hands in them at one point." I shrugged my shoulders. "But before I left the studio I made a point of asking everyone who'd been around up until she died if the envelope belonged to them."

"And no one claimed it?"

I shook my head. "Not one."

"So it really might have belonged to Elisabetta…"

"Well I certainly can't rule out the possibility…on the other hand it could have been in the studio, unnoticed by whoever worked there yesterday or the day before."

"True…but say someone working in the studio within the last few days had lost it there. Don't you think they would have asked the studio about it? I mean, they might be valuable if they're really old."

"Good point. Also, what I find odd is that there are only three of them. Where's the rest of the pack? Why are these three singled out?"

"Why don't I head over to Megastudio and look into it while you're at your casting," Sebastian said. "I can find out from the front desk whether anyone's asked about a missing envelope or some tarot cards."

"That would be great." I was silent for a moment as another thought came to me.

"What are you thinking, Holmes?"

"Elisabetta's assistant, Marzia… Out of all of us, only Marzia and I went into the dressing area all morning. None of the others had a reason to."

Marzia.

Her name circled through my mind. She'd been on her own with Elisabetta before I came into the dressing area… and she had conveniently left it just before Elisabetta died, so that I was alone with her, and Marzia was out of the way. That didn't necessarily mean anything, though. If the police were right in their belief that Elisabetta was poisoned at Ugo's party – and all the evidence seemed to point to that – then Marzia could hardly have poisoned her in the studio that morning. But could she have seen the envelope in Elisabetta's hands?

I'd asked everyone if the envelope belonged to them – but I hadn't asked them if they knew whether it was Elisabetta's. And Marzia had been in such a state after seeing Elisabetta, that it's quite likely she didn't even hear my question.

"You know what I think, Holmes?" Sebastian said as he watched me.

"What's that, Watson?"

"I think you need to pay Marzia a visit. Maybe I can search her out."

"Thanks, Watson." I nodded. "I've got an appointment tomorrow at *Amare* so it would be good to know if she'll be at the offices. Maybe I can 'bump' into her while I'm there. If not I'll have to ask Tomasso for some help…" I pulled my phone out and found Tomasso's email with all of the details for today's *Amare* shoot. "Her full name is Marzia D'Onofrio."

"Noted, Holmes. See you in a while."

"See you in a while."

Our plans made, we parted ways.

The cool air in the large courtyard of the building hit me like a soothing whisper as I stepped under the entrance arch. I gave my name at the reception desk and was directed to the first floor conference room where the casting was taking place. But I hadn't even made it as far as the stairs when I heard a familiar voice call out my name. It was Ellie.

"Perfect timing!" she said as she slipped her phone back into her large black squishy shoulder bag and put her arm through mine as we ascended the stairs. Ellie looked as fresh after a day's shooting as she had this morning. If anything, the traces of make-up smudged around her blue eyes and her roughly brushed out hair only emphasized her beauty. She looked tanned and healthy in her light, flouncy short dress with its cute red-and-black pattern. Around her waist she'd tied (literally – she wasn't using the buckle) a thick, studded, worn leather belt and on her feet she wore gold sandals. A pair of aviator sunglasses completed her outfit.

"So what have I missed? And don't say 'nothing'," she quickly added when she saw me start to purse my lips, "because it's written all over your face that you've got something major going on. Besides, your messages hinted as much. Am I right or am I right?"

I nodded. "It's about Elisabetta, and while I want to tell you everything, I'd rather we did it when we're at dinner – without any fashionistas hanging around."

"Got it. But is there anything I can do to help, here, now?" She nodded towards the open door of the casting room. "I have a fitting so I won't be seeing the same people you are, so, if you can think of something…"

"Just keep your eyes and ears open. Any information about Elisabetta could be really useful."

"Will do. Oh, and Axelle?"

"Yeah?"

"Don't forget to take your glasses off."

I was just about to tell her that I wasn't wearing them when I automatically brought my finger up to my face to push them up the bridge of my nose and felt them. "Oh, yeah, right. Thanks." Large, nerdy glasses like mine had just been all over the runway for the Gucci resort collection show, but they were still a no go at castings, especially the one I was about to do. A half-hidden face would not a career make.

I hadn't seen Kristine Abrams since she'd booked me for a couple of shows for New York City Fashion Week, a couple of months earlier, but I remembered her clearly. She was friendly, quiet and soft-spoken – especially for a fashionista; she didn't feel the need to speak in witty or catty pronouncements, like some I could mention.

I noticed her the moment I walked in. She was sitting at a long table at the far end of the large, brightly lit room. Various assistants and Fiore employees were huddled around her, animatedly discussing the model book they were looking at. Nevertheless as soon as she looked up, she caught my eye, smiled and winked.

As a casting director Kristine's job is to find models for fashion shows or campaigns. But not just any model. Casting directors – the good ones like Kristine – had an eye for the next big thing – a valuable asset to have in an industry obsessed with the new. Of the hundreds and hundreds of girls they saw in a year, the good casting directors could find exactly the ones whose looks either converged perfectly with their time, or would lead the fashion flock into the next big beauty trend.

Good casting directors also had to understand what look a particular ad campaign or fashion show needed. Looking for more edge? They'd find the right model. Need a face that hadn't been seen in a while for a luxury ad campaign? Kristine knew the perfect person. She held a lot of power and sway, and her instincts were well respected.

Not that you'd believe it to look at her. I suspected Kristine was dressed in the exact same outfit I'd seen her wear in New York: jeans, an untucked man's shirt in blue, and dirty trainers. Her blondish hair was pulled back off her scrubbed face. She didn't wear jewellery or nail polish. It was almost as if she needed to keep her physical persona detoxed from all the fashion she was constantly immersed in.

As it turned out, getting Kristine on to the subject of Elisabetta was much easier than I'd expected. As I stood in the short queue of models waiting to show their portfolios the talk turned to Elisabetta. Word was out about her death and in fact, it was all everybody seemed to be talking about.

When the model in front of me wondered aloud what had happened to Elisabetta, a shocked conversation followed, and I waited for my moment.

"There's a terrible rumour going around that she'd been poisoned," I said. Everyone looked at me, and I could feel a collective intake of breath. "They say it happened last night," I continued, "but she didn't fall ill until this morning."

Kristine's colourfully dressed assistant, Marco, turned to her. "You were with Elisabetta last night, weren't you, at Ugo Anbessa's?"

"That's where they say she was poisoned," I added.

Kristine's eyes widened. Now everyone was watching her. She took her time to answer. "Yes, I was at Ugo's, and, yes, I've heard the same rumours...how come you know so much, Axelle?"

I bowed my head a little, hoping only Kristine would hear. "I was working with Elisabetta this morning – when she...she..." I couldn't bring myself to be more precise – because suddenly everyone was staring at me. I wasn't sure what the police would think about me telling people what I'd seen – but they hadn't said anything about not discussing it. Besides, my experience was mine to share, wasn't it?

Gasps of "You saw her die?" echoed around the room.

Kristine got up. "I'm going to take five, Marco," she said as she turned to her assistant, "would you continue, please? I need to talk to Axelle."

She motioned for me to follow her out of the room and into the corridor. We walked the short distance to the large staircase that swept up from the ground level. On the wide landing at the top of the stairs was a sofa, a couple of armchairs, and, conveniently, a water machine. As if on autopilot Kristine filled a couple of water glasses for us and sat down on the sofa, bidding me to do the same. I discreetly turned on my phone recorder before taking a seat next to her.

"Sorry to drag you out of there like that," sighed Kristine, "but I'm desperate to talk to someone about it all. I still can't believe Elisabetta's gone… And I can't believe you actually saw it happen! That must have been awful! And what about the others at the studio? They must have all flipped out…"

"It was horrible…" I admitted.

"So, because you witnessed the death, you've also been questioned by the police, right?"

I nodded.

"Good. I thought that might be the case. So I'm not saying anything I shouldn't. You know, there are lots of rumours going around already…"

I nodded. "Apparently, some people think she may have even eaten poison on purpose…" I said, pushing for information. "Do you think that's a possibility?"

Kristine shook her head. "The police asked me the same thing, but no. I've known her for years; there's no way Elisabetta was depressed. On the contrary – she was full of life. I always thought of her as a warm smile on high heels. She'd had a rough time over the spring, but I never heard her complain."

"What happened?" I asked carefully.

Kristine sighed again. "She was mugged last winter,

then her apartment was broken into and…I'm not sure I should tell you this, but she did have money troubles, too. She'd mentioned it to me during Fashion Week in New York. She'd had a bit of wine with dinner and it just came out. Not that she told me any details…"

Hmm… "Well, if she didn't eat the poison herself, do you think someone gave it to her deliberately?"

Kristine looked at me, her eyes huge and uneasy. "You're sounding like the police all over again. But like I told them, no way. I mean, that implies murder…"

I looked down the stairs as I answered, avoiding direct eye contact. I didn't want her to feel that I was hanging on her every word. "It's only a theory." I shrugged my shoulders and left it at that.

"Well, it's a ghoulish one," she said. "I feel badly for Ugo, though – the police think the poison came from that plant he has on his terrace, the monkshood. I suppose she could have touched it or something…but I didn't see her stand anywhere near the plant all night."

"How deadly is it?" I asked, playing dumb.

"Very," Kristine assured me. "It can kill anyone, but I'm more at risk than most – I have a sensitivity condition that makes me lethally allergic to that family of plants. That's how I know so much about it. At least the police have crossed me off their list of suspects – the process of getting the poison would have killed me, even if I'd been wearing gloves." She gave a weary smile. "We all knew Ugo had monkshood growing on his terrace, though. I bet if it does turn out that plant provided the poison, the police will label him their main suspect."

Perfect, I thought, Kristine was giving me just the lead in I needed. "Yeah, but a person needs a strong motive to want to hurt someone that way. Did Ugo, or anyone else at his party, have a grudge against Elisabetta?"

"Not that I know of…but I mean, this is the fashion world, right?"

"So?"

"So there's no shortage of rivalry. Ginevra Mucci and Elisabetta, for instance, had a well-known, ongoing feud. And then, actually, there's Ugo, too. I mean, as far as I know – and I've known Ugo for ages – he doesn't have a grudge against Elisabetta. They are best friends. But they had some kind of argument last night and it got quite noisy – or at least Ugo did."

"Really?" Ugo hadn't mentioned a fight to me. "What was it about?" I asked. "And when did it happen?"

"Not too long after we arrived at Ugo's. I didn't notice Ugo and Elisabetta move away until I heard voices coming from another room through an open window. Ginevra and I were talking on the terrace when we heard them, but it stopped quite quickly."

"Did you hear what they were saying?"

"I have no idea what they were arguing about but we could hear Ugo saying, 'Don't do it!' He sounded almost menacing, actually, and very worked up. At one point I heard Elisabetta say, 'I have to.' But that was all I could make out."

"And then what?"

"Ugo and Elisabetta joined us on the terrace, looking as if nothing had happened. They are such old friends that I think everyone assumed it couldn't be serious – you know how old friends are sometimes... Anyway, I remember one of the others joked about the shouting but Elisabetta said that Ugo was only looking out for her and left it at that." Kristine was quiet for a moment before suddenly adding, "Alessandro was upset, I think. He went close to the window when he heard them arguing, as if he wasn't sure whether to interrupt them and stop the row."

"And did he interrupt them?"

Kristine shook her head. "No. He just listened. I understood from little comments he's made that he's jealous of Ugo and Elisabetta's friendship – the one they had, I mean."

"Alessandro was jealous?"

Kristine stood back up and ran her hands over her head. "Yes. Alessandro Matteo and Elisabetta were seeing each other, you know. And he'd become quite possessive recently – always wanting to know what she was up to and who she was seeing. In fact, Elisabetta told me about a month ago that it really bothered her the way Alessandro was always following her around and asking about everything she did."

Again I wondered why Ugo hadn't mentioned their relationship even though Francesca had.

"I've never seen Alessandro so taken with a girlfriend," Kristine continued.

"Will he be coming here for the casting?" I asked.

Fortunately Kristine was too busy with her own thoughts to find my question odd. Without hesitation she answered, "Yes. He should be here at any moment."

Perfect, I thought.

Kristine suddenly stood up, distracting me from my thoughts. "Listen, Axelle, I'm sorry I've talked your ear off, but, apart from the interview with the police, I've been bottling this up inside me all day." She stopped and looked at me. "This whole thing is so, so sad. Anyway, thanks, Axelle, for talking…" She stifled a sudden sob, blew her nose and continued, "Time to get back to work, now." She took a deep breath and we headed back towards the casting room. While we walked the talk turned back to modelling. "By the way, I have to admit, I'm not sure you're right for this show, but you are on option for the Lei-Lei show on Friday. Lei-Lei love you, so they should confirm tomorrow. But show us your walk here anyway. You never know, you might be suitable for Fiore next season."

I walked (in my own clothes) up and down the length of the room for Kristine and the team. Then I went to the impromptu photo set where an assistant was taking a quick photo of each model at the casting. The photos would be used as memory aids by Kristine and her team; they'd be printed immediately via Bluetooth and then pinned on the casting board where everyone could see them. While I waited in a short queue for the photo, I took out my phone and looked up Alessandro online.

Alessandro was Italian, slim, blue-eyed and boyish, with long, dark-blond hair. There were many images of him working for various magazines and catalogues, although, from what I read it seemed he was attempting to phase out of modelling and into acting.

Finally it was my turn to be photographed. It was literally one snap and then, as I walked off set, Alessandro walked in. Perfect timing!

He looked incredibly distraught, but he was a well-known face and a murmur of recognition rippled through the room as he waved at Kristine and headed towards the casting board. While he perused the photos pinned to the board I walked up and introduced myself.

"I'm really, really sorry about Elisabetta, Alessandro. I wouldn't bother you if it wasn't for the fact that I was at Megastudio this morning. I was...I was the last person to see her alive..."

His blue eyes widened as he looked at me. "Oh my God." He took hold of my hand and led me to a quiet corner of the room. "So you saw her just before..." He stopped and took a long, slow breath. "Did she say anything? Did Elisabetta mention me?" He continued to hold my wrist as he spoke. He looked intense, his voice soft, with a lilting Italian accent.

I shook my head. "No, I'm sorry. She'd said she was feeling ill, but we were talking about the shoot and then she gave a kind of cough and just stopped breathing – I didn't realize what had happened at first."

Alessandro suddenly dropped my wrist and leaned back against the wall. "I still can't believe it. We hadn't been together for long, but already she was a huge part of my life. She was a very special person. Everyone loved her…"

"So I've heard."

After a moment he asked, "Did she by any chance mention her plans for tonight?"

His question took me by surprise. "That's funny," I said. "I was about to ask you if *you* knew about her plans for tonight…"

"Ah! So she did say something. Can you tell me what?" He was looking intently at me. Kristine's comment about Alessandro being possessive of Elisabetta came to mind.

"She only mentioned that she had something important to do…"

"That's it?"

I nodded. "I thought you might know more; it might be helpful for the police to know where she was going."

"Yeah, well they've already asked me questions. And I have no idea what important thing she had planned." I saw his fists clench. "She could be secretive, you know. Anyway…" He didn't say more.

"By the way," I quickly asked, "did you hear the argument between Elisabetta and Ugo last night? At his after-party?"

"Yes, I did. We probably all did. Ugo was always interfering in Elisabetta's life. Anyway, how do you know about it?"

"One of the other guests mentioned it." He was restless now and keen to go. Much as I wanted to question him further, I couldn't keep him any longer without raising his suspicion. Hopefully I could find out more about him from other sources. At that moment my phone buzzed. It was a message from Ellie; her fitting had ended. As I put my phone away a Fiore showroom assistant suddenly motioned for Alessandro to follow her, but before leaving he leaned close to me. "Listen, Axelle, if you happen to hear anything more about Elisabetta or what she'd been planning on doing, would you call me?" He quickly dug into his rucksack and pulled out a card with his name and number on it. "I really loved her. I'd appreciate hearing any last memories she may have shared." I watched him as he walked away. His words, I thought, sounded loving, but did his intentions match? Hmm…

I slowly turned, waved to Kristine, and left.

Ellie was waiting for me on the landing where I'd sat with Kristine earlier. "So did you hear anything?" I asked her as we walked down the smooth stone steps.

"Yes, lots actually. Everyone's talking about it. They're saying she was poisoned. Is that true?"

I nodded. "It seems so. At least that's the theory the police are working on. All her symptoms point to it."

"How horrible," Ellie whispered. "And have you found out anything else?"

"Yes." I nodded slowly as I sifted through the information Kristine and Alessandro had shared. Some of the things Ugo had told me – like the fact that Elisabetta hadn't been near the plant – were confirmed by Kristine. But Ugo had neglected to tell me about his argument with Elisabetta. This revelation threw a different – more suspicious – light on Ugo. After all, if he was as innocent as he claimed, why not tell me about their row? Maybe he thought no one else had heard it? Regardless, he was still withholding information – and that always smells fishy. But surely the police would have found out about it from Kristine and Alessandro? And they'd mention it to Ugo sooner or later…I'd have to have a word with him.

But first, dinner – Italian style. I was starving. Besides there was something in particular that I really wanted to try…

* * *

Sebastian and I chose a tiny neighbourhood dive to eat at. It was just around the corner from the Fiore offices and although Ellie had a glamorous fashion party to go to – something Dolce & Gabbana was throwing – she had just enough time to have a quick bite with us before going back to our flat to change. She slid into a chair opposite me at our small table. "I want to know everything," she said. "The D&G party can wait."

As I looked at the blackboard menu of the day the one dish I'd been hoping to find leaped out at me: bruschetta with tomatoes and basil.

"You really want to eat that? From the little you've told us, I'm not sure I can stomach it at the moment," Ellie said as her lips formed a nervous smile. "Besides, the bread won't be gluten free, so I really can't stomach it." I could see she was relieved to have an excuse.

We ordered and then didn't waste any time in diving right into talk about the new case. I started by quickly going over the basics of what Ugo had told me.

"And do you believe him?" Sebastian asked.

I nodded. "I think I do," I said slowly. "But I also have the feeling that he's holding something back – maybe it's to do with the argument? Whatever it's about, though, it kind of fits with the fact that he even called me in the first place."

"How do you mean?" Ellie asked.

"Well, he's a suspect, of course, but beyond that, he's

already convinced that Elisabetta's death is due to foul play – granted that's a theory the police seem to agree with – but, still, he seems so sure about it that it's almost as if he knows something he's not telling anyone."

"Like a reason someone would want to poison her?"

"Yeah, something like that. Only time will tell. But if he's asked me to look into it then he must believe that there's something suspicious about her death...maybe something he doesn't think the police will pick up on. Anyway, what I find interesting is that neither Ugo nor Kristine believe Elisabetta would have intentionally killed herself. And they both say she never went near the plant on Ugo's terrace."

"Which brings us back to the theory that she was intentionally poisoned," Ellie said.

I nodded. "At the moment, the police think she was poisoned last night at around midnight, at Ugo's house." The bruschetta arrived just as I finished speaking.

"Perfect timing," Sebastian smiled.

The bruschetta was tangy and sweet with a nice toasty crunch. The mixture of garlic, olive oil, tomato, basil and thick home-made bread was a good one and I could see why it worked as a snack – the dry bread kept your fingers clean and the slices could be cut to bite-size. Furthermore, as far as foods to hide poison in go, you could do much worse than bruschetta. Ugo was right about the garlic – it would take a strong flavour to override the taste.

"So who could have poisoned her?" Ellie asked.

I pulled out the list Ugo had given me from my rucksack and pushed it across the table towards Ellie and Sebastian. "These are the names of all the people who were at Ugo's party last night. However," I said as I opened my notebook to the second, shorter, list I'd also written earlier, "these are the names I think we should concentrate on first, because these people stayed on after the food had been brought out." We studied the shortlist carefully.

Ugo Anbessa
Francesca Ventini
(Kristine Abrams)
Alessandro Matteo
Ginevra Mucci

"Why are there brackets around Kristine?" Sebastian asked.

"Because she has a condition that makes her lethally allergic to monkshood. Apparently, if she'd given any to Elisabetta she'd have died while handling it – even with gloves on. And, in any case, Ugo didn't see anyone wearing gloves. Also, I've dropped Ugo's housekeeper Maria from this list, even though she stayed late, because my gut tells me she's not the one – at least for now."

"So you've spoken to Ugo and Francesca and you've seen Kristine Abrams," Ellie said.

I nodded. "I also spoke to Alessandro Matteo briefly. And I have an appointment to see Ginevra Mucci tomorrow."

"I've met Alessandro a couple of times," Ellie said. "But I've never worked with him or talked to him. He's hot, though, isn't he?"

"He might be hot but there was something a bit odd about him. He was very curious and in fact a bit upset about the plans Elisabetta had made for *tonight*, whatever they were…" I explained.

"Tonight? But she's dead. Why would her plans for tonight still interest him?" Ellie asked.

"That's exactly what I'm asking myself." I stopped for a moment, remembering the intense look in his eyes as we'd talked about her plans. "Kristine says that Alessandro is the 'jealous type', and that he'd become quite possessive of Elisabetta."

"So maybe Elisabetta had plans to meet someone else? Plans she wouldn't tell him?" Ellie said.

"Maybe," I agreed.

"Well it seems a bit extreme to stay jealous even after someone's died…" Sebastian said.

"The only gossip I've heard about him lately is that he has money trouble. Transitioning into acting hasn't been easy for him," Ellie said.

"That's funny, I heard that Elisabetta was having money trouble, too…Kristine mentioned it."

"Well, I can ask around about him," Ellie volunteered.

"That would be great." I gave Ellie a thumbs up. "I'd really like to know more about his relationship with Elisabetta."

"And I know they're not on your shortlist, but Coco Sommerino D'Alda and her mother, Lavinia, were at Ugo's too, weren't they?" Ellie said.

"Yes, but they left before the food arrived," I said.

"I could help you meet them if you'd like. Maybe they could shed a bit more light on last night?"

"Yes please, Ellie, that would be great. I need to hear as many details about the party as I can."

Ellie nodded. "No problem. I know Coco well; she's always at the big shows – designers love her – and we're often at the same parties. I can call her and set something up for you. In fact, why don't I send her a message now?" Ellie said, taking out her phone.

"Are you going to ask Ugo about his row with Elisabetta?" Sebastian said as he helped himself to the last slice of bruschetta.

"Yes, I must. I'll call him later tonight," I said. "In the meantime did you find anything out about the cards or Marzia?"

"I thought you'd never ask," Sebastian smiled.

I showed the cards to Ellie as Sebastian began. "First of all," he said, "I told the girl on reception at Megastudio that I'd been in Studio Three last week and had lost a grey envelope. As far as she knew no one has said anything about missing any cards – or even just the envelope. Because the studios are kept empty, except for a few pieces of basic furniture – they don't have a lost and found. Anything left behind is normally spotted straight away by the clean-up crews."

"And what about yesterday – Monday? Was the studio busy then?" Ellie asked.

"Yup, there was a small group shooting," Sebastian answered. "But no one has called them to ask about a missing envelope."

Sebastian pulled his notebook from the inside pocket of his leather jacket. "It was beauty products. No live models. The dressing room wasn't used."

"So it seems likely the envelope was forgotten today."

Sebastian nodded. "And if no one has reported them missing, it seems even more likely that they belonged to Elisabetta."

"I agree. I mean, if they're old and valuable they might be part of a collection, and surely, if that's the case, someone would have come forward to claim them?"

"I asked the receptionist to give me a call if anybody mentioned them," Sebastian said. "I don't know if she'll do it, but like you say, it would be interesting to know if anyone does ask after them."

"But do you think the cards have some connection with Elisabetta's death?" Ellie asked.

I shrugged my shoulders. "Who knows? At this point I have no way of linking the two. But it is odd that I found the cards in the studio just next to her. Maybe they *were* hers. Maybe she liked tarot?" I said as I pulled the black card with the dancing skeleton out from behind the other two and pushed it across the table towards Ellie and Sebastian. "And I know enough about tarot to understand that this card represents death."

Ellie looked at me wide-eyed. "Spooky," she said.

"It's called coincidence, Holmes." *Typical Sebastian*, I thought, *ever cool and collected*. "Besides, it's just a card. It looks black and morbid because it was made to give people the creeps."

"True, Watson." I shrugged my shoulders. "But as for it being a coincidence, hmm…" My grandfather's words swirled through my mind.

An incident that appears to be coincidence is often some kind of plan masquerading as chance.

For a few moments we each sat lost in our own thoughts. The sight of the grinning skeleton seemed to cast a spine-tingling shadow over our table. Abruptly, I reached for one of the other cards and covered the figure of death with the blonde lady on her white horse. I took a quick breath and straightened up. "Whatever these cards were doing in the studio this morning, if they're valuable someone might be looking for them. So…"

It was time to start on some research. As our pasta

arrived, I pulled my tablet out of my rucksack and typed "tarot cards" into the Google search window.

"You said 'so', Holmes, but never finished your thought..." Sebastian said, as he speared a few penne onto his fork. Even in the harsh lighting of the restaurant he looked sun-kissed. I forced myself to ignore his tanned forearms and concentrate on our conversation.

I smiled. "True, Watson. What I meant to say was, so, either the tarot cards and Elisabetta are two separate mysteries, or..."

"Or?" Ellie asked.

"Or they're one and the same..."

As we ate, Ellie and Sebastian discussed different theories about Elisabetta's death, while I spent most of the time researching tarot cards. I clicked on "images" first. The cards came in all sorts of different designs, and, rather amazingly, the ones I'd found resembled some of the earliest cards still in existence, dating back to the fifteenth century.

Could they really be as old as that? I wondered. The thought that I might have been carrying something so precious around in my rucksack all day, was quite shocking. I stopped searching on my tablet for a moment, and stared at the cards.

"Earth to Axelle," Sebastian said. "You look like you're zoning out. What's going on?"

"Look," I said, handing him my tablet.

I watched as Sebastian and Ellie studied the images on

the screen. "Wow. They're a lot like your cards," Ellie said.

"And like on your cards, the imagery on these is also very medieval," Sebastian said.

"Precisely. Now scroll down and read what's there."

Sebastian read out loud:

"The Arcimboldo-Crivelli deck of tarot cards was commissioned by the rich Milanese banker, Galeazzo Arcimboldo to celebrate his marriage to the Venetian beauty and aristocrat, Nicolosia Crivelli, in 1445. The cards were painted by the famous Florentine painter, Piero Vasari. Today, thirty-seven of the original cards from this deck are part of the collection of fine art at the Pinacoteca di Brera, in Milan, Italy. Twenty more are at Yale University, USA, with the known remainder in private hands. The original deck probably consisted of up to seventy cards. Originally a card game for the nobility, tarot became popular as a tool for divination in the eighteenth century. The Arcimboldo-Crivelli deck, together with the Visconti-Sforza deck of 1443 (also Milanese), is considered to be the direct ancestor of today's tarot cards."

Ellie and Sebastian both looked at me with wide eyes.

"I know, right?" I said. "What if those cards," I pointed to the middle of the table, "are that old? They even look as if they could be a part of that deck." I quickly and carefully put the cards away – the last thing they needed was tomato sauce splashed on them.

"And what a coincidence that that deck was made here, in Milan," Ellie said.

"Actually, according to the articles I've just been reading, the first known documented tarot cards were from Milan. I think we should start trying to find out more about these cards. I wonder if there's a tarot expert somewhere in the city…"

I picked my tablet back up and did a quick search, but the names I found were only for experts at tarot card *readings*.

"Well it could be fun to give it a go," Ellie laughed. "You could ask them if you're going to solve this case!"

"Ha ha," I said, I rolling my eyes. "Seriously, though, I have to have the cards appraised by an expert." I continued to search as I spoke. "If they are as valuable as I think they might be, then why hasn't their owner stepped forward to claim them?"

"Maybe because their owner is dead?"

"For someone who believes in simple coincidence, it sounds to me as if you're starting to see life in more complex patterns, Watson."

Sebastian smiled as he leaned back in his chair and watched me through half-closed eyes. He looked totally yummy – until a vision of him with Francesca came to mind, that is. I felt a fleeting pang of jealousy (yeah, I could sort of admit it – but only to myself).

Ellie finished her plate of gluten-free *linguine alle vongole* and got ready to leave. "I won't be back late tonight, Axelle. I've an early start tomorrow morning for the new Armani

Exchange campaign. See you later, guys." She dropped some money on the table, slipped her large slouchy bag over her shoulder and left the restaurant, oblivious to the admiring glances that followed her.

Sebastian immediately brought the subject around to Elisabetta's assistant, Marzia. "Okay, so after Megastudio I dropped into the *Amare* offices – they're not that far from here. Marzia will definitely be in tomorrow."

"Great. So I'll make sure I 'bump' into her while I'm there."

At that moment Sebastian's phone rang.

"It's Francesca," he said, looking at the screen with a smile. "I'd better take it quickly if you don't mind."

"But we're discussing the case," I said, trying not to sound snappy.

"Yeah, well she might have some more information," Sebastian said as the phone continued buzzing in his hand.

"What could she possibly say to you now that she couldn't have said earlier?" Now I definitely sounded irritated. I kicked myself for it.

"*Pronto*, Francesca," Sebastian answered.

What? Now he was even talking in Italian to her!

"Yes, I'm alone," he said into the phone as he smiled at me and headed towards the door of the restaurant. I heard the bell chime as the door shut behind him.

Grrr!

Sebastian came back a couple of minutes later. "Sorry about that but we had to make plans. We're going to meet tomorrow at three. There's more she'd like to discuss."

"Like what exactly?"

Sebastian shrugged his shoulders. "If I don't meet her I won't know, will I?"

He leaned back and smiled looking thoroughly pleased with himself. "Even you have to admit that the more I find out the better."

I stopped myself from rolling my eyes. "By the way, three is not great. We were thinking of checking out the Parco Sempione then, remember?"

"Oh…right. Well, I'll have to take a rain check on that, Holmes. I think it's more important to concentrate on this case, don't you?" His brow creased and he looked genuinely concerned. So he was still playing that game!

It took all of my self-control to calmly say, "Fine, Watson. You meet Francesca at three and I'll go to the park on my own and then carry on with my castings."

"Good."

"Fine."

After a moment of awkward silence, which was only broken by the group getting up from the table next to ours, Sebastian and I decided to go.

"And by the way," I said as we left the restaurant, "I'd like to ask Francesca a few more questions myself. Maybe tomorrow?"

"You don't seriously think you're going to find out more than I will, do you?" snapped Sebastian.

I stopped to look at him and then threw his own words right back at him. "If I don't meet her I won't know, will I?"

Annoyance flashed in Sebastian's eyes. He started to say something but then thought better of it. Finally he muttered, "Fine."

"Good."

Mrs B was waiting up for me. As Sebastian and I drove up to the door I could see the curtain twitch in her sitting-room window next to the street entrance of the building. In the darkness, I could just make out a blurry face peering from behind the curtain.

The street was quiet and things were awkward again between Sebastian and me. I know Ellie is always telling me that my mysteries are complicated...but, seriously, if you ask me, it's *guys* that are complicated.

I pulled off my helmet and handed it to Sebastian for safekeeping until tomorrow. "She's still watching, isn't she?" I said with a nudge of my chin towards the window.

Sebastian nodded as he slipped his helmet off, too. "I'll walk you to the door."

I was still too cross to want to kiss Sebastian at this point – although, for all I knew, maybe he didn't want to kiss me either. In any case, I never found out what his intentions were because as we walked towards the door his phone buzzed again.

"It's from the receptionist I saw at Megastudio." He looked at me, his eyes wide.

"And?"

"She's only just left – one of the studios was shooting late. She says she had a call from someone wanting to know if they'd found some tarot cards, possibly in a small packet, in Studio Three today…"

I stared at Sebastian. "So someone really is after the cards. Any idea who?"

Sebastian shook his head and handed me his phone. The message ended with a relatively friendly *you asked me to let you know, so I am*. Then there was a smiley emoji and that was it.

I was about to ask Sebastian to call her back, but he was on it before the words were out of my mouth.

"No name was given and the voice was unrecognizable," reported Sebastian as soon as he came off the phone. "Daniela – that's the receptionist – couldn't even be sure whether it was a man or a woman who'd called. The whole thing lasted about ten seconds and the caller hung up as soon as Daniela said that nothing had been found."

"Well it was nice of her to let us know…"

"She likes me," Sebastian smiled.

Yeah, and she's not the only one, I thought, as a vision of Francesca's sultry glances came to mind.

"Anyway, Watson, knowing about that call really gives this case a whole new spin."

"How so?"

"Well, if the person who called owned the cards then why didn't they say so? Why not say, 'Hi, I'm so and so and I lost some tarot cards this morning in Studio Three. If you see them please call me on this number so that I can pick them up.' But the caller was anonymous and didn't say anything like that. It was all cloak-and-dagger. Anonymous, mysterious, and, therefore, I can only think, suspicious."

"Good point, Holmes. I agree, anyone with any kind of legitimate claim to the cards would have given their name and number."

"Exactly. So who is interested in the cards?"

"And why?"

"And how did they know that the cards were in the studio this morning if it was someone else who lost them?"

My mind was racing. Someone knew about the cards and someone wanted them enough to risk raising suspicion by calling Megastudio on the same day that Elisabetta had died.

"I've got to find out what's so special about those cards." I stood, silent for a moment, remembering what I'd read earlier while at the restaurant.

"What are you thinking, Holmes?"

"I'm thinking that I should start my day tomorrow by checking out the antique *tarocchi* cards at the Pinacoteca museum. I think I read that it opens at eight-thirty in the morning. Will you meet me there?"

"Would you like me to?" His eyes held mine.

"Yes, I would."

His eyes didn't soften, but he did smile. "Good, then I'll see you at the Pinacoteca at eight-thirty. Anything I should look into?"

"Actually…yes. Kristine mentioned something about Elisabetta being mugged this spring – and her apartment was also burgled. And she said Elisabetta had some money trouble, but she didn't know any details."

"So you want me to look into those three things?"

"I'd appreciate it, yes."

A lock turned as I spoke and Mrs B's face suddenly peered out at us from behind the door to my building – she didn't look to be in a particularly friendly mood.

Without another word, Sebastian and I went our separate ways. Our day was over as quickly as it had begun. Before going to bed, however, there were a couple of phone calls I had to make. I opened my list of contacts and found the New York number I needed. I hadn't seen her in a while, but I was sure she'd spare me the time to answer a few questions.

"Hey, Axelle, Ms Detective! What's up? I'm in Miami – woohoo, *Miii-ami*! Just landed. What about you?" Rafaela Cruz, the caramel-eyed, long-limbed New York City native and tattooed supermodel gave a hoot of laughter at the other end of the phone. I could practically feel her clap my back in that way she had. I'd forgotten how she'd taken to calling me Ms Detective. When we'd worked together this spring in the Big Apple she'd been convinced that I'd been helping to find a missing diamond. In fact, she'd been right, and her instincts about my reasons for questioning her had been spot on. Not that I confirmed it then – and I certainly wasn't going to now either.

"Hi, Rafaela, I'm in Milan, working...but something has happened and I'm hoping you can help me..." I briefly explained about Elisabetta.

"Wow. That's horrible. No, I hadn't heard about it," she said. "I've only just stepped off the plane." For a moment she actually sounded at a loss for words. "I can't believe it – I was with her last night. I went by Ugo Anbessa's after-party before leaving to catch my night flight here..." She went quiet for a moment. "Oh, wow, I've just spotted some emails from my Milan agency – they're asking me to contact the Milan police as soon as possible."

"They'll want to ask you about Ugo's after-party..."

We chatted for a while and Rafaela confirmed that she'd heard the fight between Elisabetta and Ginevra. "Then again," Rafaela added, "so what? It was just a fight, we all do it sometimes, you know what I mean?"

She hadn't, however, heard the disagreement between Ugo and Elisabetta. She'd left early, with her boyfriend 5Zentz and hadn't even seen the food arrive. And she definitely hadn't seen Elisabetta touching Ugo's monkshood plant.

"What about 5Zentz? Did he see Elisabetta touch the plant?" I quickly asked, hoping she wouldn't get suspicious of my questions.

"I don't know – but here, why don't you ask him? My suitcase has just come out on the carousel. I've gotta go!" I was abruptly handed to 5Zentz.

I briefly introduced myself, and asked him if he'd seen Elisabetta go near the monkshood plant. "Nah! But then again, I was checking out Ugo's place. That is one super-cool crib! He's killin' it!"

Not a great choice of words, I thought, considering that Ugo was a prime suspect. I asked if he'd heard the fight between Elisabetta and Ginevra. He had, but only because he'd been checking out a painting on the wall near them. "They were fierce – woowee, Italian women can be feisty! And speaking of feisty, here comes—" 5Zentz didn't get a chance to finish his sentence – Rafaela's voice suddenly boomed down the line.

"Axelle? You still there?"

I thanked her for her time and tried to get off the phone before she turned the questions on me, but I wasn't quick enough. Before I managed to end our conversation she said, "I can smell something, Axelle, I'm telling you. You were acting like Nancy Drew in New York and now you're doing it again. Hmm…one of these days I'm gonna have to get the whole story out of you. You're hiding something and I can feel it…" She laughed, but I admitted nothing.

This wasn't the time to feed her fire.

"I was there when it happened this morning," I explained, "that's all."

"Uh huh. Sure. And I've never walked down a runway." She laughed at her own joke. "Well, I look forward to hearing what happened from *you*. I have a feeling it won't be long before you know more about it than anyone else – including the cops." Then she laughed again, told me to call her when I was next in New York, and we hung up.

Next I called Ugo.

"Progress, already?" he said.

"Actually, Ugo, I have a couple of questions for you… First of all, why didn't you tell me that Elisabetta and Alessandro Matteo were going out together?"

I could practically feel him roll his eyes over the phone line. "Probably denial on my part. I can't stand the guy, to be honest. And, anyway, Elisabetta, *grazie a Dio*, was on the verge of breaking up with him. He was the stereotypical jealous Italian guy, you know? He always wanted to know where she was going and what she was doing. It really started to bother Elisabetta – that's why she wanted to break up."

"How long had they been going out? And where did they meet?"

"They met at Falco's. Falco loved Alessandro, you know, he booked him for all of his shows and campaigns. They got together when they were working on Falco's last collection. And they were inseparable while Falco was in hospital. In fact, they often went there together."

"So in the beginning, anyway, she was happy with Alessandro?"

"I think so. We didn't talk about it that much at first – I think for Elisabetta he was just a fun affair. But then he always wanted to be with her, to know about everything she was doing."

Thinking about love as a powerful motive for murder, I asked, "Did he know that she wanted to break up with him? Had she told him?"

"Yes, I think she'd tried to, but he'd gone bananas so she was waiting for the right time before making the final break."

I wanted to ask Ugo about his argument with Elisabetta, but I thought maybe that was best handled in person so that I could judge his answers more carefully. So I thanked him and we agreed to meet the following day.

I took my tablet and notebook and slipped into bed. I checked my emails – Tomasso had managed to squeeze another go-see with a photographer into my schedule for the next day. I quickly noted the details and then started background searches on the suspects on my shortlist. I didn't get far though. I was asleep faster than you can say *lip gloss*.

WEDNESDAY MORNING

Flirting with Danger

I woke up early, the vision of Elisabetta's glassy stare jolting me from my sleep. I'd been so tired last night that I'd slept dreamlessly. But as I slowly surfaced, yesterday's events began to rewind in my head.

To push away the rising sense of panic I told myself that everything was fine, that I was in Milan, in a flat I was sharing with Ellie – who I hadn't even heard come in last night. I took a deep slow breath and stretched. My bedside clock said 6 a.m. I got out of bed and padded out of my room and across the corridor to Ellie's door. I opened it quietly and saw, with relief, her long, slim limbs sprawled across the bed. Her thick, nearly waist-length blonde hair spilled across her pillow and I smiled as I looked at her face, without a trace of make-up. Ellie always said, "Rule number one for good skin is to remove all make-up before going to bed – always."

Feeling better, I shut Ellie's door

and went back to my room. Despite the blackout blinds on my bedroom window, the early morning sun leaked in around its edges. I pulled up the blind and smiled as the Milanese sun flooded my bedroom. Nothing could dispel uneasy thoughts more rapidly than sunlight, I thought, as I opened the window to let in the morning air.

I slipped on my blue kimono dressing gown (a present from my dad last Christmas) and grabbed my tablet. After settling down on my bed with my pillows stacked behind me I clicked online and, sure enough, quickly found the first reports of Elisabetta's death – and an email from my mum asking me about it. She was trying to seem casual, but I could read between the lines: she hoped I wasn't getting involved. I quickly wrote back, praying to the detective gods that Mum would buy my claim that Italian culture was eating up all my free time. Which it sort of was – if you included poison and murder as culture. As I emailed Mum I made a note to myself to take some selfies with monuments or paintings in the background that I could send her as proof. Then I turned back to the reports of Elisabetta's death.

There wasn't a lot of detail – it seemed the police hadn't released anything other than the most basic information about the case. The various reports I read mentioned that she'd died while working on an *Amare* photo shoot, that it had been sudden and that cause of death was still to be determined. No other details of the shoot were given – although there were plenty of pictures: Elisabetta at the fashion shows, editorials she'd styled for top magazines, and Elisabetta together with various fashion industry hotshots – including Ugo and Falco Ventini.

After I'd read a number of reports, I resumed the background checks that I'd started last night – not that I found anything helpful. Even after carefully sifting through masses of information not one single rumour came up suggesting bad blood or any weird tensions between the suspects on the list and Elisabetta. I found a piece about the feud between Ginevra and Elisabetta – but from the way it was presented, it didn't sound serious. And although there were a few pictures of Elisabetta and Alessandro together, there was no suggestion of his jealousy or their impending break-up. And yet surely one of them must have had a motive? One of them had wanted her dead.

Time flew past and when I stopped to look at the clock on my tablet it was already 7.30. I had to meet Sebastian at the Pinacoteca in an hour. I quickly scanned my to-do list.

Wednesday:
8.30 a.m. Meet Sebastian at the Pinacoteca di Brera for tarot card research
10 a.m. Cutie-Pie fitting
10.45 a.m. Meet photographer Antonio Moretti
11.30 a.m. Amare go-see with Ginevra Mucci (and try to see Marzia)
12.15 p.m. Meet Sebastian. See the Duomo? Have

lunch. Parco Sempione (alone). More sightseeing?
4 p.m. Miu Miu casting (for campaign)
4.45 p.m. Italian Elle *general go-see*
5.30 p.m. Gucci casting (for campaign) – plus
possibility of tracking down Alessandro for further
questioning?

My day would be busy but there was some time in between the various appointments to follow up on whatever new leads I might find over the course of the day – and to squeeze some sightseeing in with Sebastian. Before and after his appointment with Francesca, at least.

I stopped any thoughts about *her* from bubbling to the surface and rushed to get ready. I hopped into the bath, grabbed a quick breakfast and, before leaving, I stopped and made plans to meet up with Ellie later.

"Well, I'll be on location all day, but don't forget that we're going to Rocco Rosa's book launch tonight. It starts at 7 p.m.," Ellie said as she towel-dried her hair.

I'd already completely forgotten!

Now that Ellie had said it I sort of remembered Tomasso mentioning the launch on Monday. It was one of *the* parties of Milan Men's Fashion Week, and I hadn't planned on going, which probably explained the memory lapse. Ellie watched me purse my lips.

"Show me your list of names again," she said. I pulled it out of my rucksack. "Well, Ginevra Mucci will definitely be there and so will Coco – and her mother Lavinia. Oh yeah! I saw Coco at the Dolce & Gabbana party last night. She's *so* talkative – it shouldn't be a problem to grill her for information on Ugo's after-party."

"Great! Then I guess I will go tonight after all."

Ellie laughed. "I swear you're the only person I've ever met who has to be dragged along to anything that seems even the least bit glamorous. My little sisters and their friends would give anything to go tonight."

"Well, so would I – as long as there's a suspect there," I laughed.

Ellie threw the towel she'd been drying her hair with over my head. "See you tonight. We can go together from here."

I hadn't washed my hair, but it was all right. The humidity in Milan kept it bouncy so I wasn't going to encourage the frizz by washing it until I really had to – that was something I'd learned. As a model you're supposed to arrive at your location with clean hair in the morning, but, often, if I'm working with the same crew for a couple of days, the hairstylist will ask me *not* to wash my hair for the second day because, actually, hair with a bit of grime in it is easier to work with and has more texture. With that thought in mind I ran my hands through my hair as I hurried down the stairs, hoping it would look good enough when I got to my castings later.

As I flew out of the building and into the courtyard I

caught sight of myself in the large mirror at the bottom of the stairs. I was wearing light, loose-fitting khaki trousers that Ellie had found for me at a New York Army and Navy store, a fitted T-shirt in pale, washed-out peach, Converse (white, and with some DIY doodles I'd drawn on them) and I carried my black leather quilted rucksack on my back. Of course, I was wearing my glasses. And I still had the dark purple nail polish I'd used for the shoot on Monday. My mum would have made me change into something more dressy, but one good thing about modelling is that the clients actually like it when models show up with their own sense of style intact. It said something about your personality.

I was running late so I hopped into a super-clean underground station. Everything in Milan is a lot smaller than at home in London so it takes a lot less time to find your way around. Within fifteen minutes I was climbing the stairs out of the Montenapoleone station, right in the heart of Milan's chicest shopping district, and in another five minutes I was standing outside the formidable-looking tall brick exterior of the Pinacoteca museum.

Sebastian was waiting for me. And although we were both clearly keen to start hunting down clues, yesterday's awkwardness still hung in the air between us. We kissed quickly and hurried inside. "I'm super excited about seeing the tarot cards," I said. "I really hope they can shed some light on the case."

We walked silently through the large entrance of the

former convent and looked around. An enormous bronze statue of Napoleon Bonaparte standing on a plinth (he was all ripped muscles and naked apart from a strategically placed fig leaf) was positioned in the middle of a dazzling white quadrangle. Open galleries ran along the four sides of the inner courtyard. And because the Pinacoteca is also a university, it was buzzing with people.

We crossed the quadrangle (I took a selfie on the way) and entered a large doorway opposite the main street entrance. There I found a woman at a desk and told her we were looking for the Arcimboldo-Crivelli deck of tarot cards; she'd heard of the cards, but had no idea where they were. She suggested I go to the library and waved her hand at the corridor just behind us.

"Time is ticking and I want to see those cards," I said as I pushed my way through the throng of people.

"Well, let's hope they're in here," Sebastian said as we passed a sign that read *Biblioteca Nazionale Braidense*. We climbed an imposing staircase and then turned into a small wood-panelled antechamber. There a clerk directed us to the most astonishing library I've ever seen. It was like a ballroom – lined with books. It felt as if I was stepping onto a set for *Beauty and the Beast*. Wooden bookcases lined every wall from floor to ceiling and they were full to bursting with old leather-bound tomes. A spiral staircase led to a gallery that ran along all four sides of the room. High above us hung two enormous crystal chandeliers, their electric candles blazing with light. I had to take another quick selfie.

In the middle of the library were old-fashioned wooden display cases. Sebastian and I split up and took a look at everything in them – but still no cards. I glanced at my watch. It was just past nine – I had to speed this up, I had a fitting at ten. I searched for help and finally found it in an equally impressive reading room just off the library. The librarian in charge, however, wouldn't let me in. I'd need a day pass to read and study in the room.

"Actually," I said, "I'm here to see the tarot cards in the collection."

She didn't understand me. I tried mentioning Arcimboldo-Crivelli and the librarian said, "Ah! *Tarocchi!* You want to see the *tarocchi* cards?"

Normally, she explained, only experts had access to the cards and even then special permission was needed. I didn't know what to say. I had to see the cards!

"*Ma siete fortunati,*" she continued with a smile, when she saw my crestfallen expression.

I had no idea what she meant but I suddenly heard Sebastian's voice behind me. "*Fortunati? Come?*"

"*Sì,*" she said excitedly, continuing to speak Italian at top speed. I watched as Sebastian spoke with her – good thing he was there to translate.

"She says you're lucky because the cards from the collection are on display at the moment in the Palazzo Reale.

They're part of an exhibition about the great Renaissance patrons of Milan and the artwork they commissioned."

I couldn't believe my ears! We thanked her for the information and three minutes later Sebastian and I were briskly walking out of the Pinacoteca.

"By the way, Watson," I asked as Sebastian opened our guidebook at the map of the city centre, "since when did you speak Italian?"

"I don't. But I studied Spanish in school and they are quite similar." He smiled and pointed in the direction we had to go. "Let's walk there. It's very close and at least we won't have to worry about parking the scooter."

The Palazzo Reale, or Royal Palace, was next to the Duomo. As we hurried along the tiny pedestrian streets just outside of the Pinacoteca I asked Sebastian if he'd found out anything about Elisabetta's mugging, flat burglary and financial trouble.

"Yes to the first two," he answered. "She did report the mugging and break-in but there were no details apart from the dates – and yes, both happened this spring. Neither were really pursued. I got the feeling she only filled in the paperwork for the sake of her insurance and to renew her ID."

I nodded. "And her finances?"

"I'm still working on that. There's nothing online about it and, of course, I can't get hold of her bank records. But I'll keep digging."

"And I'll keep asking."

We were walking briskly through another pretty pedestrian street when I caught sight of a small card table set up on the pavement. A sign on the tattered red tablecloth covering the rickety table read: "Tarocchi/tarot".

"Want to come back for a reading later?" teased Sebastian.

I was about to answer when I caught the eye of the brightly dressed woman (with equally brightly coloured hair) sitting at the table. She was obviously the reader. And while, for all I knew, she may have been the best reader in the world, her black eyes, set like dark stones in her wrinkled face, scared me. I felt as if she could read my mind, and didn't like what she saw.

"Actually, Sebastian," I said, "I think I'll pass."

At the Palazzo Reale we found the posters for the exhibition. Sebastian laughed as he watched me take yet another selfie in front of the palace entrance. "What are you doing, Holmes? I've never seen you take so many selfies! Are you finally falling in love with modelling?"

"Ha, ha, very funny, Watson. Clearly, if your powers of deduction were up to scratch, you'd have guessed that the pics are for my mum. If I show her all these photos she'll relax and assume I'm taking in the culture for once… I don't want her to get suspicious."

"Good thinking," he laughed as he took my phone and took a couple of pictures for me.

We made our way inside the former palace and entered the exhibition space. It was composed of a series of linked rooms, with walls painted in dark, dramatic jewel-like tones, while the lighting stayed dim to protect the artwork. Each room was dedicated to a particular form of art: paintings, tapestries, jewellery and more – but still no tarot cards. I was starting to worry that the librarian had made a mistake when we walked into one of the last rooms. There, in a glass display case that took up almost an entire wall, were the tarot cards.

The metallic paint of the images twinkled like tiny jewels – even in the dimmed lighting. Angels, cherubs, castles, queens, knights, jokers, ivory towers, white horses, magicians, devils, huntsman and hermits – the cards seemed to cast a spell through the thick glass, their visual power still potent despite the passing of nearly six hundred years.

A tingle of excitement crept up my spine as I realized that the cards I'd found looked identical in style and size to the ones on display – at least as far as my untrained eye could tell. The article I'd read had said that a few of the cards from this deck were still in private hands. Maybe some of the missing cards were in my hands?

"They really look like the ones you found," Sebastian said as he stared at the display case.

I nodded. "They do. No wonder someone wanted to claim them… But if they are very valuable, why were they left at the studio yesterday? We've got to find an expert who knows about antique *tarocchi*."

I was frustrated that we hadn't found any useful information in the exhibition, but as we left and walked through the gift shop, a table selling modern-day packs of tarot cards caught my eye. Some of the packs were quite cheap and the size of normal playing cards, but others were expensive, deluxe versions printed on very thick paper – copies of the antique *tarocchi* we had just seen. I looked more closely at the stickers on the boxes and realized they were all supplied by the same store in Milan – a store that specialized in tarot cards. I went to find a salesperson.

"Yes, the store is just near here," she said in perfect English. "It is the most famous *tarocchi* shop in Milan." That was all I needed to hear. Thirty seconds later Sebastian and I were outside and running.

Tarot decks of all kinds were arranged around the store and books about tarot and the occult lined one entire wall. The shop even advertised lessons in how to read tarot and the names of professionals who would give a private reading.

The owner introduced himself in heavily accented, but very correct and careful English. He reminded me of Rumpelstiltskin from the fairy tale. Bent at the back, with a long white beard and whiskers coming out of his ears, his vivid blue eyes nonetheless twinkled with interest at my question. And this time I spoke straight away of *tarocchi* – and not tarot.

"An expert in *tarocchi*?" he said slowly as he pulled at his beard. "If it was straightforward modern tarot I could help you, but you mean the old cards, I think – the antique ones?"

I nodded.

"Then there's only one person in the city who really knows about them." He opened up an old, dog-eared address book and wrote down a name and address on a slip of paper. "Here," he said. "If he can't help you, no one can. He's in the Brera, in a small office at street level. It's only open in the mornings – he closes at 12.30. He's actually a world authority on Italian Renaissance art. *Tarocchi* is only a side interest for him, but he'll be happy to help you if he can. He knows his stuff. Some of my clients are serious collectors; I send them all to Thaddeus."

Thaddeus Greene, PhD, D.A.
Professor of Renaissance Art

That, I thought, explained why I hadn't found him. As an expert in Renaissance art of course he wouldn't have come up under listings about tarot cards.

"Greene isn't a very Italian name," I pointed out.

"That's because he's American – it's his wife who's Italian."

So at least he speaks good English, I thought. I thanked the shopkeeper and we left. I had exactly fifteen minutes to get to my Cutie-Pie casting. Luckily we were only two minutes away from the subway I needed.

"So when should we meet?" Sebastian asked.

"How about 12.15 at Professor Greene's office? I should have just enough time to get there after my *Amare* appointment at 11.30."

"Why don't I pick you up at *Amare*? I can be outside the building by quarter to twelve."

"Perfect," I said.

We reached the subway. "And is there anything else I can look into while you're at the meeting?"

"Yes please," I said. "I need background checks. We've got to dig deeper. Somewhere there must be a motive that explains why Elisabetta was poisoned at a party full of her friends."

I slipped my rucksack over my shoulder and waved to Sebastian as I ran down the stairs and into the subway.

Tomasso called me as I reached my platform. "Axelle, what a beautiful day for doing castings! Sunny and not too hot." (Clearly he wasn't English – *I* found it very hot!) "If you have any problems with anything just call me – oh, and don't forget to check your email for updates! And I'll text you if something important comes up, okay?" With his heavy Italian accent, Tomasso's "okay" had three syllables – *o-kay-ay*. "Good luck with your Cutie-Pie fitting. *Ciao bella!*"

I was already confirmed for the Cutie-Pie shoot and it was scheduled for the next day, but the client had called me in to make sure that the clothes fitted me well. This way, if anything needed adjusting, they could do it in time for the morning. As it turned out they'd been right to call me in – the clothes were enormous.

"Hmmm…" said the stylist as she stood back, looking at me, her hand grasping a handful of fabric at the back of the jacket I'd been asked to try on. "You are so small, Axelle."

I am so small? How about the clothes are cut way too big?

A model has to deal with this kind of comment all the time – and, of course, it's never, ever the client's fault. It's always, *You're too big for our clothes* or *You're too small for our clothes. Your feet aren't big enough,* or *Your feet are too large.* Even worse is, *Hmm…your skin's too dark for this job* or *too light.* I'd even heard, *I'm not sure about the shape of your mouth.*

It's enough to make me scream, *SHUT UP! I'M PERFECT AS I AM!*

The worst is that the comments are often made right in front of you as if you don't exist. Like now.

"You really are small," the stylist continued as I rolled my eyes and held my tongue. I wanted to say that she and the powers-that-be at Cutie-Pie had already seen my zed card, with my measurements clearly printed on it, *before* they booked me, so they all knew *exactly* what size I am!

She finally stopped her belly-aching, called an in-house seamstress and started pinning a little bit here and there until all the clothes I'd be wearing on tomorrow's shoot had been sent away with the seamstress. Finally, after three-quarters of an hour I was free to go. "See you tomorrow, Axelle," the stylist said with a wave as I turned and left. "It should be a great campaign."

Whatever.

I was now running late for my appointment with Antonio Moretti, the photographer, but Tomasso called to warn him that I was still fifteen minutes away, so it wasn't a problem. Antonio's office was located in the lively Navigli district of Milan just outside the old city centre, an area criss-crossed with old canals.

We had a bit of a chat, and Antonio carefully went through every photo in my book. He took a couple of pictures of me to show a client he had for an upcoming job and that was it.

I only had one more appointment before lunch, and that was at *Amare* to see Ginevra Mucci and hopefully, Marzia, too.

Ginevra Mucci was the exact physical opposite of her now dead arch-rival Elisabetta Rinconi – and their personal styles couldn't have been more different either. Tall and lanky with broad shoulders and thick, dark, shoulder-length hair, hers was a tough, no-nonsense style – in contrast to Elisabetta's, which could be described as light, charming, even whimsical. She was dressed in black jeans: a black silk blouse and black stiletto-heeled ankle boots. A very cool skinny belt shimmering with metal studs circled her waist. This, too, contrasted Elisabetta's more Bohemian approach, I thought, remembering the outfit Elisabetta had worn at the studio the day before.

Ginevra wanted to see me for an upcoming *Amare* editorial she was casting. It was a story about coats – but inspired by the style of famous female rock singers from the 1960s and 70s like Joan Jett, Janis Joplin and Stevie Nicks (yeah, I'd had to google them, too). Apparently, Ginevra seemed to think that I'd be a natural fit for channelling Joan Jett in particular. "There's something about your attitude," she said as she went through my book.

Ah! I thought. *Just the lead I need.* Remembering what I'd heard about Ginevra accusing Elisabetta of copying her I said, "Ginevra, I love your magazine editorials, you know. I don't really understand how people can confuse your way of styling with Elisabetta Rinconi's. There's been a lot of talk about it online since she…" I quickly looked up to the ceiling and asked the detective gods to forgive me for talking about Elisabetta like this, but I had to get information out of Ginevra. "Anyway, I know some people think that you might have copied Elisabetta's ideas but it's often looked to me as if she copied you."

The rivalry Ugo and Kristine had told me about was

obviously still alive and kicking because Ginevra immediately responded.

"Yeah, well, people will say things. But I started styling before Elisabetta so, naturally, I'm sure she was more than a little influenced by me – not that *she* ever admitted it. In fact, a lot of her well-known campaigns were directly inspired by editorials I'd already done. Like the all-red campaign she styled for Cutie-Pie – that was *completely* lifted from an all-red story I did years ago for *Dazed* magazine. *Completely*." Ginevra said all of this calmly; her tone of voice didn't change as she slowly and methodically turned the pages of my portfolio. And yet when she looked up and handed me my book, her hatred for Elisabetta still lingered in her expression, like a simmering cauldron of, well, poison. I grabbed my book and pulled my hand back from her as quickly as I could. She suddenly made me think of Halloween. I swallowed and pushed forward with my questions.

"You were at Ugo's, weren't you, on Monday night, the night she was poisoned? How horrible to have witnessed it all!"

"Actually, there was nothing to see," Ginevra said as she grabbed her desk phone and called her secretary. She barked a few orders down the line and continued our conversation as soon as she put the phone down. "We went to Ugo's, we had fun and then we left. End of story."

"They say that someone must have tampered with the

food. Put something into the bruschetta, for example, and given it to Elisabetta."

"Please! It's all so preposterous. The food wasn't served until quite late and then it was on the table in front of us all, so I don't know how they think someone could have just slipped some poison onto the food unnoticed. Even then, how could they make sure Elisabetta took the poisoned food and no one else did, because no one else was affected?

"No, if you ask me, I think Elisabetta went on another one of her famous benders. She must have gone home and done some drugs or something. Anyway, I'm sure it will all come out in the tests they're running."

"But I heard she hadn't partied hard in years."

"Right. And Valentino claims he invented the colour red."

Clearly, I thought, the idea that Elisabetta had cleaned her habits up in the last few years hadn't made much of an impression on Ginevra.

She stood up from her desk and motioned for me to follow her to the door. "I have to go now. But it was good to see you – I'll call Tomasso about the booking."

As soon as Ginevra left, I headed back to the reception desk and asked to see Marzia. A minute or two later the receptionist led me down a corridor through a door to a large room with clothes everywhere, in boxes, hanging on racks, or waiting to be steamed. This was obviously the space where clothes were packed and unpacked after a shoot or when they arrived from a fashion house.

"Axelle!" Marzia said as soon as she saw me.

"I was here to see Ginevra and thought I'd just come by and say hello and see how you were feeling after yesterday."

She nodded and gave a weak smile. "Thank you, I should have stayed at home today really, but I can't relax wherever I am. It was all so horrible, so shocking. But really I should be asking you how you are doing – you saw her die!" Marzia's eyes began to fill with tears. "What a terrible day. I will never forget it, never."

Neither will I, I thought, as I felt my guts churn with the memory of Elisabetta's glassy stare. I took a quiet breath and forced myself to concentrate on the task at hand; if I didn't, I'd never get anywhere with Marzia. "I'm okay Marzia, thanks," I said slowly. "Although, like you, I'm still shocked... Listen, though..." I added as gently as I could. "I also came to see you because I was wondering if you'd noticed an envelope in the studio yesterday? A grey one? I thought it might have been Elisabetta's. Do you know anything about it?"

Marzia took her glasses off and rubbed her eyes. "But didn't you show me an envelope yesterday at the studio?"

"Yes, yes I did. I thought it might be hers and asked around but no one claimed it. I still have it so I thought I'd ask you again seeing as I'm here."

"Well, no, it's not mine. And I didn't see Elisabetta with any envelope. *Certo*." Marzia seemed genuinely disinterested in the envelope so I dropped the subject. I followed her as she walked to the steam machine and started to work on a sleek, silk-satin halter dress in a deep petrol colour.

A new thought suddenly entered my mind and, without thinking, I said to Marzia, "By the way, I was wondering if Elisabetta used tarot cards?"

Marzia looked surprised. "Tarot cards? You mean like the ones for telling the future?"

I nodded.

"No. Elisabetta didn't go in for that sort of thing. She could seem kind of ditzy and absent-minded but she was actually very, very sharp – and not at all gullible. I know for a fact that she didn't like tarot or horoscopes or numerology. She always said that the best way to predict the future was to be precise with your actions today."

So maybe they weren't Elisabetta's cards after all. And yet who else could they belong to?

"I never once heard her mention tarot – except to scoff at it," Marzia continued. "We have a lot of tarot here in Milan, you know. There are even tarot readers on the streets."

Hmm…time to try another tack. "You know, I just saw Ginevra Mucci. She really didn't like Elisabetta, did she…?"

Marzia shook her head. "She was always accusing Elisabetta of copying her. And actually, she was furious about Elisabetta winning Editor of the Year at the Moda Awards."

"How do you know?"

"She told me – and that was *after* I'd already heard her insult Elisabetta when we were on our way to Ugo's. Everyone knows Ginevra's feelings about Elisabetta. People were surprised that Ginevra even agreed to hire Elisabetta – but then one or two were quick to note that Ginevra could control, and even destroy, Elisabetta's career if she was under her thumb. Anyway, there was a lot of malicious gossip about them…even I don't know the truth."

Marzia was on her knees, carefully aiming the nozzle of the steamer at the hem of the long dress. As I thought about what she'd just said I couldn't help but notice that she was wearing white Converse – my favourites. At the sight of them, however, something in my memory was jogged. It took a moment but finally I remembered what it was they reminded me of. I was surprised I hadn't thought of this detail earlier because the existence of the sneakers I was thinking about went against all that I had heard so far. But maybe Marzia knew something about them that the others didn't? It was worth a try. "You know, you, me and Elisabetta all have something in common," I said brightly.

"And what's that?"

"White sneakers," I said. "Elisabetta had a pair with her yesterday. Did she wear sneakers a lot?"

Marzia's eyes widened and she looked up at me, laughing.

"No, not at all, Axelle. Elisabetta never wore sneakers. She loved her heels too much!"

"But I saw her with a pair yesterday. She had them in her basket."

Marzia shrugged her shoulders. "Elisabetta only wore heels. Even after a full day at the fashion shows she'd still be wearing heels in the evening. I don't know how she did it."

"So it was unusual for her to have a pair of sneakers with her?"

"I didn't even know she owned any."

"Maybe she was planning on going to the gym, or running, after work?"

Marzia laughed out loud. "You didn't know Elisabetta. She thought exercise was a waste of time. The only thing she lifted regularly was her lipstick! But who knows, Elisabetta was full of surprises. She may have decided to start working out, but she certainly didn't say anything about it to me."

So, she didn't believe in tarot and yet those cards had probably belonged to her. She didn't wear sneakers and yet I'd seen a pair in her basket. What did it all mean?

"She also told me she had something important to do last night. You don't happen to know what it was she was planning on doing, do you?" I asked.

"I have no clue." Marzia sighed. "I was her styling assistant – not her personal assistant. My job was the clothes, not her calendar. She probably could have used a personal assistant though, she was always so busy."

Marzia hung the halter-neck dress on the rack next to her and started work on a beautifully tailored Alexander McQueen coat. "It always feels odd to work with these heavy winter clothes when it's so warm outside," she said. "But that's fashion for you – out of sync with the weather!"

I thanked Marzia and after saying goodbye I turned to leave. I could hear the steamer hissing and spitting behind me as I left the room. My mind was whirling. Who did the tarot cards belong to if not Elisabetta? And who had called Daniela at Megastudio asking about them? And what about the sneakers? I'd *definitely* seen a pair – I'd even helped Elisabetta pick them up off the floor and put them back in her basket. Why would she take them to work with her if she only ever wore heels?

A warm smile on heels, that's how Kristine had described Elisabetta. And Marzia, who had worked with her all day, every day, never, ever saw Elisabetta out of heels. I considered my last question to Marzia…what had Elisabetta been planning on doing last night? And was it something so unusual that the sneakers could have been a part of it?

I dashed out of the *Amare* offices and, true to his word, Sebastian was waiting for me. He handed me my helmet and I quickly pulled it on, slid behind him onto the seat of the scooter and locked my arms around his waist. We peeled away from the kerb and five minutes later we were in the Brera neighbourhood and parking on a street close to Thaddeus Greene's office. With exactly ten minutes to spare, we half-ran, half-walked the rest of the way.

We found the office quickly. A simple brass plaque on a narrow front door confirmed it. A large window looked in on a small room lined with bookshelves and religious paintings. A few globes of various sizes and brown with age added antique flavour to a room that was packed to the ceiling with papers, books, paintings, sculptures and boxes of who knew what. This was unmistakably the professor's office, but it didn't look like anyone was in.

"Maybe he's through the back?" Sebastian said.

"There's only one way to find out," I said as I pushed the door open and walked in.

I could hear someone rustling around in a room at the back. The door to the room was slightly ajar, so I walked up to it and gave it a sharp rap with my knuckles. "Professor Greene?" I called. "Hello?" I waited a few seconds and then called out again.

"Coming," said a muffled voice and two seconds later a tall, broad-shouldered man with dark hair walked into the room. He was carrying a heavy load of boxes piled so high that I couldn't see his face. Sebastian and I waited as he set the boxes down on the floor and stood back up. He was dressed in old blue jeans, a shirt, untucked, with the sleeves rolled up, and trainers. His arms were tanned and muscular. He also had an apple in his mouth and the most amazing green eyes I'd ever seen. He looked about the same age as Sebastian.

"Are you Professor Greene?" I asked, surprised.

Honestly, I'd been expecting some kind of stereotypical professor: stained tweed jacket, steel-rimmed specs perched on the end of a long thin nose, and an absent-minded manner. I certainly hadn't anticipated the totally hot apparition in front of me. This guy looked as if he'd just stepped out of some big Hollywood action film. A cross between an archaeologist and an adventurer.

"Actually, Professor Greene is my father," he said in flawless English (with an American accent) as he took the apple out of his mouth and reached for my hand. "My name's Lucas and I'm just cleaning up around here while Dad's away on holiday. Sorry about the dust." I could feel him watching me in a way that made me nervous, or giddy, or both.

"Professor Greene is away?" I asked. I should have been disappointed, worried that it would set my investigation back, but none of that was registering yet. I was too surprised. By Lucas.

"Yup, 'fraid so. He'll be back in a couple of weeks, but if there's anything I can help you with…?" He left the question hanging in the air for a moment as our eyes met and we held each other's gaze. Apart from a quick nod hello he'd hardly even registered Sebastian. As Lucas smiled, I noticed that his eyelashes were very long and nearly black, like his hair.

I smiled back, trying not to stare.

Get it together, Axelle, I thought to myself. *He's not that gorgeous... Actually, yes he is.*

Before I could say anything, Sebastian cleared his throat loudly and stepped forward. "We have a question concerning some tarot cards." Lucas turned away from me and looked at Sebastian and it was as if some kind of spell had been broken. Or was I imagining things?

"No problem," Lucas said to Sebastian before shifting his focus back to me. "I'm really interested in tarot myself. What's your question?"

"We'd like to—" Sebastian and I spoke at exactly the same moment. I suddenly felt the way I had yesterday at Ugo's when Sebastian had let Francesca think I was his assistant – and it was a feeling I didn't like.

I cleared my throat as I stepped in front of Sebastian and rested my rucksack on the table. I pulled the cards out. "I just inherited these from my godmother," I said. "She died suddenly and didn't leave any information about them. I was hoping your father could tell me a little bit—"

Again Sebastian interrupted. "Like how old they are and maybe where they were made?" he said loudly.

Was Sebastian trying to hijack this appointment from me? *Dream on.* This was *my* case, after all. I gave Sebastian an icy smile and simultaneously kicked him in the shin. I was wearing Converse so it couldn't have hurt, but if his look of surprise was anything to go by it seemed he got the message.

"These are pretty incredible," Lucas said. He was bending over the table, peering closely at the cards; a second later, he disappeared into the back room without a word.

"What was that kick for?" Sebastian hissed as soon as Lucas had left.

"What do you think, Watson? This is *my* case and *I* found those cards so I'd appreciate it if you'd let me do the talking!"

"But Lucas is totally hitting on you!"

"No, he's not," I hissed back. "And even if he is, so what? Who cares? I'm here to find out about the cards. Unlike some people I know, when I'm on a case *I'm on it.*"

"Well you could have fooled me with the way you're looking at him all moony-eyed."

"You mean like the way you had your eyes all over Francesca yesterday?"

"Francesca, in case I need to remind you, is an important part of this case."

"Yeah, well, so is Lucas."

"Fine."

"Good."

Lucas returned just as suddenly as he'd left, holding two pairs of white cotton gloves. "These tarot cards are so old,

I think it's better if we handle them with gloves," he said as he passed me the second pair.

Carefully he lifted one card after the other. "Yes, definitely Milanese. And here," he said as he pointed to the bottom edge of the card with the lady on horseback, "there's a pair of initials worked into the scrolling along the border. Can you see them?"

"PV?"

Lucas nodded. "For Pietro Vasari. And this is typical of the way he included his initials in his work."

"Didn't Pietro Vasari work on the Arcimboldo-Crivelli tarot cards?" I asked. I was trying to remember if I'd noticed the same initials on the cards I'd just seen at the Palazzo Reale. I kicked myself for not having noticed them before.

Lucas nodded. "I'm not sure you needed to come here – it seems you already know quite a bit yourself." I could feel the colour rise to my cheeks as his eyes caught mine. I quickly reached for my notebook, pencil and glasses, studiously avoiding Lucas's hypnotic eyes.

As I put my glasses on and opened my notebook I steadied myself and, then, turning once more to Lucas I said, "So can you tell us anything more about them?" He was holding the card with the grinning skeleton up to the light and peering at it through a magnifying glass.

"To be honest, three things occur to me about your cards," he said as he set the death card down and picked up the one with the magician.

"Yes?"

"First of all, these *tarocchi* are very, very old. I think they must date from at least the 1450s, maybe earlier. Secondly, they are quite valuable. Of course, any tarot cards of that age will be worth a lot, but what singles these out in particular is that, thirdly, I actually think there is a very strong chance that your cards are from the Arcimboldo-Crivelli deck. I've never seen anything like these tarot cards outside of my dad's books or the Pinacoteca's collection."

"We've just seen the ones from the Pinacoteca's collection in the exhibition at the Palazzo Reale. And they do seem identical in style…"

Lucas nodded excitedly. I heard Sebastian tut under his breath. "Interestingly," Lucas said, "the majority of the cards still in existence from the Arcimboldo-Crivelli deck belong to two famous collections. One you saw, at the Pinacoteca, and the other is at Yale University in America. But neither of these collections has the magician's card or the death card. Experts believed – if they were ever painted – that these cards must be in private hands. You might just have them. I'm amazed your godmother never told you anything about them. Did she have more?"

"Um…no. Not that I know of… Why? Are you looking for more?"

"Sort of…the thing is, funnily enough, you are the third person since yesterday evening who's asked about old *tarocchi* cards… The other two people were looking to buy, though. They gave me their numbers and asked me to let them know urgently if I heard about three antique *tarocchi*, belonging to the same deck, going on sale. I told them that we'd definitely help them if we could, but that it was highly unusual for any antique *tarocchi* cards to come up for sale, let alone three from the same deck."

A shiver ran up my spine and the room suddenly felt cold. I tried to keep my voice steady and indifferent as I said, "What did they say specifically?"

"Both said a 'friend' was missing three cards from their collection and wondered if I'd come across them. It sounded to me as if the cards had been stolen and put up for sale. Actually, they both also mentioned wanting the card of death. That's why I asked you where you got them." Lucas was suddenly quiet as his eyes searched mine. Did he think I'd stolen them?

I laughed lightly. "Well, now you know. My godmother was very generous."

"I guess so," he said, in a way that made me doubt he believed me. "I thought that perhaps, if you are the mysterious friend with the supposedly missing cards, then you're playing a very good trick on them. Or…" Lucas trailed off and turned to busy himself with some papers.

"Or?" I said as I leaned across his desk, my eyes boring into his back.

He turned round and his eyes searched mine again

slowly as he ignored my question. "Anyway," he said finally, "what a coincidence, right? Old tarot cards, three of them, and the death card, suddenly appear after two enquiries yesterday…"

There was that word again. *Coincidence*. Somehow I didn't think it was a coincidence at all. "I don't suppose you can tell me who these people were?"

"My dad's really strict about client privacy. I couldn't tell you even if I'd seen them."

"*Even if* you'd seen them?"

Lucas nodded. "Yeah – they both phoned up. And to be honest, I couldn't even tell if they were male or female, old or young. They were just a couple of people calling up with about an hour or so between them. Weird, right?"

It certainly was. Sebastian and I looked at each other, any sore feelings forgotten for the moment. I knew we were both thinking about the call Daniela had received at Megastudio yesterday. The hairs on my arms stood up; someone was definitely after these cards.

In fact, *two people* were after these cards.

"I'm sorry I can't tell you more, but if they call back I'll let you know. Which reminds me, maybe you should give me your number?" Lucas asked.

I saw Sebastian roll his eyes. "Sure," I said as I wrote it down for him.

"And, by the way," Lucas said as he dug around in a filing cabinet just behind him, "take care of your tarot cards.

Here," he said as he turned and passed me a fresh envelope, "this is acid-free. Those cards are valuable. You should try to slip the envelope into some sort of case for protection. The colour and metallic pigments on the *tarocchi* are very sensitive."

"Thank you." I packed the cards into the new envelope and after loosening the drawstring on my rucksack I slipped them in between the pages of my modelling portfolio. *That*, I thought, *should protect them nicely.*

Lucas quickly looked at the clock on the wall behind him. "I have to get going now, but I'm free at around three this afternoon, if you'd like to talk some more about the cards?"

"Actually—" Sebastian started but I cut him off.

"Actually, Sebastian, aren't you busy at three?" I asked.

"Um, yes, but—"

Before Sebastian could finish I said, "Lucas, three o'clock would be perfect."

"Great. Then why don't you meet me here and I can show you some other cards and then we'll take it from there."

"That sounds great." I slipped my rucksack over my shoulder, shook Lucas's hand and turned to leave.

"What do you think you're doing?" Sebastian asked as soon as we were out in the street.

"Nothing more than you are."

"Oh, so this is about Francesca, is it?" Sebastian said as

he turned to me. "You know, every time her name comes up you get frosty. You're turning her into a much bigger deal than she actually is."

I carried on walking and looked straight ahead. "I'm not turning her into anything. You have an appointment with her at three and now I have one with Lucas. Where's the problem?"

Sebastian was about to answer me back when I suddenly put my arm out and yanked him into a darkened passage just next to us.

"Hey!"

"Shhh!" I said as I put a finger to my lips and motioned to Sebastian to flatten himself into the shadows. Light from the open courtyard behind us filtered into the passageway, but didn't reach us. I held as still as possible and slowed my breathing as best I could. I wasn't sure I could believe my eyes. Had I just seen who I thought I'd seen? Or was my mind playing tricks on me? What was he doing here? He couldn't be on this narrow street purely by coincidence?

That word again!

Coincidence?

Or part of a plan?

I heard footsteps coming up to us now. They slowed down as they came alongside the alley, then carried on past.

As the footsteps echoed down the street I stepped away

from the shadows and peered out of the alleyway just in time to catch a glimpse of Ugo at Professor Greene's door. Lucas was just leaving the office. And although I couldn't hear their conversation, I did see Lucas shake his head. Then he and Ugo headed off in opposite directions. Again, Sebastian and I flattened ourselves into the shadows of the passageway as Ugo walked past.

I motioned to Sebastian that we should follow him. Back on the street, we stayed on the shady side, as flush to the walls as possible. We traced his steps to the crowded and busy square of the Duomo.

I wanted to know what Ugo was up to and where he was going next. It could *not* be a coincidence that he'd stopped by Professor Greene's. "Didn't we have some sightseeing we wanted to do today?" I said.

Sebastian nodded. "And the Duomo was on our plan for right about now."

"In which case, this is perfect timing, Watson. Let's go."

WEDNESDAY AFTERNOON

Dressed for Death

It was just past one and the sun was high. The square in front of the Duomo was dazzlingly bright. No tree or building cast a shadow over its vast open space, filled with a mix of tourists, bustling business people, noisy, aggressive street vendors and even a group of nuns. As my eyes adjusted to the sounds and smells I searched for Ugo but couldn't find him. Where was he? We'd seen him approach the square, but he'd vanished amongst the thronging crowds.

"There," said Sebastian excitedly as he pointed up ahead. Both of us ran towards Ugo, but he was walking quickly. We separated slightly, moving parallel to each other, keeping Ugo in sight. But he moved easily through the crowds and I wasn't able to get closer. A large group of art school students suddenly came between Sebastian and me. We were just pushing through them when they all pulled out their large sketchbooks, found a space to sit down and started drawing. By the time we climbed our way around them, Ugo was long gone.

Argh! "I can't believe we've lost him," I said as I stood there, exasperated with myself for letting him get away. Yesterday I'd had the feeling that he'd been holding something back from me... Did he know something about those cards? Something that had to do with Elisabetta? Despite the sweat I could feel trickling down the back of my neck a chill ran through me as a new thought formed in my mind... How much did Ugo really know about Elisabetta's death – *and how much did he have to do with it?* I'd have to find him at his home or office and confront him as soon as I could. In the meantime, I took a deep breath.

"Look," Sebastian suddenly said as he put his hands on my shoulders, "Ugo's gone now. Okay, so it would have been good to see what he was up to, but maybe you can ask him outright later – put him on the spot? I can find out where he'll be from Francesca..."

I rolled my eyes – there was no need to involve Francesca when I could just call Ugo direct to make an appointment. But perhaps Sebastian had a point. I needed to see Ugo face to face when I asked him about why he'd been at Professor Greene's, and in fact it might be best to find out where he'd be later, and then surprise him.

"My point is, we're both here, so we might as well check out the Duomo now and then grab a quick bite to eat before we track him down, don't you think? And look…" Sebastian pulled two white slips of paper out of his wallet. "I pre-booked tickets for us. And they include the rooftop, by the way. They're valid for the whole week – repeat visits included."

"With an offer like that, Watson, I can't refuse." I took one of the tickets and we headed towards the signs pointing to the Duomo entrance. My mind was swirling with thoughts of Ugo's strange behaviour, whether I'd see him at the party tonight, and how best to confront him about his visit to Professor Greene, all of which meant it took me a moment to notice that Sebastian had stopped at one of the street vendors for a bottle of water. I was standing on my own waiting for him when a large group of Chinese tourists appeared. Like a loud, babbling stream they surged around me on all sides. Sebastian caught my eye and was just making his way towards me when I felt myself yanked from behind. Thinking someone had bumped into me I tried to step forward – but someone or something was holding me back. I saw Sebastian suddenly wave his hands and start struggling towards me, but, too late, I realized that someone was trying to steal something out of my backpack.

"Your wallet!" shouted Sebastian. I turned just in time to see a fast-moving, black-clad figure disappear into the crowd.

Sebastian caught up with me. "Did they take your wallet?"

"I don't know – I haven't had time to check!" But suddenly another more worrying thought came to mind. "The tarot cards!" I said as we pushed our way through the crowds after the figure.

"You check your bag, and I'll follow the thief," Sebastian said as he pushed ahead.

I kept moving, slowing only long enough to examine my backpack. The clasp on the flap that closes over the rucksack was open and the drawstring underneath was loose. Someone had definitely tried to get into it – but the tarot cards were safe! I'd slipped them into my modelling book – and it was impossible to pull the portfolio out of my rucksack without loosening the opening completely. My wallet, on the other hand, would have been easy to reach – and yet it was still there...had Sebastian alerted me just in time? Or was the thief only after the tarot cards? And if so, how did they know I had them? There was only one way to find out – we had to catch them.

I put on a burst of speed, pushed my way through the throng and reached Sebastian just as a large group of American tourists stepped out of the Duomo. At that moment the distant black figure changed direction and headed past a sign marked "Duomo Tickets". Maddeningly, whoever it was, was wearing sunglasses and a regular black baseball cap. Their clothes were basic and totally androgynous; it was hard to see whether we were chasing a man or a woman, but there was no way I was going to let them slip away from me – not after I let Ugo vanish so easily. Then again – maybe it was Ugo? In which case, he must have come prepared with the cap and sunglasses. So maybe he *had* seen me earlier? Or maybe he'd been following me all morning?

The fleet-footed figure disappeared into the queuing crowds waiting to buy tickets. I elbowed my way through an endless line of tourists. To our right was the north side of the cathedral and to the left was a long ticket booth. We were effectively corralled into a rectangle with the lifts to the rooftop in front of us. The only way back into the square was behind us.

The person we were following must have realized the same thing because, suddenly, up ahead, I saw a flurry of activity near the doors of the lift that had just opened.

"It's the thief!" I said to Sebastian. "Going up – trying to lose us. If they go up to the rooftop then they don't have to go past us to get out!"

I pulled out the ticket Sebastian had given me. "I'll follow them up. Can you get your scooter? They'll have to come down at some point."

"Got it. I'll find the rooftop exit and wait there." Sebastian turned and ran.

I pushed my way through the crowds separating me from the rooftop lifts as aggressively as I dared – the last thing I needed was for someone to call security. But as I finally reached the head of the queue, the lift doors shut just in front of me – and for the second time this morning I was stopped in my tracks. I glanced up at the top of the cathedral. Heights aren't my thing, but I wasn't about to let the thief get away.

I showed the guide my ticket and waited for the next lift, which came less than a minute later. As I got in, I could only hope that in the time it took me to get to the roof the thief wouldn't have come back down already.

I had to know who it was. I mean, of all the people to target on the square, why had I been chosen? I didn't exactly look as if I was loaded with jewels and cash – and my wallet had been left untouched even though it was lying on top of the things in my rucksack. My gut was telling me this was about the tarot cards. Was I chasing one of the people who'd called Lucas about the cards? My stomach suddenly lurched. But if Lucas had insisted on client privacy for them, then surely he'd protect my identity too…?

So, who besides Lucas knew that I had the cards? Again, very possibly Ugo. But was there someone else who knew? And if so, how had they found out?

As soon as the lift doors opened at the top I darted forward. To my left the steeply pitched roof climbed higher still, and to my right the cathedral plummeted downwards in one sheer straight line to the square below. I was so high up I couldn't even see the ground unless I went right up to the balustrade. This was no time to indulge my fear of heights, I thought, as I pulled back quickly. In contrast to the crowds below, up here it was quiet – peaceful even.

As quickly as possible I followed the only designated path through a rooftop forest of spires, saints and gargoyles. Finally I was directed up a stone staircase that followed the steeply ascending roofline over the Duomo's main entrance. I figured that as long as I held on to the railing, I'd be all right. But when I hazarded a quick glance through the spires, I felt sick – far below me the people on the square looked like coloured pinpricks. I felt my legs start to buckle. *No, no, Axelle!* I turned away from the view below and forced myself to climb as quickly as I could.

The rooftop over the nave of the cathedral was surprisingly small. Some people sat on the slanting sides of the roof while a few others walked along its flat spine. A couple of guides were talking to each other at one end of the rooftop as they kept an eye on visitors. But no one was running. And there was not a black baseball cap in sight. So where had they gone? I balled my fists up with frustration. Time was ticking – I had to move.

I turned and followed the signs that led off the nave roof and on to another staircase – the mirror image of the one I'd ascended. At that moment a flash of movement below caught my eye – a figure in black running along a different roof level far below me. I leaped down the stairs two at a time, praying I wouldn't fall. The figure was still within sight, moving between the spires below me. But before I reached the bottom they disappeared between the cathedral's buttresses and then vanished through a stone doorway.

Ignoring a guide who tried to slow me down with a wave of his arm, I sprinted along the roof, past more stony gargoyles and under the gaze of the golden Madonna. I grabbed a statue for balance as I turned sharply through an arch that led to a lower level. A moment later I reached a dead end in front of the lifts. I slid to a stop just as the lift doors shut in front of me for the second time. Argh! I pushed the button to stop it but to no avail.

Frantically I looked left and right. A sign next to a small arched doorway read, "Stairs to the exit". Which way had they gone? Down the lift or the stairs? I hesitated, wondering whether or not to wait for the next lift. But if the thief was on the stairs there was a good chance I might catch them yet. Without further thought I entered the turret and started my way down the narrow, spiral staircase.

To my relief I heard the pattering of fast-moving footsteps ahead of me. The footsteps stopped for a moment. Were they listening to see if I was following? After a quick pause they resumed. The chase was back on!

The steep stairs were clearly the less popular option for getting down. I passed no one and heard no other footsteps behind me. As I concentrated on not slipping, I kept my ears tuned to the footsteps up ahead. Then suddenly they stopped.

I came flying out of the stairwell, all senses alert. I was about to exit onto the square when I saw a shadow flit quickly between the enormous marble pillars to my left into the cathedral.

The loud chords of the organ vibrated throughout the church. My heart was beating as I searched the crowds, elbowing my way past groups and interrupting photo sessions until I caught sight of the figure again, heading towards the exit. Hot on their trail, I followed them, but when I came out of the Duomo, I could see no sign of the figure. Where had they gone?

At that moment I heard Sebastian call me. He was on his scooter to my left, my helmet in his hand. I ran over and threw myself behind him, pulling on my helmet as we sped away. I'd lost sight of the figure, but Sebastian hadn't. He'd been waiting and watching the exit. As we zoomed in and out of the traffic I realized we were following a taxi, but within two minutes Sebastian cursed as we were forced to screech to a stop at a red light. The taxi had just made it through. Luckily we caught up with them two lights down and from then on we followed closely behind. It wasn't easy. We were still in the old part of Milan and had to navigate our way around a maze of ancient streets.

Finally, a monument I recognized from my guidebook loomed into sight. We raced past the grand Columns of San Lorenzo, sped to the Porta Ticinese and from there to the canals of the Navigli. We turned towards Porta Genova and then drove on past it. The taxi seemed to slow as it made a few more turns through the warren of one-way streets that ran along the canals. Then, suddenly, it stopped outside what looked like abandoned old government buildings. As we drove up the thief sprang out of the taxi and raced towards a graffiti-covered doorway. The taxi sped away just as Sebastian and I screeched to a halt. We jumped off his scooter and I quickly stashed my rucksack in the locked compartment under the seat. "The cards are probably safest locked up here," I said as we took off on foot in the direction of the abandoned building.

Inside the building the walls were covered in old signs and faded, curling notices with all manner of official stamps and warnings and lists. As we ran down corridors and jumped across debris, we concentrated on staying as close behind the running figure as possible. We entered a courtyard choked into darkness by a jungle of overgrown plants and trees. As we moved past the graffiti-covered façades and decaying interiors a door slammed up ahead. We burst through it and found ourselves facing a vast tarmacked courtyard surrounded by huge concrete buildings with broken windows. We ran to the first door we came to and pushed it open.

We stood in a large, empty, hangar-like space. Sunlight filtered through the filthy, broken windows, throwing strange shadows on the floor and walls, making us turn left and right thinking we'd seen someone. Then, suddenly, we heard footsteps from behind a high pile of debris in the far corner. We took off in the direction of the noise and followed it down a dark stairwell. I noticed we lost phone connection as we descended but it was too late to stop and call for help now. Using our phones as torches we continued downwards, but we didn't seem to be gaining on the figure. On the final step, we came to another doorway, pushed through it and found ourselves in a chamber of some kind. We stopped – the footsteps had stopped too. Had we lost them? We looked at each other questioningly. The silence was absolute. We advanced further into the darkness but still nothing moved or made a sound. Where had they gone? And that's when we heard it: the sound of a heavy metal door shutting behind us. We turned and instinctively threw all our weight against the door, pushing and pressing up against it with every ounce of strength we could muster. We kicked and screamed until, finally, engulfed in darkness and breathing hard, we had to admit the obvious. We were trapped.

"Only one torch on at a time, we've got to save our phone batteries," Sebastian said as he reached over and turned mine off.

"Argh!" I kicked the earth and screamed out loud.

"I never even got close enough to tell if it was a man or a woman we were following!"

"I couldn't tell, either. But whoever it was they're fit."

"And they know the city well."

Sebastian scanned our surroundings with his torch – not that we could see much. The air was damp and very humid. The smell of earth was overwhelming. Drops of water fell from above, and when the beam of the torch finally landed on a wall it looked slick with moisture.

"Do you think they're coming back for us?" Sebastian swept the beam of his torch overhead, but only revealed more blank concrete. In front of us was pure darkness.

"No. We were led here for a reason. Someone wants something. Or wants to keep us away from something."

"The tarot cards?"

"Maybe." I took a sharp breath. "I hope the cards will be all right locked up in the scooter?"

"Should be. We parked on a busy street."

"And we saw people walking past. Anyway we won't find out anything if we keep standing here." I took a quick breath. "Maybe there's another opening into this place? You take that wall and I'll take this one. We have to find a way out."

I tried to sound upbeat even though I was screaming inside. I was angry at my own stupidity. One thought in particular came to mind: the taxi had slowed down when we'd entered the Navigli district and that should have warned me – why would it do that in the heat of the chase…unless the occupants wanted to make sure we were following?

Yeah, well, too late now, Axelle.

There were walls to our sides and, behind us, the shut door. But the beam from our torch was too weak to allow us to see far ahead. At first we advanced cautiously, sure that we'd come to a wall, but it soon became clear that we were in some kind of underground passage.

We moved forward as quickly as we could. I wanted to run but we decided it was too risky because there were wooden stakes and large pebbles on the ground – the last thing we needed was for one of us to twist an ankle or worse… At one point I tripped on a bar of some sort. I thought it must be another wooden stake, half buried. But it wasn't wood – it was iron.

"I think this must have been a railway for coal or supplies or something." Sebastian swung the beam of his torch towards my feet. The bar did indeed appear to be connected to some half-buried and very narrow tracks.

The tunnel continued with frustrating predictability. There was no ladder leading upwards; no fork in the road, not even a boarded-up door. How long was this tunnel? It seemed to go on for ever! I took a deep breath and figured we might as well use our time wisely. "Watson, did you manage to get any background checks done while I was at my castings this morning?"

"Yes, I did. But I'd completely forgotten about all that." His voice carried a little way along the tunnel. He quietened to a whisper. "We've been running non-stop since I fetched you at *Amare!*"

True, I thought. This morning already seemed like a whole week ago. "Did you find any trace of Elisabetta having double-crossed or fallen out with any of the suspects on the list?"

"Apart from Ginevra and Elisabetta's well-documented feud I couldn't find a trace of a grudge or vendetta or anything. Zero. The group at Ugo's party really do appear to be friends. From what I could see none of their paths crossed until they started in fashion, which for most of them was when they were in their late teens. Then their paths crossed all over the place. But without incident."

I stared into the gloom, thinking carefully. "Yet there must be something that links one or more of them to Elisabetta; something more than just fashion or their friendship with Ugo..." I sighed and brought the conversation back on track. "Ginevra's quite fiery and strong. I could see she hated Elisabetta, but enough to want to poison her? I think she loves the plum position she has at the top of *Amare*'s masthead too much to risk it."

We walked on in silence for a moment. Then Sebastian said, "It's funny though how Elisabetta's career has followed Ginevra's so closely. Both started as freelance stylists, took their styling skills up a notch by working at Falco Ventini

– Elisabetta as muse and in-house stylist and Ginevra as studio director – and then from there jumped ship, as fully fledged editors, to *Amare*."

"The Milan fashion scene is small," I said as we continued along the tunnel. "Like, I read this morning that Alessandro was also part of Falco Ventini's inner circle before he died. And Kristine Abrams, the casting director, started out doing bookings for Falco."

"And," Sebastian said, "Coco Sommerino D'Alda – remember, she was at Ugo's party? – is a brand ambassador, although that only started once Ugo took over after Falco's death. But Coco's mother, Lavinia, knew Falco well. She was his in-house publicist for many years. According to what I read online, she was with Falco from the very beginning, and stayed until he died."

I was silent for a moment, rapidly going over the details in my head.

"Hello, Holmes? What are you thinking?"

"Well it's interesting, Watson…" I began. "All of the people who stayed late at Ugo's after-party have worked for Falco."

"So? As you said yourself, Milan is small and Falco Ventini is a prestigious fashion house that every fashionista wants to work for. We can probably find groups of friends all over Milan who've all worked for Prada and Armani, too."

"Most likely, yeah." I paused and a drip of water splashed

noisily to the ground. "But right now I'm looking at *this* group, and everyone in this group worked for Falco at some point in their career. It's a link and it's in their past – I'd say it's worth looking into. Maybe there's a secret in there somewhere? Maybe something happened and Elisabetta tried to blackmail one of them?" I was excited to finally have something to sink my teeth into and it was fun to run with my idea for the moment, though it wasn't going to be of much use as long as we were stuck underground.

"Well, it's definitely worth digging into," Sebastian agreed.

We continued walking. The strength of the phone torch wasn't great and we couldn't see that far ahead, but it seemed this tunnel had no end, and there was still no trace of a phone signal.

"How much did they overlap at Falco's?" I wondered aloud. "Like, were they all working there together, at the same time? Can you remember any details? I know that Elisabetta was still there for Falco's last collection, before he fell ill – I've seen pictures of her at the show. Ugo was already there, too. I think they both joined at more or less the same time, which was about two years before Falco died."

"Kristine was around at that time, too," said Sebastian. "I think she started casting for the Ventini shows a few years before Falco died. And she still casts for Ugo today."

"Yes, and I've seen photos of Alessandro working for

Falco right up to the end – he even went to the hospital sometimes with Elisabetta when she visited Falco. In fact, I think they met at Falco's." I was starting to feel that there had to be something in this.

"And I'm pretty sure," Sebastian added, "that Ginevra worked at Ventini up until Falco's last collection. Then she jumped to *Amare*. Elisabetta left for *Amare* a bit later – right around the time Falco died. I'd have to double-check but I think I'm right."

"Don't forget, Watson, like it or not, Francesca was there, too."

"Ha ha, Holmes. Yes, she was."

"She was designing on the accessories team." We walked on into the darkness.

"Okay, so if we're remembering everything we researched correctly, Ugo, Elisabetta, Kristine, Francesca, and Alessandro all worked for Ventini, in different capacities, at more or less the same time. And Ginevra, who'd started with Falco, had already moved on by the time Ugo took over."

"That sounds about right," Sebastian agreed.

"So, apart from the general facts that they all work in fashion, and that they are all friends of Ugo's, the one and only thing we know that links the group who stayed late at Ugo's specifically, is that they all worked in some kind of professional capacity for Falco, within the last five years of his life." I was silent for a moment as I thought about that.

"I know it's not much, but so far it seems to be the most interesting link I can find between them. We should do some digging into their Ventini days. You never know…" Though I was beginning to wonder whether we'd ever get the chance…

We stopped to catch our breath for a moment and check if we had phone signal. We didn't, so Sebastian turned his torch back on and we pushed forward. I was just about to speak when I was forcefully yanked backwards. Something grabbed me from the side and wasn't letting go. With a sharp intake of breath I reached out for Sebastian with my right hand. "Sebastian! Stop!" He turned quickly and with a sweep of his arm shone the torch onto me. I covered my eyes with my hands as the light blinded me. Something was still holding me back. I was desperate to free myself.

Suddenly Sebastian laughed. "It's all right, Holmes, it's nothing…no, wait…actually, it's a door!" I'd been so close to the wall on my left that I'd brushed up against some sort of doorknob and it had caught on one of the pockets of my military trousers. I nearly laughed with relief. I unhooked myself as Sebastian swept his torch beam down the tunnel in front of us and then back onto the door beside me.

"So, Holmes, tunnel or door? Our batteries won't last for ever. We've got to decide which way to go – at least we have an option now."

I stared into the black void of the tunnel. Who knew how long it was or where it led…? On the other hand, the door was tight shut and probably fused to its frame with rust, but it seemed to hold more promise.

"Let's try the door, Watson. We should at least see what's behind it." Together we turned and pulled on the knob, but despite some creaking, it didn't budge. After a few minutes of fruitless effort I picked up a wooden stake from the ground. "Give me some light, will you?" I said as I slipped my phone into my back pocket and grabbed the stake with both hands. I started running the sharp end along the door frame, jamming it under the lip of the door wherever I could. While Sebastian held the torch with one hand, he kept working on the doorknob with his other, alternately turning it and pulling on it. Within minutes we were both panting from the exertion.

"What I love about being with you, Holmes, is that even in cities packed with all kinds of attractions we always get to see and do things that are totally non-touristy – like trekking through this incredibly fascinating tunnel."

"Just think of it as urban authenticity, Watson," I quipped. "You're lucky to be getting a taste of the real Milan."

"Thanks – er, I think."

At that moment the door gave a brittle, raspy creak.

"That's it, Holmes, I think it's coming loose! We just have to keep trying…" Excitedly I worked the stake even harder as Sebastian continued to pull on the doorknob.

"By the way, don't you have your date with Francesca right about now?"

"It's not a date, and you know it – besides what about you? Shouldn't you be getting all moony-eyed with Lucas?"

I didn't answer because I suddenly felt the door loosen. "Turn the torch off," I said. "Then we can use our four hands to pull on it." We did just that, and slowly, very slowly, the door came loose from its frame until suddenly, with a loud snap, it swung back heavily on its rusted hinges.

Sebastian and I jumped to the side and let go of the handle just in time, to avoid being hit by the door. But before I could react, high-pitched screams filled our ears.

"What on earth was that?" I raised my hands to my ears and *felt* something swooping in close to me. The hairs on my arms and neck stood up. I could hear the screams in one place but then they'd move to another. It was like standing within the vortex of a flock of angry, swirling birds.

A scream choked in my throat as I felt something catch in my hair. Panicking, I hit at my head and tried to free it. And that's when I felt fur – fur attached to a small wriggling body. My hand snapped back in horror as wings beat against it – but they weren't bird's wings, I now realized. This was something else entirely, with wings, but fur instead of feathers – *a bat.*

I managed to free it, but this time I couldn't stop the scream, and pressed a hand over my mouth in case one of them tried to fly in. I could feel the bats darting in and out of the doorway as they lurched through the air all around me, their high-pitched squeals echoing off the tunnel walls. "Stand still," Sebastian yelled. "They'll fly away soon. And don't turn your torch on. Just stay calm."

The last thing I felt was calm. I bent down and huddled into a ball, my head tucked down. I tried to breathe as slowly as possible – not an easy task with wings beating all around my head. But Sebastian was right – after a few minutes the screeching subsided and, with a last collective swoosh, they receded as quickly as they had come. I was still curled up on the ground, though, as I slowly opened one eye and peered out from behind my arm.

Sebastian turned on his torch, stood up and came to my side. He pulled me to my feet and we shook ourselves off as best we could before stepping through the opened doorway. And, by the light of the torch, we saw we were in another tunnel.

"I think we should continue along the first tunnel," Sebastian said. "This doesn't look like a better option." As he swept the torch over the ceiling above us I saw hundreds more bats, huddled together in clusters, hanging upside down from the ceiling. Their grinning faces seemed to mock us and their glittering black eyes followed our every move. They hung calmly, turning only their tiny heads as if to get a better look at us. "Besides," he continued, "look how low those bats are hanging. Do we really want to risk upsetting them again?"

I was suddenly reminded of a biology lesson at school;

we'd learned quite a bit about bats. "Actually, Watson," I said carefully, "I think the bat tunnel just might be our best option."

"Really?" Sebastian stood, hesitating at the doorway.

I took my phone out of my back pocket and switched on my torch. "Save your battery, we'll use a bit of mine now," I said as I aimed my light beam forward, through the doorway and down the tunnel. "The thing is, I don't think there are any bugs down here. I haven't seen any flying around I mean. Or felt any. Have you?"

"No. Why?"

"Bats eat bugs and if they don't find them here in the tunnels – and it doesn't seem likely they do – it means they must hunt them outside. They live in this tunnel, but go hunting outside, probably over the neighbourhood canals – they'd find plenty of bugs over the water."

"So they must have a way in and out of here – an opening that leads outdoors?"

"Exactly. The question is, could we squeeze through an opening they fly in and out of?" I remembered my biology teacher, Mr Hawkes, lifting up his hand in front of the class, his thumb and forefinger touching to form an "o" shape. "Bats can fly through the smallest of openings – that's how they get into all sorts of buildings and rooftops and sleep in crevices in between walls and roof rafters."

"Well, there are an awful lot of bats in here, so let's hope the opening is a large one! Lead the way, Holmes."

Surprisingly the bat tunnel was in better shape than the one we'd just left – there were train tracks here too, and though they were rotting and rusting, they were still in place and not half-buried as they had been in the first tunnel. After a hundred metres or so and a bend in the tracks, there was a sudden, if barely perceptible, change in the air.

"Somehow it feels like we're getting closer to an opening, doesn't it?" I said as we broke into a slow run.

We would have carried on running forward if Sebastian's shoe hadn't hit a stray stone. We heard it rattling loudly ahead of us before an eerie silence seemed to swallow it. A second later we heard a distinct "plop". At that, Sebastian and I both held our arms out to stop each other from advancing.

Sebastian turned on his torch, and we swept the two beams of light in front of us. Then we jumped back with a yelp; we were right at the edge of a huge underground pool. The water was still and unmoving. We had no way of knowing, but its forbidding blackness suggested it was very deep.

"That was close, Holmes," Sebastian said, sighing with relief.

But something else had caught my eye. "Look at that…" I said as I pointed across the water. At some distance, but directly opposite us, a weak shaft of light was just visible. "It must be an opening!"

We stood gazing across the quiet surface, with both torches illuminating the scene. The pool was rectangular in shape and enormous; its sides were steep and straight. I had no idea how to cross it – we could jump in and swim, of course, but the water looked filthy, and I wasn't confident we'd be able to climb out on the other side.

"It's not a natural pool," Sebastian said. "It's an aqueduct or reservoir of some sort."

I nodded. "My guidebook says that the Romans built a maze of canals and aqueducts under Milan. They were used to store and carry water to all parts of the city, but a lot of the old Roman canals were paved over in the 1920s. Only a few are still open. I think they have special tours to see some of the older aqueducts and canals. The ones underground, I mean."

"Like this one." Sebastian suddenly said, "Look down there, Axelle." He was pointing to the left. I followed the arc of his finger and saw what looked like a stone ramp that led directly into the water. And at the top of the ramp lay something I couldn't quite make out. We hurried along the edge of the pool until we reached it. A dirty old tarpaulin hid the shape from view. Sebastian pulled off the cover in one swift movement. Years of dust blew up in our faces, and, once again, frantic shrieks filled the air. I screamed as a colony of rats awoke and scurried away, their long tails dragging behind them. I jumped as one ran over my Converse.

"Smooth move, Watson."

"Just testing your reflexes, Holmes."

"Thanks."

Underneath the tarpaulin was a ramshackle old wooden rowing boat. One oar was still attached but the second one had rotted through. A small metal case held a couple of mouldy, half-decayed life jackets and what I guessed was a map of some sort. I said as much as I handed it to Sebastian.

"It's not a map," Sebastian said. "These are instructions for opening and closing the various valves in this reservoir. It's a kind of maintenance manual. Anyway," he continued as he threw the instruction booklet back into the metal case, "this boat's our best ticket out of here. In fact, it's probably our only one," he added.

There were no walkways along the sides of the aqueduct, and I didn't see any openings in the high walls surrounding it. It was certainly better than trying to swim across. "Then I think it's all aboard, Watson."

We pulled the decrepit boat down the ramp and to the water. I hoped it would hold up. Once we'd pushed it into the pool Sebastian held the sides while I got in. Then I held the single oar as he followed me in and soon we were on our way. Sebastian got on with rowing while I sat at the front and helped guide him.

The boat was small and now that we were waterborne its flimsy build was even more apparent. After a few metres water started seeping in. I did my best to scoop it out with my hands, but it wasn't enough. The boat was sinking.

"If we don't speed up, we'll have to swim the last bit," Sebastian said.

Just the thought of getting into the dark, cold water made me nervous. But no matter how quickly I scooped it out, more seeped in. "We'll have to jump, Axelle," Sebastian finally shouted. "Give me your phone and get in."

I thought of the swimming lessons I'd had at home in London. I hadn't enjoyed them.

"Go, Axelle, go! The boat's about to go under!"

Argh! Sebastian was right. I shut my eyes and slipped overboard. I tried to keep my head above the water and more or less succeeded, but it was absolutely freezing.

"Here, take the phones," Sebastian said, handing them to me. "Hold your hands up high, so they're out of the water and kick with your legs."

Sebastian dived into the water, easily clearing the remains of the sinking boat.

Getting to the other side of the pool was slow going – we had to paddle and bob all the way, but by each holding an arm up and out of the water our phones stayed dry, and eventually we climbed onto a docking ramp, next to another small boat, at the far end of the pool.

We were exhausted. It took all of our strength and concentration just to breathe. We both sat shivering on the ramp slowly catching our breath before deciding our next move. Out of the corner of my eye I saw Sebastian watching me. He smiled and ran his fingertip slowly from the top of my forehead down to my chin, tracing my profile. Despite being soaked and feeling shattered, his touch felt warm on my skin and for a second I forgot everything but him.

"You all right, Holmes?" he asked gently.

"Yes I am, Watson – although I could have done without the bats." I turned and caught his eye.

"I'm glad being locked up and possibly left for dead didn't bother you." He laughed and I grabbed his finger. Then he helped me to my feet and we set off towards the light.

This side of the pool didn't have a tunnel leading out of it – or any other easily accessible opening that we could see. It did, however, have an abandoned industrial lift – although it looked like only the cage-like shaft was left, leading directly to the ground above. The light we'd seen earlier had come from here, and was now streaming down.

"This must be where the bats fly in and out," I said.

"Yeah, it's a shame we can't follow them."

"True, Watson…"

"At least we can open this one easily," Sebastian said as he pulled on the rusted metal bars of the old lift door. "Door" was actually a sophisticated word for the dilapidated, scissor-style gate in front us. And even if we hadn't been able to open it, we probably could have squeezed through its widely spaced bars. We stepped into the shaft and craned our necks upwards.

The lift that must have fitted the shaft once upon a time was long gone. "But maybe..." I looked up. Just above our heads was a protruding U-shaped metal bar, one of many that seemed to lead right to the top of the shaft. They were heavily rusted but still securely fixed in place – originally put there for maintenance presumably – and, with some luck, climbable. "We've been running and swimming but we haven't done any climbing yet. Shall we?"

"Funny, Holmes."

Sebastian crouched low and I clambered up onto his shoulders. Once he was standing I easily reached the first bar and pulled myself up. I climbed a bit higher and leaned back down. Sebastian jumped up and grabbed my wrist, placing his feet against the wall as he did so. I managed to pull him up just enough that he could reach the first bar with one hand, and we began to climb.

It wasn't easy. Some of the bars were missing and it took all of my concentration not to look down as I stretched to reach the next one. It was only the thought that if I fell, Sebastian was just below me to catch me, that enabled me to continue. Finally, though, after one last effort, I pulled myself up and out of the shaft. I rolled onto the ground and closed my eyes.

The heat was surprising. After being underground for so long, and now dripping wet, I'd forgotten that it had been a warm day up above. As our eyes adjusted to the light, we gazed at the abandoned buildings around us, but there was no time to lose. It took us a short while to navigate our way out of the complex and eventually, after scrambling over a low wall, we found ourselves on a busy road. Sebastian flagged down a taxi almost immediately. The driver threw us a few suspicious looks in his rear-view mirror – we hardly looked like the average tourists, but he only asked us if we were okay. Sebastian managed to reassure him in his broken Italian.

Luckily, from the short description we gave him, the driver was able to find his way back to Sebastian's scooter. After Sebastian found some coins in his pockets, he paid the driver and we ran to the scooter. It was still parked where we'd left it, but the seat looked slightly wonky, and marks around the bodywork made it plain someone had tried to break the lock. Fortunately they hadn't succeeded. Perhaps a passer-by had interrupted them?

"Whoever decided to show us underground Milan was probably the one who did this," Sebastian said. "And I bet they'll try coming back here later on, when it's dark, to open it properly."

"Well, then they'll have a nice surprise when they see it's gone."

"Yeah, but when they realize their little plan didn't work, won't they decide to have another go at us?"

"They might – so I guess we'll just have to be more careful from now on, Watson."

Sebastian's phone had no more battery left, and mine

was running very low. He attached his to his scooter charger while I checked mine for messages and emails. Now that I was back on the street and had a signal again, an assortment of notifications came pinging through. But I had so much running through my mind about the case, that it was difficult to change gear and think about what I'd missed while we'd been underground. How long had we been gone?

Tomasso had been calling like mad. And so had Lucas – and Ugo! Ellie had also called a few times. Argh! I'd completely forgotten about my appointments – not that I could have done anything about them. But Tomasso would be furious. And Rocco Rosa's fashion book launch party! It started at 7 p.m. – I checked the time; there was only half an hour to go!

I thought about the party – Ellie was going to introduce me to Coco Sommerino D'Alda – and who knew who else might be there. Ugo perhaps?

Maybe Sebastian could come with me? He gave me the thumbs up when I asked him. It was a book launch, after all, and the invitation had been for me *plus* a guest. I gave him the address, and then called Ellie.

I told her we'd had a rough afternoon and that we'd have to meet her at the party. I couldn't help but purse my lips as I looked down at my clothes though. They'd definitely seen better days – and no doubt so had my face and hair, but I needed to go the party and I really didn't have time to go back to the flat and change. Because it was a cocktail-hour book launch, it wasn't as if the guests were going to be hanging around for ages.

Ellie suggested we meet at the Park Hyatt hotel just around the corner from the book launch and agreed to bring clean clothes for me and to call by Sebastian's *Pensione* and pick up a few things for him too.

Next I called Tomasso. "Axelle! *Oh mio Dio*! I cannot believe it! And I was just about to call the police! Seriously! Where have you been?"

It took me a couple of minutes to calm Tomasso down and assure him that I was still in one piece. "I'm getting too old for this job! *Madonna!* What you've done to me today is not funny!"

I apologized and told him that I'd fallen ill while sightseeing.

"Well, o-kay-ay, no problem, Axelle," Tomasso said. "I'm just thankful that you are fine. So we are back at the square one. I'll reschedule the appointments you missed for tomorrow or later in the week. Take it easy and I'll email you your details for tomorrow's Cutie-Pie booking now."

My shoulders slumped as I came off the phone to Tomasso, I was so relieved he'd bought my story. But a moment later I was standing straight again as I remembered that I had to call Lucas!

"And I have to call Francesca," Sebastian said as if reading my thoughts. With our backs turned to one another, we made our calls.

"Lucas is meeting me straight after the party," I said as I hung up and turned around.

"And Francesca is meeting me there. She was going *anyway*," Sebastian made sure to add pointedly.

I listened to the messages from Ugo – he'd left me two – but I was reluctant to ring him back. I wanted to catch him by surprise when I asked him about Professor Greene. I needed to see his reaction face to face, and judge his honesty for myself.

Sebastian started up his scooter, while I checked myself out with my mirrored compact. What I saw wasn't great – I'd have to wash up at the hotel. Sebastian was all set to go, so I hopped onto the scooter and we left.

The plan was to meet Ellie at the ritzy Park Hyatt Milan hotel, where she usually stayed when she was in Milan for the shows. She was meeting a group of her fashion friends there before heading over to Rocco's party. "It'll be easiest if you change at the hotel," she said. "And don't worry, they know me well, so it won't be a problem. I'll be in the bar in the main lobby. If you don't see me then just ask for me when you walk in."

Ellie might only be a couple of years older than me, but sometimes, like now, when she talked about the most glamorous hotel in Milan as if it was just some kind of casual crash-pad, I realized what five years of modelling – with the last two at the top – can do to a person. Not that she was obnoxious about it – but to her, glitz and glamour were just part of her everyday life – at least when she wasn't hanging out with me or her family in London.

From the outside, the hotel is so sober and discreet that its nineteenth-century stone façade, with no tacky signs, was easy to miss. Only the sight of four dark-suited security officers standing outside with earpieces signalled that the building was not exactly average. According to Ellie, the First Lady of the United States, an A-list Hollywood actor and Naomi Campbell had all stayed there in one week.

The liveried doorman nodded hello as we walked through the hotel entrance. I saw his eyes widen just a touch – our soggy clothes, perhaps? – but he was too polite to show more than mild surprise. Ellie saw us immediately. She was with her friends, sitting at a table under the enormous glass cupola that soared upwards from the lobby. She handed us our clean clothes and linked an arm through mine, ready to lead me to the Park Hyatt's bathrooms.

"Don't forget, Elisabetta, Ugo, Francesca, Ginevra, Kristine and Alessandro." I ticked the names off on my fingers as I reminded Sebastian. "We need to know exactly when they worked at Falco Ventini." Sebastian had offered to double-check a few facts and dates once he'd got changed.

"That shouldn't be a problem. I'll see you in a minute." He headed off in one direction and Ellie led me in the other.

Once in the bathroom, I pulled out the clean dress and Converse she'd picked up for me.

"And you forgot this," Ellie laughed as she handed me the thick invitation to the book launch. "You can't get in without it. Tomasso sent it over to Mrs B's this afternoon."

I changed in a stall while she asked me about my day and although I didn't have the time to go into detail, I filled her in on the basics.

"Wow! Honestly, Axelle, you're lucky to be in one piece – and out of there. It sounds like someone was hoping you'd get lost for good."

"Well, today wasn't their lucky day…" Now that the nightmare was over, I wasn't particularly keen to talk about it. Ellie seemed to understand and asked, "So your background checks and asking around haven't led to any big discoveries?"

"Annoyingly not," I said as I pulled the dress on – it was black, sleeveless and pretty cool. "The only thing that the suspects have in common – independent of the fact that they are all Ugo's friends and all work in fashion – is that they've all worked for Falco Ventini, in one capacity or another. More specifically, with the exception of Ginevra, it seems they were all working for him at the time leading up to his death. Sebastian is double-checking that now. I have no idea whether this is important or not, but at this point it's the only lead I have that connects them all to each other at a specific place and at a particular time."

"Okay. But what can that possibly have to do with Elisabetta being poisoned?"

"I have no idea, but I won't know unless I look into it. Like I said, it's all I have for now. Well, that and the sneakers…"

"The sneakers?"

I explained to Ellie about how Elisabetta had had a pair of sneakers in her basket yesterday.

"Maybe they were someone else's?" Ellie said.

"Maybe. But while she was talking out loud to herself she said she had to do something important that night – meaning last night. And then she died. And the more I think about those two things the more curious I am about them. The trainers, especially, are out of character – at least according to Marzia. And what was it that she had to do that was so important? Could it be that she needed the sneakers to do it?" I thought of my afternoon and how I'd had been chased, followed, trapped and more. "Or did she simply have to do something that required some kind of physical effort?"

"Good questions, Nancy Drew. Ooh, perfect!" Ellie cooed as I stepped out of the stall. "I love that dress."

"H&M, High Street Kensington, in case you're wondering."

"Thanks for the info."

I went to the mirror, took my make-up bag out of my

rucksack and tried to clean up my face and hair as best as I could. Surprisingly, my hair didn't look too bad. The mixture of tunnel grime and aqueduct water had somehow congealed to give it fantastic texture. It fell in chunky strands to just past my shoulders – and without any frizz!

"Your hair looks amazing, Axelle," said Ellie. "Good choice of product."

I didn't say anything.

But my face was a different matter. Using a moist tissue I wiped away the dirt and spiderwebs. Then I added some powder, mascara and lip gloss, and brushed my eyebrows with some eyebrow gel. I added some blush for good measure, too. It was as good as it was going to get.

"We better get going," Ellie said. "You have to meet Coco and this party isn't going to last long."

"Ellie, can you introduce me to Coco's mother, too? Didn't you say she'd be at the book launch?"

"Yeah, she'll be there. And she's really cool. Why?"

"I need to ask her about Falco Ventini and his last few years there."

"Well, she'll know all about that. Come on." Ellie linked her arm through mine and we walked back to the lobby. There we met up with the others, including Sebastian, and together we walked the short distance to the book launch party.

WEDNESDAY EVENING

Couture and Cards

Rizzoli Galleria is located in one of the oldest shopping malls in existence – the stunning Galleria Vittorio Emanuele II. The high-vaulted ceilings glittered far above us in the soft evening light that streamed through its glass roof. Fantastic mosaics ran along the top of the buildings, made of gold and coloured tiles that twinkled gently. And although many of the stores, like Prada and Louis Vuitton, had closed for the day, the galleria was still busy and crowded. A hubbub of laughter and chatter could be heard from the busy terraces where people were eating and drinking.

Though the Rizzoli bookstore was closed to the public, inside it was clearly running on full steam. Dazzlingly bright, its interior was white with clean spare lines, high ceilings and dark wooden floors. Bookcases lined every wall and a simple staircase, right in the middle of the store, led to the various floors.

The fashionistas were out in full force and a number of paparazzi were waiting outside, but fortunately Ellie and her friends quickly became the focus of the photographers' lenses, so Sebastian and I were able to slip in unnoticed – and I made sure to keep my rucksack with the cards in it tucked tightly underneath my arm.

"What did you find out?" I asked Sebastian as we headed towards a quiet corner away from the crowds and the bar.

"Well, it turns out *all* of them were working for Falco right up until his death." Sebastian stopped as he took a couple of orange juices off a passing tray. "Also, it seems there was a lot going on in Falco's last year. Apparently his last collection was his most intensive and beautiful – ever. And then he became very ill just after showing it. And his business was struggling too. So good stuff and bad stuff. It must have been a tough time." Sebastian took his phone out and showed me various articles he'd saved.

"Wow, his last show was a real biggie…" Sebastian clicked on a video of it. I admired the rich, Byzantine fantasy of bejewelled dresses and accessories. The hair and make-up were stunning too. The models all looked like princesses from an extravagant dream, their hair lustrous and either pinned high or left long and loose. On their heads they wore jewelled crowns of varying sizes and styles – and sometimes flowers too; rich, dark-red carnations and wine-coloured roses that matched the deep tones of their matt lipstick. But the dresses! They were a lavish parade of shimmering tunics, sparkling shorts, jewelled corsets and gem-encrusted lace gowns and more spectacular than any I'd ever seen.

"Amazing, right?" Sebastian said.

I nodded as I surfed through the other articles he'd bookmarked for me to read.

"Can you send me all of these articles?"

"Will do. By the way, all the reviews for his last show were amazing. And when you read the articles they all say that he'd never worked harder. Of course, his financial difficulties might have motivated him."

I nodded. "When I was doing my background reading on Ugo I came across a lot of information on how close Falco was to bankruptcy. It seemed he spent too much – he thought of himself as an artist first and foremost and totally ignored the business side of things…"

I suddenly felt that excited buzz that comes over me when my detective gut feels it's onto something. I still had no way of tying any of this to Elisabetta's death, but my instinct was humming – and that felt great.

As if picking up on my vibe Sebastian asked, "So what's your plan for tonight?"

"I'm going to meet Coco – although now it's actually her mother I'm more interested in."

"To ask about Falco's last year?"

"Exactly. And then I'm hoping that Ugo might be here,

although I'd like to surprise him somewhere quiet. He's so smooth that if he sees me first, or if we're distracted by other people, he'll have time to plan what he wants to say. And then let's see who else I bump into."

"Like Lucas?"

"Yes, like Lucas. Although I won't be bumping into him *in* here – he's not invited so I'll have to keep my eye out for him. He said he'd be at the entrance later. I do need to find out more about the tarot cards…"

"And I bet Mr Moony-Eyes would love to answer."

"If it helps me with the case…"

Sebastian rolled his eyes.

"By the way, check that out…" I nodded in the direction of the entrance. Cameras were flashing and everyone was staring as Alessandro entered.

"Do you see what I see, Watson?"

Sebastian nodded. "He's limping."

"Exactly. And he definitely wasn't when I saw him at the casting yesterday. I'm going to need to find out how that happened. As soon as he's worked his way further into the room, I'll 'bump' into him."

"Absolutely, Holmes."

We watched for another minute and Sebastian asked, "And what's my objective for tonight?"

"Listen out for rumours. Anything to do with Falco's last year or that last show or whatever. Keep searching for anything that might give one of the suspects a motive. We also need to find out what Elisabetta wanted to do last night and why she had those trainers in her basket – not that I know how I can find out anything more about them without looking through her personal effects."

"Which, no doubt, are still in the hands of the police."

"Probably."

Sebastian was smiling at me.

"Care to share what's on your mind, Watson?"

"It makes a change, you know, to see you without a bat in your hair."

"I'm glad your humour is intact, even after the day we've had."

"But, seriously, your hair looks nice…"

Our eyes locked for a moment – and then Francesca's voice rang out from behind us.

"Sebastian!" she cried excitedly. "There you are!" She looked stunning, in a short red dress that hugged her curves. High, gold platform heels and some long beaded drop earrings added a touch of fun and funk to her outfit. Her dark wavy hair was loose and in her hand she held a leopard-skin clutch.

Looking at Francesca I couldn't help but think that just as some of us are born with frizzy hair or the need for glasses, Italian women are born stylish. Honestly, the city was packed with chic women. "Oh, you're here, too," she said when she saw me. She was looking at me as if I could give her some kind of disease just by standing near her.

"Yes, I'm here, too." I forced myself to smile. "I hope you've had a good day?" I looked around me hoping Ellie was free to introduce me to Coco. The last thing I wanted was to stand there listening to Francesca – she really brought out the worst in me. But if Sebastian found her *that* interesting then he was welcome to stay where he was. I sighed with frustration as I thought that she was actually the perfect person to ask about Falco's last year. I told myself that before leaving the party I'd have to ignore her attitude and question her. First things first though.

"If you don't mind I'm just going to find Ellie," I told Sebastian. I watched as Francesca took a nibble from a passing tray and greeted another guest.

"Go ahead," Sebastian said. Then he leaned into my ear and whispered, "And don't worry, I'm on the case."

I rolled my eyes. "Just make sure you ask her about Falco's last year."

"Promise. And I won't get all moony-eyed."

"It looks like it's too late for that." As soon as I said it I kicked myself for sounding so annoyed. Luckily at that moment I spotted Ellie waving at me from the other side of the room. I mumbled a quick "See you soon, Watson," then turned and left. As I made my way towards Ellie, though, I was stopped by Benoit, the hairstylist from Tuesday's shoot.

"Wow wow wow, Axelle," he crooned as he reached out and touched my hair. "*J'adore!* What have you done to your hair? It looks a-maz-ing!" He was standing in front of me, reaching out with both his hands to twirl strands of my hair around his fingers. "How did you get this fabulous texture?"

"Um…" I didn't know what to say. In truth it was down to a mixture of spiderwebs, dirt, aqueduct water, possibly bat poo and definitely tunnel slime. "Well, you know, it's a little bit of this and a little bit of that. Something I mixed myself."

Benoit narrowed his eyes. "I don't believe you, *non, non, non!*" He wagged his finger at me. "I will get your secret recipe out of you next time," he laughed.

"By the way, Benoit, can I just ask you something? You told me you were an old friend of Elisabetta's, right? That the two of you go way back…"

Benoit stopped smiling and nodded. "We were very good friends, yes – even if I didn't see her as much as I used to. She lived here, I live in Paris, but still, during the fashion shows we'd catch up and since she started working at *Amare* she booked me whenever possible. She was sweet that way, very loyal. I still can't believe what happened yesterday."

"I know. It's terrible."

"Yes, and everyone is talking about it, which makes it even worse. They seem to think she was poisoned…"

"It's hard to believe. But listen, do you know by any chance if Elisabetta liked tarot?"

"*Tarot*? You mean the cards that tell the future?"

I nodded.

"No. She never went in for any of that kind of stuff. Never. She used to laugh when she saw me reading my horoscope. Why?"

"Just wondering." I moved on before he got more curious. "And I'm also wondering whether she liked to work out?"

Benoit laughed. "No way. She liked to eat healthily and look after her skin and weight, but otherwise it was like she was allergic to the gym, running or anything that made her sweat."

"You never saw her in trainers then, I guess?"

Benoit shook his head. "No way! I don't think she even owned a pair."

"But there was a pair in her basket yesterday."

"Okay…that's funny." Benoit shook his head and looked at me quizzically. "Unless they belonged to someone else? Or she decided to turn over a new leaf and was keeping it a secret?"

"Maybe," I answered. "I don't suppose Elisabetta mentioned anything to you about something important she had to do last night?"

Benoit started to shake his head but then stopped abruptly. "You know, it's interesting you should say that because we actually had dinner plans for last night. We'd spoken on Monday about it and I'd suggested that we grab a bite to eat straight after the shoot. But she told me she'd have to meet with me a bit later because there was something else she needed to do first. Maybe that was the important thing? I have no idea what it could have been, though."

"Me neither...but that's what she said just before she died. It seems so sad, she never got to do what she'd wanted to do..." I hoped he'd buy this as an excuse for bringing up the subject.

I watched as Francesca and Sebastian swept past us, her hand on his arm, but I wasn't going to let that distract me. I ignored them and turned back to Benoit. "You know, I'm writing a fashion article for my school magazine. I thought I might do it on the Ventini brand and some of the interesting people who've worked there – like Elisabetta. She was there for some time, wasn't she?"

He nodded. "I think she met Falco through a summer school experience programme. They really hit it off. Falco loved her – but then, who didn't? I saw her a lot when she was a freelance stylist, in Paris and New York. But then she decided to move back to Milan. She went straight to work for Ventini and stayed there until just after he died. She was part of the team that put together his last collection – she was Falco's most trusted in-house stylist. He ran every stylistic decision past her – much to Ginevra's annoyance! Ugo didn't mind, though – he valued her opinion too. Anyway, Elisabetta got me in to do the hair for Falco's last show. What an amazing night that was!" As I listened to Benoit, images of those incredible jewelled dresses came to mind.

"Falco was so happy when she moved back from NYC – she was like family to him. He depended on her a lot, I think. He could ask her for anything and she'd help him. One person was really put out when Elisabetta returned though. You know, of course, that Francesca is Falco's niece? Well, she was very jealous of the relationship between Falco and Elisabetta. I could tell from the way Francesca looked at Elisabetta…she saw her as an interloper.

"Anyway, after Falco died Elisabetta was lost for a while, but then she got the chance to move to *Amare*, and becoming a fashion editor, well it was like a dream come true for her. "

"Wasn't she worried about working under Ginevra Mucci?"

Benoit shrugged his shoulders. "She always said she could handle Ginevra. And you know, the thing is, Milanese fashion is a small world – she could never have avoided Ginevra – unless she moved away again."

Ellie suddenly appeared. "Axelle, here you are. I wanted to introduce you to Coco Sommerino D'Alda."

I said hello to Coco and the four of us chatted for a few minutes before Benoit excused himself. Like me, Coco was just sixteen. Tall, gangly and friendly, she had a funny way of laughing: she'd thrust her neck out and show a lot of teeth. And while that may not sound too attractive, somehow it fitted her coltish looks. Her skin was flawless, her hair long, dark and glossy and she had enormous expressive eyes. She was beautifully dressed, too, in a short candy-pink Ventini dress.

Ellie stood listening while I explained to Coco that I'd seen Elisabetta die, and had even been questioned by the police. As I'd hoped, this led her to tell me about the after-party at Ugo's.

"I've known Elisabetta all my life," Coco explained. "She was a good friend of Mum's. I can't believe I'll never see her again."

"You must have known Falco too?" I asked.

"Since I was a baby," she agreed. "He was like an uncle to me."

But I quickly established that Coco knew little of Falco's day-to-day work life.

She was still at school, after all. The excitement I'd felt about making progress with the case was flattening out now. I didn't seem to be getting anywhere. But then Coco's mother suddenly swept down upon us.

"Hello, darling," she said to Ellie before turning to me. "I'm Lavinia, Coco's mother." She was very grand and very polite. She too had long thick brown hair and Coco had clearly inherited her mother's large eyes. I knew that Lavinia had modelled when she was younger, and, besides working in PR for Falco Ventini, she'd married the scion of an old Milanese banking family. According to Ellie, she was half Venetian and half Brazilian and very well connected. "She knows everyone who's anyone in Milan," Ellie whispered in my ear.

"Are you having fun, girls?" Lavinia breezily waved a ring-laden hand.

"Yes, we are, thank you," Ellie said. "Lavinia, my friend Axelle is a huge fan of Ugo Anbessa's work for Ventini—"

"So are we," Lavinia interrupted as she waved her other ring-laden hand to indicate herself and Coco.

"But Axelle is also curious to know what Falco's work was like. She didn't start modelling until this spring, so she never saw him."

"I especially like his last few collections," I added, hoping to steer the conversation in a helpful direction.

"Ah," said Lavinia. "Falco was an artist, you know. Very old school – he was the last in a generation that included Oscar de la Renta, Yves Saint Laurent and Hubert de Givenchy. They had great reverence for craftwork and design. Falco did all of his own drawings too, you know. Half of the so-called young designers today – especially the 'lifestyle' designers in America – don't even know how to hold a pencil. They have 'design teams' to discuss ideas with. I'm not saying that's bad – it's just different. Falco could also sew – he was very good at embroidery. I was stunned the first time I saw him personally take a needle and thread to make a last-minute correction to a dress before it headed out onto the runway. Very few designers are capable of doing that, you know."

"I heard he had some money trouble towards the end of his life?" I said.

"It's true," agreed Lavinia. "Falco was a lousy businessman. Thank goodness Ugo has taken over. He's doing a marvellous job."

Fortunately Lavinia liked to talk and didn't question my interest so I continued asking her about the general atmosphere of the design studio during Falco's last days, pushing her for as much information as I could get.

"It was interesting," Lavinia explained. "I mean, it was so busy – and so sad. You know, Falco's last haute couture collection was his best – ever. The fashion world was raving about it, and those dresses – they were *stupendo*! You know, the last one, it was a spectacular red-jewelled evening gown?" I could picture the dress as she spoke. "He did most of the sewing on it himself – sent the exhausted seamstresses home early while he stayed on in the atelier and continued to work on it on his own. He loved that dress! Then again, who didn't? It was covered in precious and semi-precious stones and cost a fortune. And if you're wondering how I know, it's because I handled all of Falco's haute couture sales personally. That dress was on the cover of I don't know how many magazines the month after it went down the runway. Anyway, it's sad, but despite all of the beauty he was creating, and the rave reviews, the rest of his life was a mess. His business was close to collapsing – and then he fell ill. And, well, it all ended very quickly."

"When did he find out he was ill?"

Lavinia shut her eyes and shook her head. "He'd probably tell you that it was in the cards. But the thing is, for a long time he'd had stomach pain that just wouldn't go away. When he finally went to the hospital to get it checked it was too late. The cancer had spread; it was inoperable. He died three months later."

Although I listened to everything Lavinia said, one comment was still ringing in my ears. *He'd probably tell you it was in the cards.* What did that mean? Did she mean it literally? Had Falco used cards to read his future? In which case could it be that he did it with tarot cards?

"Lavinia, what did you mean about Falco saying his illness was 'in the cards'?"

"Oh, nothing. Just that Falco loved *tarocchi*. You call them *tarot* in French."

"And in English," I said.

"Well, he loved it. And he absolutely believed in the power of the cards. He had a reader he saw regularly – but not one of these street readers. No. Falco's was someone he'd found in the south of Italy, in Bari. I always called her his personal witch. He would fly her up from Bari and she would stay just long enough to do his reading and then she'd fly back down. She was quite chic, actually. Not at all what you'd expect. She was very softly spoken, too. But there was a look in her eye…"

I smiled. "What do you mean?"

Lavinia drew closer. "It was as if she could see right through you…"

Just hearing that Falco consulted a tarot reader suddenly had me buzzing again. He believed in tarot and I'd found tarot cards!

"Did Falco have any tarot cards of his own?"

"Oh, yes. He collected them. His niece Francesca inherited them, I believe. Although for his readings, Signora Ferrera always used her own cards."

Now I was really buzzing. I still didn't know why I'd found those three tarot cards at Megastudio on Tuesday but maybe they were somehow connected to Falco? But how? And what kind of collection did Francesca inherit? Did it include any very old cards? It was even more important now that I talked to her. Questions were pinging around in my head. Meanwhile Lavinia was getting ready to move on. She waved at a group nearby and then after quickly double air-kissing Ellie and me, and telling Coco to let her know if she ended up leaving with friends, she was gone.

I had to find Francesca. I had to ask about her uncle's tarot card collection. I said I had to use the loo and I left. Ellie winked at me as I went.

It didn't take long to spy Francesca through the crowds. Surprisingly, she was on her own – and she was talking on her phone. I walked up to her and cleared my throat loudly. She turned around and pursed her lips when she saw me. I jumped in as soon as she ended her conversation.

"Francesca, would you mind answering a few questions for me? I'm writing an article for my school magazine—"

"How cute – your 'school magazine'," she said as she reached for a meatball from a passing tray.

I ignored the jibe. "Yes. And I've decided to write about Falco Ventini – the man and the brand. I know he was your uncle…"

She rolled her eyes. "Please, everybody knows. It's a burden being related to someone so famous. I'm never seen as being my own person, you know. It's lucky I have the personality to handle it."

I said nothing although I knew from what Ugo had said that she never let anyone forget she was a Ventini. I cleared my throat again. "I wanted to find out some unusual facts about your uncle…I know he liked *tarocchi* – Lavinia was just telling me he left you his collection."

Francesca turned to me, her eyes slightly narrowed. "Yes, he did. He taught me all about tarot – the cards and the game. He was practically an expert. Do you know anything about *tarocchi*?"

I decided to play my card. "Yes, actually, I do. I've got a few antique ones. Maybe you've got some similar ones in your collection? Mine are Milanese and date from about 1450…"

"Really?" She was playing with the straw in her drink. "Well, unfortunately, I don't have any in my collection that are quite that old."

"Oh...that's surprising. I'd heard your uncle had some antique cards, too." I hadn't really, but just wanted to see her reaction.

"Yes, but nothing as old as that. At least not in what I inherited." I watched as she looked over my shoulder and into the crowd, her eyes darting around the room. Clearly she'd had enough of my questions. I grabbed a last chance to press her for more information. "You must have been very close to Elisabetta?"

"Well, she worked for my family..."

"Someone was saying earlier that she was like family to your uncle..."

Francesca pursed her lips for a moment. "Yes, they were close...had been for a long time. She visited him every day when he was in hospital – but so did I. And my uncle had many other friends, too. But a blood connection means so much more, you know. Anyway, Axelle, nice talking to you but I have to go now." She turned to leave then but stopped and looked back over her shoulder at me. "By the way, if you ever decide to sell your cards, let me know – maybe I'll add them to my collection." Then she laughed and quickly disappeared into the crowd.

I wasn't at all sure what to make of our exchange. But I didn't have time to think about it – at that moment I felt a hand reach out for me and grasp me around the waist. "Hi there, beautiful."

I turned; it was Lucas.

"I've been looking for you."

"I didn't think you had an invitation."

"Coco let me in."

"You know her?"

"Milan is small – don't forget. And over the years my dad has helped Coco's parents with their collection of Renaissance art."

"But no tarot cards?" I hugged my rucksack closer to me at the thought of the valuable *tarocchi* hidden inside.

"No, no tarot cards. There are very few collectors of the antique *tarocchi* – which makes you all the more rare."

I felt myself blush and quickly looked into my rucksack for my lip gloss. Anything to avoid his eyes. Then I apologized again for my earlier no-show. I gave Lucas the same excuse I'd given my agency – a sudden illness.

"Well you look amazing now," Lucas said. "Clearly an upset stomach suits you."

I laughed, but I could feel my colour rising again. I'd heard Italian (okay, so he was half American, but still) guys were huge flirts, and so far, Lucas seemed to be bearing that out. "Come on, I'll get you a Coke with a lemon slice in it. That's always good for stomach trouble." We got our drinks and walked to a far corner of the store. I noticed Sebastian watching me, but I avoided making eye contact.

He'd spent time with Francesca uninterrupted, and now it was my turn to spend time with Lucas – he was important to the case after all. I was wondering about the best way to ask him about Ugo's visit this morning, when he brought it up himself.

"Listen," Lucas whispered as he leaned in close to my ear. "I wanted to tell you what happened after you left this morning. Someone else – the third person, now – told me that if someone called Rinconi came looking to sell antique *tarocchi* cards that I was to inform him as soon as possible. He offered to buy them immediately – and at any price. He seemed quite desperate to have them."

"This third person," I said carefully, "was he wearing dark clothes, bracelets and a gold watch?"

Lucas was adamant he couldn't reveal his clients' identities, but I could see by his reaction that the description had rung true.

I couldn't believe it! How did Ugo know about the cards? And why say someone called Rinconi would be selling them? Rinconi was Elisabetta's last name. And of course he knew Elisabetta was dead.

"But unlike the other two people," Lucas continued, "this third person asked me specifically about *three* antique *tarocchi* cards. It can't just be coincidence…"

No, I thought, *it can't.*

I had to see Ugo as soon as possible and get some answers out of him. He was definitely holding back some information from me. *But what?* And why didn't he tell me – especially as he was the one who'd asked me to solve this case?

"By the way, I'd be interested to see any other cards your…*godmother* might have…" His eyes were curious. Did he still think I'd stolen them?

I decided to play it cool. "There are no others. But thank you, Lucas, for telling me about the third caller. And I promise that if I decide to sell the cards you'll be the first know."

He smiled, and I tried to the stop colour rising in my cheeks again by asking another question. "By the way, you didn't happen to notice anything especially unusual about my cards, did you? Besides that they're old and possibly famous?"

He shook his head. "No. They looked to be in good shape, no strange marks or, worse, tears – that can really hurt the value of a card. But just let me know when you'd like me to look at them again. Or, I could tell you more over dinner and maybe show you around Milan a bit?" He saw the doubt in my eyes and quickly added, "Of course, if you've been feeling sick then you're probably not hungry or in the mood to sightsee. But maybe we could go out for a drink or something?"

He'd been flirting with me earlier, but still his question caught me by surprise.

In the event it was easy to back out. I told him I had to

work tomorrow and that it was better I had a good night's sleep; my agency would probably drop me like a hot potato if I had to cancel again tomorrow.

Lucas totally understood and we made tentative plans to meet up the next day – to talk about *tarocchi*. If he was hoping this would lead to more than just *tarocchi*, well, I'd cross that bridge when I got to it.

"At the very least, though, why don't I walk you home?" Lucas had just asked this question when Sebastian suddenly appeared at my side.

"Axelle, I'm going to take Francesca home quickly. You don't mind, do you?"

Actually I do, I thought. I wanted to ask him if driving her home had anything to do with the case, but with Lucas standing in between us I kept my thoughts to myself. Instead I said, "Don't worry about me, Sebastian. Lucas has just offered to take me home." I smiled at him.

Sebastian looked annoyed. "I can come right back…"

"Don't worry," Lucas said smoothly.

Ignoring Lucas, Sebastian quietly said to me, "If that's how you want it…"

"Yes."

"Fine."

"Good."

"Have fun."

"You too."

I made plans to meet Lucas again fifteen minutes later.

I hadn't seen Ugo, but I had to speak to Alessandro before I left.

He was surrounded by people; it was difficult to get close. But I was certain he'd seen me – though he'd quickly averted his glance. What was that about?

I pushed my way towards him. "You again?" he asked. He had a drink in one hand and was clearly enjoying himself.

"Yes, I'm here with friends. I saw you and just wanted to know how you're getting on."

"Not well. I miss Elisabetta. I don't even know why I'm here."

"I know, it must be very hard for you," I said, trying to sound sympathetic. "I guess it's good to keep yourself busy."

"Sure," he said impatiently.

"I noticed you were limping earlier. What happened? Are you okay?" I tried.

"I twisted my ankle going down some stairs. Nothing major." He was watching me. "How about you? How are you doing?" He crushed some ice in his teeth as he waited for me to answer.

"I'm well, thanks. Work is going great – but I hardly have to tell you how busy Milan can get."

He pushed his long blond hair behind his ears and leaned close to me. "What about Elisabetta?" he whispered in his sing-song, accented English. "Have you heard anything else about her? I still haven't figured out where she had to go on Tuesday night – have you?"

I shook my head. "But why is it so important to know what she was planning on doing?"

I saw my question took him by surprise, but he hid it well. "For sentimental reasons." He pulled back and watched me again for a moment. "Anyway," he said, his manner suddenly brisk, "keep me posted, all right?"

"Sure." I watched as he quickly turned and joined the large group standing beside us.

Some questioning! I hadn't gleaned much, but his sudden limp made me wonder. As did his persistence in following up on Elisabetta's whereabouts on Tuesday night. "Sentimental reasons" he'd claimed. Hmm…

I suddenly felt hungry and tired. I'd been running on adrenaline all day and hadn't had a proper meal since breakfast. I also had plenty of new information bubbling in my head. Around us the party was fizzling out. Many people had left and others were heading out of the doors. I looked at my watch. I had just enough time to get back to the flat before Mrs B started looking out for me.

I waved goodbye to Ellie and she mouthed that she'd be leaving in a few minutes. Then Lucas and I headed out of the door and into the night.

It was a short walk to the model flat. We quickly fell into an easy rhythm as Lucas led me down side streets and across quiet squares. Along the way he pointed out churches and buildings where famous people lived. Inevitably, however, the subject returned to the tarot cards.

I asked him about the meaning of my cards.

"Ha! It is not straightforward. To be a good reader you have to know the cards, but you have to have intuition, too. Good intuition is vital to bring nuance to the reading and also to foresee problems. Also, don't forget that as you lay the cards out on the table a card's strength and positivity can be made weaker or stronger depending on which cards are next to it. Even the way a card is laid – with the picture facing the reader or facing the person having the reading? – has an effect on the outcome…"

"Wow. I had no idea there was so much to it," I said. "I thought the pictures told a clear story. I didn't know there was such detailed interpretation involved."

"Most people don't realize that. It's why good tarot readers have an almost magical aura around them."

"Okay, but in general, what is the basic meaning of the cards I have? Surely every card has a sort of intrinsic meaning that remains the same no matter how it's interpreted?"

Lucas nodded. "Yes, absolutely. So for instance, we talked about the death card that you have, with the grinning skeleton."

"Yes…"

"Well that card always refers to mortality. But, again, depending on the cards that are laid out next to it during a reading it can also be interpreted to mean a drastic life change of some sort – or even a fear of some kind. It doesn't always refer to a death."

I nodded as I took in everything he said. "Okay…and what about that man who looks like a magician? Does he refer to magic or fortune?"

"That's actually called the magician card. He's a kind of magician in that he is working with his hands and can seem to make something out of nothing. So the magician can also refer to manual skill."

Funnily, when I heard that I immediately thought of Falco and what Lavinia had said about him being very good with his hands – how he would draw and even sew his own clothes.

"And what about the lady on horseback?"

"She's more difficult to interpret. The image has no obvious clue to the meaning. It would help if I had the other cards in the deck – then I might be able to figure her out by a process of elimination. But she could refer to a love of art or productivity, to various roles associated with medieval women. Something like a wife or mother, queen or heiress. I'm sorry I can't be more precise…"

We were standing outside my building now and facing each other. He was tall. I looked up and into those green, green eyes of his. There was an easy elegance in the way he dressed and styled himself that definitely marked him out as Italian – though to hear him speak English, you'd think he was one hundred per cent American. *That's the advantage of being both*, I thought.

His look was flirtatious, but his curiosity about the tarot

cards was genuine. As we approached the flat, I wasn't sure quite what he intended, but in the event he smiled, stepped back slightly and said, "I'm serious about helping you, Axelle. Let me know if I can, all right?"

I was relieved not to have got into any kind of awkward romantic situation with Lucas. I thanked him for bringing me home and we confirmed our plans to meet again tomorrow. His insight was invaluable – I definitely wanted him to have another look at the cards. But in the meantime, I really needed to climb into bed and get a good night's sleep. I had the feeling tomorrow was going to be another busy day.

The main thing I would need to do was confront Ugo. I was sure he was hiding a missing piece of the puzzle and somehow I'd have to get it out of him. But when and how?

I had my Cutie-Pie booking all day. But I also needed to move forward with this case and my instinct told me that Ugo was the key to that. I had to see him in person – and if the messages he'd left on my phone were anything to go by, he was curious about how I was doing...

I quickly texted him saying that I was sorry I hadn't called him all day but that I'd been working the entire time and hadn't been alone for one moment (that much was true). I also added that I would contact him first thing in the morning – he just didn't know that it would be at his house and in person!

THURSDAY MORNING
Looks Can Be Deceiving

At 6.30 a.m. my alarm clock roused me from a deep sleep. I felt great and stretched lazily in my bed. I missed Halley, my West Highland White Terrier. At home she slept on my bed and in the mornings it was her cute little fuzzy face with its two black button eyes and wet black nose that woke me. Okay, sometimes her bad breath woke me, too, but, still, I missed her. I reached over and stopped the alarm. *No time for online research this morning,* I thought. I had to get up and go to Ugo's.

Last night after getting back I'd debated for some time before finally phoning Sebastian to ask him whether he could find out for me what time Ugo left his apartment in the mornings. The only reason I'd hesitated was because I definitely did not want him thinking I was just trying to find out if he was still with Francesca. In the end, though, I phoned, because a case is a case is a case, and with lives and reputations on the line, it had to come first.

It turned out he was at his *Pensione*. He apologized for not walking me home and asked me if Moony-Eyes had been nice. And it turned out he knew from Francesca that Ugo worked out in the mornings at his home gym. He usually left his home at around nine.

I had to get to my booking at nine, so I figured if I was at Ugo's by 7.30 at the latest, then I'd have at least a good hour with him before I had to head off.

I quickly got up and out of bed and put myself together. After yesterday, trousers – and not a dress or a skirt – would definitely be the key component of my #OOTD again. I pulled on a pair of old skinny white jeans – they were faded and soft and thin – a loose grey T-shirt, a studded pair of blue Converse high-tops, and a tiny black leather jacket. My rucksack completed the outfit. I had a quick breakfast and told Ellie I'd call her from the shoot. Then I ran to the metro station and caught a train to Moscova, the stop nearest Ugo's apartment.

Ugo was indeed surprised to see me. It was Maria who answered the intercom and I waited while she found him – she wouldn't let me in without asking him first.

"Axelle, is that you?" Ugo's voice blared out through the loudspeaker.

I assured him it was and he buzzed me through. I took the lift to the top floor where Maria was waiting for me at the door. She led me straight to his gym.

I'd already decided to jump right in so I hadn't even set my rucksack down before I looked at him and said, "Ugo, why were you at Professor Greene's yesterday?"

He was breathing hard, his legs and arms pumping as he worked on his cross-trainer. "I wasn't—" he began.

"Ugo, please," I said, "don't deny it. I saw you! I *was* there." I was glaring at him.

He hopped off his cross-trainer and wiped the sweat off his face with a towel. "So I did see you."

"Yes, you did. But I need to know what you were doing there; if I'm going to solve this case, I need you to be straight with me, Ugo."

"I was checking about some Renaissance art. Professor Greene is the best expert in Milan and I needed some advice." He avoided looking me in the eye. I watched him as he went to a bench press and started lifting weights. He wasn't unfriendly but he was definitely trying to brush off my questions.

"Ugo, come on," I said as I walked across the room and stood over him. "You're keeping something back from me and I won't stop until I find out what it is. So unless you want me to follow you around all day I'd start spilling the beans. Now. You asked me to help you find out what really happened to Elisabetta. Fine. But you seem to have your own theory – one you don't want to share. Why not? What is going on?"

"Nothing. I swear." Ugo looked uncomfortable. "I don't know more than you do."

"I don't believe that, Ugo. And you know something else? If you're looking for three antique tarot cards that belonged to Elisabetta, then you're wasting your time at Professor Greene's because *I have them*."

That finally surprised him. He set the weights down and looked up at me. "You do? Are you sure?" He looked confused. "But how can *you* have them?"

"Come clean with me about everything and I'll tell you. I ended up trapped in a tunnel yesterday because of this case, you know – it's a miracle I escaped." My anger was rising and I paced in front of him as I let him have it. "That's the real reason I didn't call you back yesterday. Someone is after those tarot cards – and it's not just you."

I was really angry now. All of my frustration about yesterday's wild-goose chase and my lack of solid leads bubbled to the surface. "I risked my life once to help you but I'm not going to do it again. And if you don't tell me right now what is *really* going on, then after I leave here I'm going straight to the police with the cards – and I'll wash my hands of all of this. Is that what you want? Some friend of Elisabetta's you are."

That last volley stung him. He rose up angrily and flung his towel down to the ground. "All right, I'll tell you what I know."

"*Everything* you know?"

"Yes, everything I know – but you have to promise me that it won't go beyond this room. Please." He took a deep breath and stood with his back to me, hands on hips.

"First of all," he said, "what I'm about to tell you is a rumour – and I'm not sure how much of it to believe. Elisabetta believed it – in fact, if there's any truth to it, it might be why she was killed…but, again, I have no way of knowing. So, I'll start at the beginning…"

He motioned for me to sit in a leather armchair. Then he began. "At the time that Falco became seriously ill his business was in very, very bad shape. Basically, he was as close to bankruptcy as you can get without it becoming official."

"You already told me that."

"*Esatto*. Well, at that time there were a lot of rumours going through the Ventini atelier and one of them concerned the dresses from his last collection."

"And…?"

"Well, the most spectacular dresses in that collection were embroidered with jewels – real ones. Like, I mean precious and semi-precious stones – rubies, sapphires, peridots, amethysts and many, many more. You see, Falco was very good with his hands. He could really sew!" I let Ugo know that I'd already found that out. "And in the lead-up to what turned out to be his last show, he was in the atelier until very late every night, either working alone or together with the seamstresses – for hours on end. He did this before every show. But for this collection he worked even longer hours than usual and regularly sent everyone home so he could work on them – especially the grand showstopper dress – alone. Granted, the dresses in his last collection had much more embroidery than usual, but, still…this caused some of the in-house jokers to suggest that he was probably exchanging the real stones for crystal and glass replicas…"

My mind was whizzing. Lavinia had said that Falco had done much of the sewing on the most bejewelled dress *alone*. Because he'd loved it. Now I couldn't help but wonder if the "jokers" had been right. "You mean, he swapped the stones so that he could sell on the real jewels?"

Ugo nodded. "That was the gossip, anyway. That he was going to use the jewels to save his business."

"But that sounds mad…"

"Yes, but Falco almost had a touch of madness about him. It was the kind of thing I could imagine him doing… Whether he actually did it or not, I have no way of knowing. But I think Elisabetta believed he had. Again, I have no proof. But she hinted at it."

"But how would *she* have known, when nobody else did? There are lots of people going in and out of the atelier just before the shows start. Surely if Falco had switched the jewels someone would have seen him?"

"Not necessarily. Falco liked to work alone and he was fast with his hands – and he was the boss. No one ever questioned him. And, as you know, Elisabetta and Falco were very close. She was his in-house stylist at Ventini, but in a sense she was more like a muse to him – he asked her opinion on everything and he loved to have her around. Both had unhappy family backgrounds; each found a kindred spirit in the other. So if any of this is true, I can imagine that if he told anyone anything about it, then he would have told Elisabetta. He really trusted her, you know – and for good reason. She was very loyal and more like family for Falco than Francesca ever was. He knew Francesca traded on his name and he didn't like it." Ugo stopped to shrug his shoulders. "As far as the jewel switch goes," he continued, "Falco always did love a good story and in the end he was taking so much medication for the pain – it's hard to know what to believe."

"If the story *was* true, have you any idea how he might have sold the jewels?"

"Well that's just it," said Ugo. "*I* don't know. But, again, I have the feeling that Elisabetta did. But then that would mean the rumour had to be true – and is it? Who knows? And the people who would know – the women who bought the dresses – haven't complained. *At all.* There hasn't been one client who has called us up to accuse us of switching the jewels on their dresses for fake ones."

"But did the client know to expect real jewels on the dress?"

"Absolutely. There was a lot of press about it – and, in part, the dresses were spectacular *because* of it. As far as I know, though, the clients have all been thrilled. I've even seen photographs of a couple of them wearing the dresses at huge balls. And some went straight to private collections – people collect haute couture, you know. Anyway, we can hardly call the clients up now and say, 'By the way, before he died Falco may have switched the real jewels on your dress for fake ones. Could you have a look for us, please?'! I could just imagine what the Ventini company board would say. Why stir up all that trouble when no one has complained?"

Checking the dresses seemed the best way to verify the rumours, I thought. But if they were all in the hands of clients – and those clients had never complained, what could I do?

"Anyway," Ugo continued, "on Monday night, at my after-party, Elisabetta surprised me by suddenly asking to speak with me privately. We went into my study and she started talking about the rumour of the jewel switch and how she had something important to do on the following evening – the night of the day she died – and that Falco's ghost would finally be happy. I cut her off immediately. I was completely exasperated with this rumour nonsense! It wasn't the first time she'd brought the subject up – but I wanted it to be the last. I told her to forget Falco and to let sleeping dogs lie. I reminded her that we'd never had any clients complain."

"What did she say to that?"

"She told me that I had no idea what I was talking about

and that everything was fine and going according to plan. Whatever that meant."

So that was the subject of the loud discussion between Ugo and Elisabetta on Monday night. I asked Ugo if he realized that the others had heard them arguing. He looked sheepish. "I may have sounded a bit forceful – but it was only because I wanted to make her think. I mean, her career had just hit a new high and here she was banging on about Falco's ghost. I know she loved him, but enough was enough!"

Hmm… It seemed that Elisabetta believed Falco had switched the jewels on his haute couture dresses. But that didn't mean it was a fact. Somehow I would have to find out… In the meantime I said, "Ugo I have to ask you again what it was you were doing at Professor Greene's office yesterday morning. I know you were asking about the tarot cards – but why?"

Ugo took another deep breath. "This is going to sound crazy…"

"Try me."

"As you know, Elisabetta died suddenly and I know she left no will. But she had mentioned to me a few times that if anything should happen to her, she had three tarot cards that she wanted to leave me. According to Elisabetta they were antique and valuable. But she never told me what they looked like or where they'd come from – in fact, I thought it was odd that she treasured them so much – she always teased me for reading my horoscope! Anyway, for whatever reason, these cards were special to her and she wanted me, and only me, to have them. Now, of course, there's no chance I'll ever get them. She only had one brother and everything will go to him, even though they were not on good terms. Apparently he's a drug addict – and I know from Elisabetta that he is always desperate for money. She'd loaned him a lot in the past – but he was draining her to the end."

So that, I thought, *is probably why Elisabetta had financial trouble…*

"I think," Ugo continued, "when he gets his hands on those cards he's definitely going to sell them. He lives here in Milan, and I contacted him to give him my sympathy. He had no idea who I was. I asked about the cards and he wasn't interested in listening to me explain why I wanted them. He told me he would sell his sister's things to the highest bidder and then slammed the phone down. I guessed that he would contact private dealers, and possibly the auction houses, to sell anything of value that Elisabetta owned. That's when I thought of Professor Greene – I've approached the auction houses, too, by the way. Anyway, I went to ask the professor to please, please call me immediately if someone called Rinconi tries to sell him three antique *tarocchi* cards. I'd like to buy them, I don't care how much they cost, because I know Elisabetta wanted me to have them."

Now I finally felt sure that the three tarot cards I'd found were the same three that had belonged to Elisabetta. I didn't have any way of proving it completely, but how else did they get into the dressing room of Megastudio on Tuesday morning?

"Why didn't you tell me all of this on Tuesday, Ugo?" I asked. "Why didn't you tell me about Falco's supposed jewel switch? Elisabetta might have been in danger because of it."

"First of all I don't believe the rumour," Ugo argued. "Surely one of the clients would have complained by now if it was true! And then, under the circumstances, it was the last thing I was going to bring up! I was already under suspicion. You should have seen the way the police were looking at me that day. I thought if I started telling them about this crazy rumour of switched jewels they would think I was totally mad. And if they believed me, they might think I knew where the jewels were or something! I might just as well have handed myself in right there and then. And what if my theory ended up being totally wrong? All I would have done was bring a ton of speculation and bad press to bear on my reputation, Ventini's reputation, and Elisabetta's. On the other hand, if I had been certain it was all true – well, that would have been a different matter."

He had a point. "So you called me."

Ugo nodded. "I didn't know what to do so I called

my old friend Cazzie and she immediately mentioned you. I thought, perfect, she's not police, no one will suspect her of anything and if she figures this all out without me saying anything then I can keep my low profile and get justice for Elisabetta at the same time."

"Well, it sounds good on paper, even I can see that. But the reality is far more complicated...someone else is after those cards and someone tried leaving me for dead yesterday. I need to know what is so important about them. And where Elisabetta got them from." The answer to the last question popped into my head as soon as I said it. Surely the cards had to have come from Falco? Hadn't Lavinia said yesterday that Falco collected tarot cards? And Francesca had inherited some.

Ugo shrugged his shoulders. "I don't know. I know that Falco was into tarot, although he never spoke about it. Maybe he gave them to her? But why give three antique *tarocchi* cards to someone who isn't interested in them? Elisabetta could be so secretive, you know – like Falco. They had that in common."

Ugo got up and poured us each a glass of water. "I promise you, now I've told you everything I know, Axelle. Really. I'm sorry I wasn't upfront about this all from day one – but I was terrified. To be honest, I've never been so frightened in all my life."

I nodded slowly and decided to take him at his word.

"But from now on I'll be totally open with you. I promise.

I really need to know the truth about why Elisabetta was killed. Please, Axelle, please…you've got to help me solve this. For all our sakes…"

"Then I need you to do something for me."

"Anything. Just say it."

"Can you call Lavinia? I met her last night and she told me that she'd personally handled the sales of the jewelled dresses from Falco's last collection. Maybe she sold one to someone living here, in Milan? If so, I'd like to see the dress up close and perhaps speak with the owner. Could you arrange that for me?" I couldn't tell the difference between a real jewel and a good fake one, but I might learn something from the owner. It was worth a shot.

"Okay, I'll call her now. I have no idea if there is still a dress in Milan but I'll ask. I know most of them went to overseas buyers."

"Well find out for sure, please. And perhaps it's best to tell Lavinia that it's for that project you and I are supposed to be doing together – so she doesn't get suspicious. I can always come clean with her later."

It was nearly eight-thirty. I had to get going. "Can you call me when you hear back from her?"

"Absolutely. Anything else?"

I was about to say no when I thought of something. "Is there a logbook at the Ventini atelier? A record of the comings and goings of the employees?"

"Yes, there is. Everyone has to sign in – not just the

employees. It keeps track of everything – deliveries, clients, that sort of thing."

"Great. Do you think you could get me the logbooks from the period leading up to the last collection until the day Falco died?"

"Yes, no problem. I'll get those for you as soon as I'm at the office. Where should I send them? Or will you pick them up?"

I was going to be busy shooting all day and I didn't want them delivered to the shoot because it could raise questions. I suggested Sebastian pick them up directly from Ugo. So he gave me the Ventini address and his direct office number, too.

"Now may I ask you a question, Axelle?"

"Go ahead."

"How is it that you have the three *tarocchi* cards?"

I smiled. "I found them at Megastudio, in the dressing area, near the spot where Elisabetta died. I tried to give them to the police – and I'll have to eventually – but on Tuesday, anyway, they weren't interested."

"So those must be the cards she was talking about…"

"Seems so."

Ugo took a long, deep breath. "Will you keep me posted on everything?" His black eyes gazed directly into mine.

"I will. And you?"

"Me too."

And this time I believed him.

I dashed out of Ugo's and grabbed a taxi. I was shooting on location today at the Villa Necchi Campiglio. And while it wasn't far from Ugo's, it was on the other side of the neighbouring Quadrilatero della Moda, Milan's chic, old-money shopping district. With only a short while remaining before the team met up, I didn't have time to waste.

Cutie-Pie was a newcomer on the international fashion stage. What had started as a local Italian store was now on its way to becoming an international brand. And an important factor spurring that growth was the high-profile ad campaigns they'd started producing a few years back.

Cutie-Pie liked to book models who were up-and-coming – they preferred young and trendy girls whose edgier looks reflected the style of their product. Their advertising campaigns were a modelling agency's dream: trendy clothes, great photographers, the best hair and make-up, good pay and high visibility in the hottest fashion magazines. And sometimes that same high visibility even helped launch a model into the big time. Ellie had done their first campaign two years earlier and on the back of that she'd been booked for her first big US *Vogue* story.

And while I wasn't sure that would happen to me, this was nonetheless a plum job. I was one of two models who would be fronting this season's campaign, although today I would be working alone. I would also be on location the whole day rather than in a studio. After Tuesday's experience I was relieved – especially because, in Milan, the vast majority of studio shoots happen at Megastudio.

It's always hard to say what a location shoot will be like. If the client is a prestigious brand or magazine, you'll be shooting in some of the most amazing places in the world. And the hotels, location buses and food will be fantastic. At other times conditions will not be so nice and you might be lucky to get a ham sandwich after having a few photos taken under a bridge on the outskirts of some industrial town.

Today I'd be shooting at the Villa Necchi, a stunning Art Deco house built by a family of wealthy industrialists. Cutie-Pie had rented it for the day.

After I arrived and said hello to everyone on the team, the first thing I did was to message Sebastian and ask him to pick up the Ventini logbooks from Ugo. I also asked him to check through them and note anything unusual. Later on tonight we'd go over them together.

The day went by relatively quickly. My hair and make-up was sleek and minimal. I looked polished, but not overdone. Dewy skin, pink lips, pretty eyes and straight, glossy hair. And because I'd already had the clothes fitted to me, there wasn't anything to pin or adjust. Plus, because the stylist had seen me in the clothes the day before, she already had a good idea as to how she wanted to shoot them – and where in the house they would look best. The bright patterns and different textures of the fabrics contrasted nicely with the cool elegance of the house's interiors. Patchwork coats made of swathes of colourful suede, patent-leather knee-high boots, and prim-looking dresses with short, short skirts gave a sleek but funky 1960s vibe to the campaign.

There was, of course, talk about Elisabetta's death – especially when I mentioned that I'd been at the shoot at Megastudio on Tuesday. But no one on the team had anything to add to what I'd already uncovered and the general assumption seemed to be that she'd died after eating a leaf from Ugo's monkshood plant by accident. There were a few muttered comments, though, about Ugo and why he'd keep a poisonous plant at his home.

I, meanwhile, thought about what I'd learned this morning from Ugo. If I went with the assumption that the *tarocchi* cards I'd found had indeed belonged to Elisabetta, then I had to wonder why anyone else wanted them so badly. Was it their financial value – or something more?

Another thing I couldn't understand was why Falco would have given the cards to Elisabetta when surely he must have known that she didn't like tarot, didn't believe in it, and even laughed at it?

Also, if they were so valuable – and Falco had probably told Elisabetta that they were worth a small fortune – then why was she carrying them around with her in a tatty envelope in her basket on an average working day? Were they somehow connected with the "important" thing she'd wanted to do that evening? Then again, why was I focusing so much on the tarot cards? It's not as if I had any conclusive evidence that linked them to Elisabetta's death. I'd just happened to find them on the day she died. They'd probably just slipped out of her basket. And yet it seemed someone wanted them badly enough to try stealing them from me – aside from Ugo, two other people had already talked to Lucas about them, too.

I suddenly thought of something else: Elisabetta had been mugged and had her flat burgled this last spring. Could those events have been connected with the tarot cards?

I quickly messaged Ugo:

Hi Ugo, when Elisabetta was mugged and burgled was anything taken? Could it have been about the tarot cards?

He replied straight away:

Hi Axelle, E told me the mugging was random. As for the burglary, nothing was taken. Elisabetta never figured out what the burglar was after – thought it might be her brother looking for money.

Argh! My frustration knew no bounds. I took a deep

breath. My hair was being restyled for the last shot before we had our lunch break, and I had just closed my eyes when my phone vibrated again. Another message from Ugo: Lavinia had tracked down one of the dresses! In fact, she'd tracked down *the* dress. That deep red, show-stopping finale from Falco's last collection. And it was here in Milan, less than a ten-minute walk away from where I was now.

It had been sold to an overseas buyer, but the client who'd bought it had an apartment here in the city and part of her haute couture collection was kept in the apartment. And, according to Lavinia, she'd been a good friend of Falco's and she'd be happy to help me with my "research". She'd even asked if I'd be able to meet her at her home that evening.

I texted Ugo back:

Perfect! I should be able to make 6 p.m.

He sent me her contact details – her name was Tavi Holt – and told me he'd given her my number. I really hoped that seeing the dress and talking to Tavi would give me a new lead. I was so excited that I could hardly stay calm during the rest of the day.

"I love your energy, Axelle," said the photographer as I stood posing next to the large marble fireplace in a small but elegant sitting room. "You're really buzzing and that's exactly what good fashion pictures need."

If only he knew. I smiled and thanked him.

"It really shows that you're doing something you love," he added from behind his camera.

Yeah, right!

"Hi, you must be Axelle, I'm Tavi – come on in. Rooster – my husband – isn't here, which is probably for the best because he can't stand talking about dresses. He doesn't understand why they give me such a thrill!"

Tavi Holt was a tall, happy dynamo of perfect white teeth, long blonde hair, non-stop chatter and curves. She also pronounced my name like the car part, and *haute couture* came out sounding like "hoot coo-chure".

"This really is perfect timing," she went on. "Because I'm only ever here in Milan twice a year – like clockwork – and only for the Ventini hoot coo-chure shows – although I come a few days earlier and order things for Rooster from their men's show. Now if you'd wanted to meet up in New York or London that would have been much easier. I'm there much more often but Rooster, he's into shipping, amongst other things, and his shipping company headquarters are here. Now, what a shipping company is doing with headquarters in a landlocked city like Milan is beyond me, but, hey, with Ventini here and Valentino just a hop, skip and a jump away in Rome, do I really need to ask?"

I didn't get a chance to answer.

"You know, I wanted to be a model. I love Kate Upton – she's my idol."

Kate Upton is the American blonde bombshell who took swimsuit modelling by storm a few years ago. After becoming a sensation who couldn't be ignored – even by the snootiest of fashionistas – she finally landed on the cover of various *Vogues* – including *Vogue* UK. I remember her cover because Jenny, my best friend in London, pinned it to her wall. "She's different," Jenny had said. "And she seems nice."

"Do you remember that video she did of her in a bikini dancing the dougie?" Tavi went on. "She posted it on YouTube and that really got her career going! Well, when I saw that I thought I can do a bikini dougie dance and post it on YouTube and launch my modelling career in the same way she did. Have you seen her bikini video? Jiggle, jiggle, it's *all* moving in that video. Anyway, in the end I had to shelve my modelling dream because Rooster saw me. He was in Kansas City on business – Rooster has more companies than I have Ventini dresses and that's saying something! Anyway, where was I? Oh yeah, so Rooster was in Kansas City on business and took his managers to see the Kansas City Royals play I don't remember who. Well get this – every time there was a break in the game, the camera would pan to me. I mean I was huge on the screen – huge! So I decided, this is it – this is my moment! And I did the dougie in my seat. And then I stood up for the next break and dougied some more and then I just kept on dougieing. The crowd was going bananas – I mean they lapped it up. Anyway, I like to say that I dougied my way into Rooster's heart on that day. And here I am."

Tavi interested me; with her relentless chatter and obsession with clothes, it might be easy to dismiss her as a lightweight – but the look in her eyes told a different story. She'd obviously grown up in a place where looks were prized more than brains, so she tended to lead with that – her eyes were kind, but sharp and determined. I liked that about her. If my instincts were right, I could probably be direct with her and get an honest answer.

Eventually we made it to the room where the dress was hanging. "This is my Milan dress archive," Tavi said with a wave of her hand. We were standing in a room that was temperature and light controlled – and roughly the size of the entire first floor of an average English house. "And this is the dress."

It was in the middle of the room, hanging on a mannequin – and it was amazing. It glittered as though it could come alive at any second. Up close the handiwork was astonishing. Tiny stitches covered the dress, so it almost looked as if it was made of rare feathers. And everywhere were exquisite jewels. It was impossible not to stare.

"Isn't it the best? I love it. And if you look closely you

can see all the fine, fine stitching. You see? I was told it took twenty seamstresses five months to make this dress. Falco Ventini actually worked on it himself. And look at this…" I waited while she flipped the dress over and lifted the lining. "The stitching is as beautiful on the reverse side as it is on the 'right' side. That's true quality. That's Ventini – Falco Ventini. I love Ugo, but he still hasn't produced a dress like this. Though I'm sure he will, and when he does I'll be waiting. Anyway, when I saw this one I knew I had to have it. It's going to be the centrepiece of the new hoot coo-chure museum I'm building back in Kansas City. It's going to be all glass and—"

I cleared my throat loudly. I realized I'd have to grab the bull by the horns so to speak or I'd never get a question in. "The archivist at Ventini told me that all those jewels are real. How amazing… In fact," I opened my notebook in an attempt to look professional (okay, yeah, and a bit older, too), "for the blog piece I'm writing I've been going through some of the newspaper articles that came out at the time of the show and this dress is the one with the most jewels. Do you have any idea how much the jewels alone are worth?"

Tavi threw her head back and laughed. "Real? All of them? Listen, Axelle, I loved Falco and all but there's no way *all* of those jewels are real. But that's just between you and me. Don't you dare tell Ugo or anyone at Ventini. Falco's dead and I certainly don't want to upset his ghost – it doesn't matter now anyway."

"How do you know they're not all real?" I asked quickly.

She rolled her eyes, raised her jewel-covered fingers and waved them in front of my face. "Because there are three things I know about: hoot coo-chure dresses, jewels and Rooster! And of the three, it's jewels that I know the most about. Don't tell that to Rooster, though!" Her throaty laugh rippled through the room.

"Can you show me how you know?"

"Of course. Stay there a moment, we need more light." She walked back towards the door and pressed a button on a panel next to the doorway. The shutters on the windows turned and the room was flooded with natural light. Next she upped the dimmer on the overhead LED lights.

"You really need a magnifying glass because some of what I'm about to show you is hard to see with the naked eye, but, here, look at this." She pointed to a sapphire – or at least what I took to be a sapphire (it was dark blue). It was one of thousands of stones on the dress. Furthermore it was small compared to most of the others and it was smack in the middle of the bottom of the back of the dress. "This one is made of glass. It lacks the depth and natural flaws that a real sapphire would have."

"Flaws?"

Tavi nodded. "Yeah, flaws. Only two kinds of gems *don't* have flaws – priceless ones and fake ones. Before I bought the dress, naturally I wanted to check that the stones were real. These are the ones I checked out first." She pointed to the collar of the dress and the cuffs; these areas had some of the largest jewels. "Now the big stones here all have flaws. A jeweller would say they're medium quality, but they *are* real. Anyway, I was like, all right, what they said is true, the jewels on the dress are real, and I didn't give it a second thought. But a while later, after I'd bought the dress, the little sapphire I just showed you caught my eye and I looked at it with my magnifying glass. I can't say why – it was just a feeling I had. It was so perfect – too perfect. And that didn't make sense – you know what I mean? If you're using a medium quality for the big stones that everyone sees, then why would you use a fantastic quality on the little stones that no one is going to see?"

It was a good point. It seemed Tavi was more of a fashion detective than she knew. I felt the hairs begin to rise on my arms, because the rumour Ugo had told me was beginning to seem more real than half the stones on the dress.

"So I had it checked," Tavi continued. "In fact, I had all of the stones on the dress checked."

"And?" My eyes were wide. Maddeningly, after having talked non-stop for minutes on end, Tavi was suddenly quiet. "What did you find out?"

Tavi threw her head back and laughed. "I found out that my gut was right – that little blue 'sapphire' I've just shown you is fake. It's made of glass – like half of the small stones on the dress." Tavi laughed again. The entire story seemed to amuse her.

"Weren't you upset?"

"No. Of course, I never told Rooster because *he* would have been upset – he'd have felt cheated, which in a way, I guess we were... But by the time I had the stones all checked Falco wasn't doing so well. He was on his deathbed. And I mean, as exquisite as it is and as beautiful as it is... well, at the end of the day, it's just a dress. You know what I mean? It wasn't worth upsetting a dying man over – especially as he probably didn't even know."

I nodded. Tavi was going up and up in my estimation. I knew that some of my school friends' mothers wouldn't be so generous; some of them looked as if they'd kill anyone who dared switch their genuine Chloe or Louis Vuitton handbag for a fake.

"Of course," Tavi continued, "when I bought the dress, there were documents exchanged that testified to the quality of the stones, and Falco did tell me that they were all real. We paid almost half a million euros for the dress – which even for hoot coo-chure is an awful lot. That was on the understanding that a good portion of the cost was because of the value of the stones... The thing is, I liked Falco – I really did. And I didn't want to cause trouble for him. He was such a character – a funny, secretive little man, almost like he might have been from a fairy tale. And he was a genius with clothes. But I doubt he'd ever have noticed if someone had switched the stones right under his nose."

My head was spinning with everything I'd just learned. While Tavi prattled on about Falco, I thought about the one and only solid clue I now had concerning Elisabetta.

I suddenly thought of something. Fortunately Tavi didn't seem to mind when I took my phone out and quickly wrote Ugo a message:

Ugo, can you find out how much Falco spent on the stones on the dress? Thanks, A

He replied straight away:

Sure can. I'll get back to you asap.

I decided it was time to be upfront with Tavi. "You know, there was a rumour at the time of Falco's last collection that Falco himself had switched some of the real jewels for fake ones on a few of the dresses in the collection…so, from what you've shown me today, I guess it's true…" I wondered whether Tavi had heard the rumour.

She looked at me, her eyes wide. "Oh, so it was Falco! Wow!" Tavi stood for a moment in silence and chewed her bottom lip. "I'd assumed it was one of the seamstresses or something but if he did it himself then…" She trailed off but after a few seconds she smiled broadly. "Actually, what a great story! Thanks for telling me. I reckon I like the dress even more now – and, if I think about it, it's probably good for the value of the dress," she added excitedly.

"How do you mean?" I asked.

"Anything collectible becomes more interesting when it has a good story behind it. And I couldn't ask for a better one than that!"

She seemed genuinely pleased.

I was also genuinely pleased. I'd come hoping to find out whether the rumour about Falco switching the stones was true – and apparently it was.

My phone pinged with a message from Ugo:

€400,000 spent on the stones.

"Tavi…" I didn't know if she'd be willing to answer my next question, but I had to try. "You told me you'd had the real stones on the dress valued…can I ask you how much they're worth?"

"My jeweller gave them a collective value of about 100,000 euros. Why?"

"Just wondering…" I was wondering all right – about where the other €300,000 worth of stones had gone.

According to the rumour Falco had wanted to use the stones to fund his business, but had he? Maybe he'd died before he had the chance. In which case, where were the rest of the jewels? Were they still hidden somewhere? Did Elisabetta know where? Is that what had put her life in danger? I pursed my lips as the various thoughts ran through my mind. It was as if I'd been looking at this case through a pair of broken glasses, and since meeting Tavi, they'd suddenly been repaired. It's not that I had any answers – I didn't at all. But Elisabetta's death now took on a whole new meaning…I finally had a motive…so which of the suspects – Ugo, Ginevra, Francesca or Alessandro – fitted it best?

"Tavi, did you know that Falco was into tarot cards?"

"Honeybun, I didn't even know what tarot cards were until Falco showed me. I had an aunt who liked to read palms but it's not really the same thing. The whole tarot card thing is pretty intense, though. Falco gave me a reading once as a birthday gift. This really chic woman, I can't remember her name…anyway, she told me that I was going to be a force for good in the world. After that I was like, oh, tarot is fun!" Tavi suddenly looked at her watch. "Listen, Axelle, I have to get going. Rooster is coming home soon and we have a dinner with the American ambassador tonight. I have to decide what to wear!"

I said goodbye to Tavi and she asked me to keep her posted if I found out anything else about the dress. "Of course, all I really want to know is what Falco did with all those stones!" she said.

Yeah, me too…

* * *

As I left Tavi's building I quickly texted Ugo:

Rumour confirmed. Will tell all in person.

He replied immediately:

Not sure that's good news. Look forward to hearing all.

Next I took a deep breath and for a minute simply stood with my eyes closed and my face tilted upwards to catch the early evening sun. It was still strong and felt wonderful. But then I remembered that I needed to speak with Lavinia. I had a question I wanted to ask her and she, having known Falco so well and for so long, might just be the only person who could answer it.

She answered on the first ring. Briefly I told her that Tavi had confirmed the rumour.

"I'm surprised," she said. "But at the same time I'm not. I'd heard the rumour…and I knew Falco was desperate to save his business, but I didn't believe he'd stoop to that. It does make sense though when I think about how much time he spent – on his own – working on that dress." Lavinia was quiet for a moment before continuing. "I'm guessing that was the only dress he sabotaged. Tavi is one in a million – I can't imagine any of the other clients keeping quiet if it turned out the gems on their dresses were fakes. Anyway," Lavinia took a deep breath, "he wasn't generally a dishonest person – I promise you. I know it must seem difficult to believe when you hear a story like that, but I can tell you that on his deathbed he was racked with guilt over bad decisions he'd made – surely this was one of them. He must have been feeling very, very desperate – far more desperate than he let on at the time – to have done something like that. Ah, Falco!" She was quiet for a moment. "Of course, it came out later that his company was very, very close to bankruptcy, which I guess explains this last-chance ploy… Anyway, tell me, how did Tavi take it? Does she want to sue? Or does she want a reimbursement? Management will love that, ugh! I'm glad I'm out of it!"

"Actually, like you, she seemed to feel sorry for Falco. By the time she found out about the switched stones he was on his deathbed, so she was reluctant to bring it up. But the receipt for the dress does stipulate real stones…"

"I know…"

"But she hasn't told Rooster."

"That's lucky. He would sue immediately. Although, having said that, for Rooster a few hundred thousand of any currency is pocket money!"

"Actually, Tavi was quite pleased that it was Falco who had switched the stones. She thought it might increase the value of the dress."

Lavinia laughed. "Well, she's right about that. She's quite clever, you know. The more I get to know Tavi the more I like her."

Funnily enough, that was exactly how I felt, too. I changed the subject. "By the way, Ginevra was still working for Falco at the time of his last collection, wasn't she? Do you think she knew about this rumour? And what about Alessandro and Francesca?"

"Definitely, yes. They all asked me about it. But I always brushed it off as gossip – and the fact that no client ever complained, for me, only confirmed that it was a rumour. Obviously I was wrong…"

"Lavinia, can I ask you one last question…?"

"Go ahead."

"Well, as we now know, the stones were switched. And it's occurred to me that if Falco didn't sell them, and since he died very soon after he took them, then they just might still be hidden somewhere. Now, knowing Falco as you did, can you think of where he might have stashed them?"

"Oh, I've no idea. But like I always say, Falco would probably tell you it's in the cards." She laughed. "I could call Signora Ferrara to do a reading for you. She might be able to lead you to them with her *tarocchi*. What do you think?" Lavinia was joking, the smile on her lips nearly audible as she spoke. But I wasn't laughing. My mind was whirring. *Falco would probably tell you it's in the cards…*

"I'm sorry I can't be more helpful, Axelle…"

"Actually, Lavinia, you've been a great help."

THURSDAY EVENING
Symbols and Secrets

I was still standing outside Tavi's flat when Ellie messaged me:

> Got another fashion party tonight – at Bulgari. But I need a break from all the male models! Also I want to know what's going on with everything...

We arranged to meet. Sebastian picked me up at Tavi's and from there we zoomed straight to the nearest deli to pick up some panini and a couple of salads. We continued straight on to Milan's largest and best-known park, the Parco Sempione, for a picnic dinner. Ellie jumped out of a taxi just as we pulled up and together we found a quiet spot on a small hillock with a picture-perfect view of the sprawling Castello Sforzesco, the ancient stronghold of the Dukes of Milan.

We made ourselves comfortable on a large blanket Ellie had picked up from our model flat and unpacked our dinner.

"So, Holmes," Sebastian asked. "Any new leads?"

"I thought you'd never ask..." I said calmly as I looked up at them both from behind my panini. Then I told them everything about my visit with Tavi, and my conversation with Lavinia.

"What a story!" Ellie said as I came to the end.

I nodded. "The jewels were definitely switched – and Falco must have done it. No one else was near that dress for long enough to swap them."

Ellie put her salad down. "So where are the jewels now?"

"That's exactly what I asked Lavinia..."

"And?"

"Her answer was the most interesting part of my day... the very same thing she told me last night when I asked her about how Falco found out he was ill. She said, *Falco would probably tell you it was in the cards*." I took another bite of my panini. "Yesterday she told me that Falco regularly flew in a professional to read for him. He seemed to look at life as one big tarot reading."

"Like you look at life as if it's one big game of Cluedo," Ellie said with a giggle.

"Very funny." I threw my balled-up napkin at her as she stuck her tongue out. "Anyway, Lavinia's words, *Falco would probably tell you it's in the cards*, keep running through my mind."

Sebastian suddenly got it. "So you think that those three

cards could be clues that will help you find the hidden treasure?"

"Possibly, yes," I said. "First of all, why else would Elisabetta have the cards in the first place – she didn't like tarot. It wouldn't be a far-fetched idea for Falco to use tarot cards to convey a secret message." As I spoke I pulled on the gloves Lucas had given me, then I took my portfolio out of my rucksack and laid the cards on top of it.

I picked them up one by one and checked them carefully yet again, but I still didn't find any kind of writing on them at all.

"What are you looking for?" Sebastian asked.

"I thought perhaps the clue to the hiding place might literally be written on the cards, but I don't see how."

"Invisible ink?" Ellie asked.

I shook my head. "These cards are so old that any kind of ink – invisible or not – would probably damage them permanently. But maybe the clues are in the images on the cards…?"

Sebastian bent forward and peered at them carefully. "Now *that* doesn't sound like a far-fetched idea to me. In fact, it sounds kind of clever…"

"How so?" Ellie asked.

"Well, first of all, because if you give someone cards as a kind of map to the treasure, it means that no written directions are necessary – and that makes it discreet and difficult to trace. You could lose the cards but still easily remember the images."

"Good point, Watson. But then what could these cards be referring to?" Briefly I repeated the conversation I'd had with Lucas about the different meanings each card represented.

We looked at the three cards: the magician, death, the lady on horseback.

"I think the magician refers to Falco himself," I said. "According to Lucas, this card also refers to manual labour – handiwork, which is what Falco was good at – and shrewdness, which is what it took to even come up with his idea of switching the stones. All of that points to Falco. And from the photos I've seen, the little magician even looks a bit like him…"

"But that wouldn't give us a clue about the location of the jewels," Sebastian said.

"Unless it's some kind of museum of magic?" I suggested. "The image does remind me of a museum I once went to, where they had magic tricks set up to look a bit like this image. Apparently they were 'antique' magic tricks."

"Okay…but why would Falco hide the stones in a museum?"

"I'm not sure," I said. "But we may as well look into it. It would help to eliminate it as a possibility."

"Right. I'll check it out now." Sebastian pulled his tablet out of his rucksack and started researching museums of magic.

"But what about the death card? And the woman on the

horse? You said Lucas wasn't sure what she represented…"
Ellie said.

I nodded. "The lady had him stumped, but he said he'd
have another look and compare her to similar cards in
other decks. Hopefully I can meet him tomorrow morning
before our show." Ellie and I would both be walking in the
Lei-Lei show, which I'd been confirmed for while I was at
my booking in the morning. "As for the death card – it
makes for a gruesome clue. I have no idea what Falco
meant by it…"

"It's as if he knew that someone would die – as if he gave
the card to Elisabetta knowing something would happen to
her." Ellie had a look of distaste on her face as she spoke.

"I can't imagine he would have given her a card that
suggested she was meant to die shortly," I said. "He loved
Elisabetta. And, anyway, how would he know she was
going to die? Unless he was directly to blame – in which
case he's a murderer from beyond the grave." I shook my
head. "No. Surely it must mean something else?"

"Hmm, old Moony-Eyes reckoned it could refer to a big
life change…" Sebastian said as he bit into his panini.
"Maybe it was the life change he thought would come after
he'd paid off his creditors and saved his business with
the stones?"

Ignoring his jibe about Lucas, I said, "Possibly, but then
we're only left with the woman on horseback as a clue to
a location – and where could she be?" I was pulling the

gloves off when I suddenly thought of something. "Those logbooks – do you have them, Watson?"

"Yes, I have." Sebastian pulled them out of his rucksack.

"I need to know if Falco did any travelling in the weeks between the time he switched the stones and the time he went into hospital."

Sebastian nodded. As he searched he explained what he'd found out so far, "By the way, the place was incredibly busy in the build-up to Falco's last collection; the records bear that out. Everyone's names are in here: Francesca, Lavinia, Elisabetta, Ugo, Ginevra, Kristine and Alessandro. All working every day and all kinds of hours. Falco, of course, never signed in – but the security staff working in the lobby made notes of his comings and goings. According to their records he was practically living at the atelier. He was there for days on end before the show – often on his own far into the night…"

Sebastian found the pages that documented the few weeks in question and handed the logbook to me. From what I could see, Falco had been at the Ventini offices every day until about two weeks after his last collection was shown. After that, suddenly, his name wasn't seen again. Presumably because he went into hospital. I'd have to double-check this with Ugo.

"Why do you need to know if he was travelling at that time?" Sebastian asked.

"Because if he didn't travel, then the stones are probably

hidden somewhere here in Milan. But if he left the country, it's possible that he took them with him and sold them overseas somewhere."

"Good point, Holmes."

"Thank you, Watson. By the way, any idea what happened to the house he lived in after he died?"

"Francesca mentioned that it was sold – along with everything else he owned. The creditors got their hands on it straight after. D'you think the stones might have been hidden in his house?"

I shrugged my shoulders. "They could have been. Maybe the lady referred to a painting or something with a safe behind it. But then if he'd wanted Elisabetta to have the stones he'd have hidden them somewhere that she could easily get to *after* his death, right?"

"Is there a statue somewhere in the city of a woman on horseback? The stones could be near that or under it or something."

"Hmm, could be," I said. "Although I hope it's not a statue on the roof of the Duomo – I'm not so keen on climbing around up there again."

"As soon as I've finished researching magic museums I'll start looking at famous statues in the city, maybe something will come up."

"If the horseback rider refers to where the stones are, then we're still left with the dancing skeleton. What does *that* mean?" Ellie asked.

Sebastian looked up from his tablet. "And if the cards are clues that lead to the jewels, then why would someone kill Elisabetta *before* making sure they had them? That doesn't really make sense – especially when they seem to have been hunting them down ever since."

"I don't know, Watson. But those are questions I'll have to answer soon – very soon."

By Saturday afternoon, I thought. I was due to fly into London on Saturday evening – and Mum would fetch me at the airport. Just the thought of anything going wrong with these plans – say, like being locked in an underground tunnel again and missing my flight – made me sweat. Mum has antennae more sensitive than your average butterfly. If she even *thought* I was working on a case, I'd be grounded for the rest of my life.

Sebastian busied himself on his tablet, then suddenly said: "There are no museums of magic in Milan. Or anywhere near Milan. At least nothing that I can find."

"Well, then, maybe we should just assume for now that the magician card refers to Falco – or more precisely to the switch he did." I looked again at the card. The little man with the impossibly large plume in his colourful hat was sitting at a trestle table. Three walnut shells lay in front of him; the prize-winning token was presumably under one of them.

Sebastian jumped in. "You're right. It *must* refer to the switching of the gems. That trick is all about switching the token – the prize – from one shell to another without anyone seeing where it ends up. And that's exactly what Falco did with the gems on that dress."

"Yes! We're making progress!" Ellie said.

"Yeah, but it doesn't seem fast enough…" I said.

My eyes moved to the other two cards – they had me completely stumped. I moved them to the side and lay down on the blanket, gazing up at the sky. Sometimes ideas come more easily if I put something away and stop thinking about it for a while.

I wondered aloud about the sneakers in Elisabetta's basket. Her friends had all laughed when I suggested she had a pair. Regardless, she had obviously intended to wear them. But why? She must have had a good reason…

"Both Ugo and I heard Elisabetta say she was planning on doing something important on the night of the day she died… I was thinking that might be what she needed the sneakers for?"

"It kind of seems like it, doesn't it?" Sebastian said. "And she hinted to Ugo that the thing she had to do was connected with Falco… And that's when Ugo told her to leave Falco's ghost alone, isn't it?"

I nodded. "Something like that, yes. And it definitely had to do with the rumour about the jewels. She also mentioned that 'everything was going according to plan'. But Ugo told her to let sleeping dogs lie and suggested she concentrate on her career." I sighed. "She must have felt she was in for an athletic evening if she'd brought those sneakers."

Ellie smiled. "Yeah, but isn't treasure hunting usually pretty physical? I mean you have to find it, then you have to dig and then you have to carry it all."

"Like a pirate?" I smiled. "There are a couple of little details that bother me, though, about the buried treasure scenario…"

"Which are?" Sebastian asked.

"Why didn't Falco sell the gems as soon as he had them? He was desperate for the money."

"Don't forget, he fell ill right after the fashion show. He probably just ran out of time," Sebastian said.

I nodded. "That makes sense…but then, if he'd told Elisabetta about it, why didn't she sell them for him?"

"Good point. I really don't know," Sebastian answered. "Maybe she didn't want to be involved? Or didn't approve? And maybe by then he thought, *I'm going to die anyway, so screw it, there's no point saving my business now, why don't I give the gems to the person I love like family, and help her out of her financial trouble instead?* Then, maybe he hid the gems in a place that Elisabetta could get to after he died, so she'd get something that the creditors couldn't take?"

"Maybe, yes." I was silent for a moment. This case had me going round in circles. "Although…"

Sebastian rolled his eyes. "Oh no. Whenever you say 'Although…' I know you're about to punch a hole right through my theory." He was laughing.

"Then make them airtight, Watson. No one's stopping you!"

"Wouldn't I like to!"

"Anyway," I continued, "Falco died about seven months ago, right? Not long after his last collection? So let's say he decided that it was too late for him to profit from the sale of the stones, and that he did indeed tell Elisabetta where the gems were, giving her, at the same time, his three cherished antique *tarocchi* as a sort of 'map'…then why did Elisabetta wait until now to find them? Especially when she had such urgent financial problems of her own? Why didn't she find the stones straight away and sell them? Or at the very least why didn't she sell the cards? *Why wait?*"

Ellie and Sebastian both shrugged their shoulders and looked at me.

"You've got us stumped, Holmes."

Another piece of the puzzle to figure out, I told myself.

It was a wonderful evening, the night warm and still. We sat admiring the view for a while, finishing the fruit salads we'd bought for dessert. Then Ellie and I went over our schedules for tomorrow.

We were the only girls in the Lei-Lei show we were booked for in the morning, and, according to Ellie (my fashion oracle), the stress level would be reduced because for once the focus would be on the guys! It also meant that it would take less prep time overall than usual, because hair and make-up would have more time for us (there wasn't *that* much to do on the guys – although they wear more make-up on the runway than you'd think). Our call time was for 8 a.m. with the show starting at 10 a.m. Hopefully we'd be out of the venue – a large palazzo not far from the park – by noon at the latest.

"And we got you a ticket," Ellie said to Sebastian. "You just have to give your name at the entrance."

Sebastian gave us the thumbs up. "I look forward to seeing you two in action."

"Yeah, well keep your eyes open, Watson, and take notes, because I look forward to seeing how your wardrobe moves beyond its usual look of jeans and leather jackets."

He threw me a punch and I ducked.

After the show I had two appointments – one to see Italian *Elle* and the other to meet a Milan-based photographer.

"I have a couple of appointments after the show, too," Ellie said, "so how about we meet up straight after we're finished?"

"Sounds good," I said.

"So which tourist sights should we check out tomorrow? Because I know we'll have so much free time…" Sebastian smiled at me as he searched for our map. "Seriously, though, maybe we can squeeze in one thing…"

"I'd love to do some sightseeing," Ellie said. "Every time I come here I'm working. All I ever see is the road from

Linate Airport to the Park Hyatt and then the road from the Park Hyatt to Megastudio or wherever else I'm shooting. I've never had a chance to get to know the city."

"Well, let's say we suddenly – magically – have a hole in our schedule..." Sebastian turned to look at me. "Obviously this is only wishful thinking at this point, Holmes. But supposing we had time without modelling or detective work, what would we do?" He laid the fold-out map of the city on the grass in front of us. There was so much to see in Milan!

"I definitely want to go to 10 Corso Como," Ellie said. She was referring to the beautiful, super-hip store on the Corso Como that was established by Carla Sozzani the former fashion editor and sister of Franca Sozzani, editor-in-chief of Italian *Vogue*.

"And I'd like to check out the castle," Sebastian said as he pointed to the enormous fortress just beyond us.

"And I'd like to..." I was about to say something about seeing Leonardo Da Vinci's *The Last Supper* (we'd missed it on Tuesday) when my eye was caught by one of the more unusual tourist sights. We hadn't planned on seeing it but I knew from the guidebooks that it was a surprisingly popular destination for tourists...and maybe...

"Yes, Holmes?"

I was staring at the map. *Could that be what Falco had meant?* Somehow it made sense... I started to get that buzz I get when I'm on the right trail. I was still staring at the map – and, if I was right, the clue was so obvious I felt annoyed with myself for not having thought of it sooner! I couldn't help but laugh – Falco was a real trickster with a smooth sleight of hand. I looked up from the map at Sebastian and Ellie.

"Oh no. I know that look," Sebastian said.

"Me, too," Ellie added.

"You know something and you're not going to share it, are you?" Sebastian was smiling.

I nodded. "I think I've figured out one of the clues." I reached for our more in-depth guidebook and searched its index. Then I opened it at the relevant pages and quickly read the information. *Yes,* I thought, *why not?* It fitted.

But before getting too excited, I needed to make a call and verify a couple of details. I pulled my phone out of my rucksack and stood up.

"*Ciao,* Axelle? Making any progress?"

"Hi, Ugo, yes, I am making some progress…" I didn't tell him that, although I was making progress with finding the stones, I was still a long way from finding out who poisoned Elisabetta – I only hoped that both strands led to the same person. "But I have a couple of questions…"

I asked him if he could remember Falco travelling at all in the time between his last couture show and going to the hospital.

"Travelling? No, absolutely not. *Certo.* He didn't have the time and he wasn't feeling well. He was around after the show because that's when the couture clients, like Tavi, buy the dresses and have their fittings. He forced himself to be present. Then he went into hospital two weeks later – and he never left. I was at Ventini every day, for hours, both in the time leading up to the show and then after the show until he went to the hospital. He had no time to go anywhere – not even for a day."

Good, I thought, *he must have hidden the stones somewhere in Milan.*

"Also, Ugo, I've been looking at the logbooks. I can see that Elisabetta left the office everyday at 6 p.m. and I've heard she visited Falco daily when he was in hospital…"

"Yes, she'd go every day, straight from the office at six, that's right. Sometimes with Alessandro."

"What about Francesca?"

"She went daily, too, also after work – and after Elisabetta."

That tallied with her 7 p.m. office log-out times.

"Have you any idea why everyone suddenly seemed to leave the office much earlier in the four days before Falco died?"

"Ah, that will be because we were told he had only a few days left…naturally, we all tried to spend more time with him."

"So up to that point there was a chance that Falco could have lived longer?"

"Slim, but yes. Everyone still hoped he'd be well enough to come out of hospital at some point."

Hmm…I ran my finger down the list of log-out times. During the last four days of Falco's life, Ginevra had left Ventini at 4 p.m., Ugo at 5 p.m., Francesca at 5.30 p.m., Elisabetta had kept to 6 p.m., and Alessandro had left at various times.

"Why are the visits so important?" Ugo asked.

"I'm trying to account for everyone's actions just before Falco died."

"But what does Falco's death have to do with Elisabetta's?"

"I don't know. I'm just being thorough."

"Of course… Anything else I can help you with, Axelle?"

"Yes, actually… Where was Falco buried?"

"Where was Falco buried? Are you joking? I thought you told me his death had nothing to do with Elisabetta's! You don't think he was poisoned, too…?" It was clear Ugo was bewildered, unsure whether to be terrified, or whether I was just pulling his leg.

"Don't worry, Ugo," I said, "and, no, clearly he wasn't poisoned. It's just a question – but I really want to know."

"He's buried here in Milan."

"Which cemetery?"

"At the Cimitero Monumentale. His family has a plot there with a small mausoleum. Why?"

"I can't tell you now, Ugo. But thanks – you've been a great help."

"I have?"

"Definitely. Now I have to go but I promise I'll call you

tomorrow – hopefully with some good news. *Ciao*, Ugo!"

I looked at the time and quickly googled the visiting hours of the cemetery. It was closed – argh! I'd have to wait until tomorrow. They opened early but I'd be prepping for the show so I couldn't go first thing – but I'd get down there as soon as we were finished.

I turned back to Ellie and Sebastian. "I know it's not on our To-See list, but I was thinking it might be fun to check out the Cimitero Monumentale tomorrow?"

"The cemetery?" Sebastian asked as he reached for the map.

I nodded, slipped one of the cotton gloves back on, and picked up the death card. As I held it high, I said, "This card represents death, right? And where better to find death than at a cemetery – particularly the one where Falco was buried!"

Sebastian and Ellie looked at me, eyes wide. "That's actually a brilliant idea," Sebastian said.

"And it makes sense," Ellie added. "But how do you know where in the cemetery to look for the gems?"

I set the card with the grinning skeleton down and shook my head. Frankly, even if the gems were in the cemetery I had no idea *where* precisely. My eye lingered for a moment on the image of the medieval lady on horseback. She was still, silent and smiling, as if hiding a secret. *She must know*, I thought.

I picked up the card and studied her more carefully. It

was an interesting image, and very flat in the way that the magician wasn't. And although the lady and her horse were obviously supposed to be in motion – one of the horse's front legs was lifted and the woman held the reins high – she looked like a statue. A glittering statue that gave nothing away.

And yet, for my purposes, if the card with the magician represented Falco and the card of death represented the cemetery, then she *must* represent the treasure...could she be a statue that marked the location of the gems? I had until tomorrow evening to find out.

It was time to go. I had some research I needed to do and I wanted to get a good night's sleep. I had the feeling tomorrow would be a busy day.

"But even if we do find the stones," Ellie asked as we folded the blanket, "how does that lead us to the person who poisoned Elisabetta?"

"Well, I think maybe it's time for me to make a move, show my own sleight of hand," I said.

"What, like flush out the killer?" Sebastian asked as he gathered our litter together in a bag.

"Exactly, Watson."

"And do you have a plan yet, Holmes?"

"No, but I'm working on one."

"Which means we won't know about it until you're good and ready to tell us. Am I right or am I right?"

"You're right, Watson."

We walked back to where Sebastian had parked his scooter. Sebastian and I didn't kiss goodbye; instead we busied ourselves confirming when we'd meet up tomorrow and then speedily said goodbye before anything got too awkward.

Even though the picnic had been great and Sebastian was being a massive help on the case, things still felt odd between us. Ellie and I caught a taxi back to our flat and Sebastian waved us off as our driver pulled away from the kerb.

"What's up with you and Sebastian?" Ellie asked. "The vibe between the two of you is kind of weird at the moment."

"Don't ask."

"It's not about the Francesca or Lucas thing, is it? That's just too stupid."

I shook my head. "It's not about her or him. There's more to it than that."

"Like what?"

"Like I think Sebastian's annoyed that I don't always put him first."

"And is he right?"

"Maybe…but how *can* I always put him first? Especially when I'm working on a case? If someone's life is on the line then that's important. Solving cases isn't just some fun hobby – they're a huge part of who I am. Does that make sense? We each have things that the other one has to deal with. And if Sebastian wants to be with me then he has to understand that the cases take priority, even when we have other plans."

Ellie nodded. "I get you. Like I couldn't be with someone who didn't understand that I might have to suddenly get on a plane the next day for a booking."

"Exactly."

"But isn't he supportive? I mean, I sometimes think he's as keen as you are to solve your cases."

"I do too, but I think this case started at a moment when he had other expectations. He wasn't keen at first, but I think now he is."

"Then why don't you two just kiss and make up?"

I shrugged my shoulders. "Because guy stuff isn't always that simple."

"You can say that again."

Ellie and I sneaked past Mrs B's eagle eyes unnoticed. Clearly she was occupied: the sound of the television was blaring from her flat. Moments later, Ellie was off, out again to her fashion party. I was happy to stay in and have some downtime on my own.

Sebastian messaged me as I walked through the door to the flat:

I miss you.

Despite my conversation with Ellie, reading those three little words made me soar. Whatever I'd been thinking or feeling was instantly swept aside while my heart did a little flip-flop dance. I felt silly and giddy all at once. Why did Sebastian have that effect on me?

I texted back:

I miss you too. À demain, Holmes.

À demain, Watson.

And we left it at that. For the moment it was enough. And maybe tomorrow we could sort things out.

FRIDAY MORNING

Catwalk Clues

I needed no alarm – I woke in a cold sweat at 6.30. Random snippets from conversations I'd had with Lavinia, Tavi and Ugo were racing through my mind, confusing and noisy all at once. It was like when my mum is driving and wants to listen to the radio but she can't get a clear signal and a few different stations come in on the same frequency with varying degrees of clarity.

I'd been dreaming of a hospital. Ugo, Francesca, Lavinia, Elisabetta, Alessandro and many more had all been there, queuing to visit Falco. Then, at some point Falco's hospital had morphed into the one at home in London where my gran died. Over and over my gran said she had no regrets and a clean conscience. She felt free and happy and very, very proud of me. And she knew I would become a detective. I woke and nearly started to cry... Why was I thinking of my gran's last moments now?

I took a few deep breaths then

grabbed my tablet from the floor beside my bed and turned it on. The best way to settle my mind was by doing some research. I had to figure out who'd poisoned Elisabetta. It wasn't just about finding the jewels – although I knew the two were tied together somehow. But how? That's what I needed to find out.

Be systematic, Axelle, I told myself. *Quiet your mind and start from one point. That's easier said than done, though. So which point – where do I start?*

I plumped for the cemetery. At the moment I knew more about the stones – and it seemed there was a chance they might be at the cemetery. It was a good place to start.

Right.

I looked at various images of the Cimitero Monumentale. The pictures gave me no idea of the size of the cemetery – on the other hand I'd never seen a place with so many statues and mini-mausoleums.

My theory was that Elisabetta had known exactly where the treasure was. Falco had told her – and given her the cards as visual reminders. It seemed to fit best at the moment.

But when had he told her? It must have been in the time between his last collection and his death. Hmm…the image of a hospital popped into my mind again. Maybe it happened at the hospital? If Falco was bedridden for his last few weeks then where else could he have done it?

Again I asked myself why, if Falco had told Elisabetta

precisely where the jewels were, she had waited so long before retrieving them. Especially with her pressing financial problems?

Argh! I still had no answers. The large digital clock next to my bed reminded me that I only had until tomorrow afternoon to solve this case – after that I'd be back in London.

I jumped out of my bed and into the shower. The previous night I'd told Sebastian and Ellie that I was working on a plan for flushing out Elisabetta's killer – and now I had it straight in my mind. But there was one person whose help I'd need. As I got out of the shower I sent Lucas a message:

Hi Lucas, can I count on your help later on today? Can you be around at short notice?

His reply was immediate:

For you I'm definitely around. Short notice is fine. What will you need?

I couldn't help smiling – although Lucas was a flirt, I was sure it was his curiosity about the *tarocchi* that really held his interest. I wrote back:

You'll need to contact someone for me...

Sounds mysterious…but no problem. I'm on call.
Anything for you!

Yeah, right! I sent him a simple thank you and told him I'd get back to him.

I pushed any thoughts of his green eyes to the back of my mind, grabbed a quick breakfast and got dressed. I'd be on the go all day so Converse and jeans were the answer. But as I looked out of my bedroom window I also decided to take my super lightweight trench coat. Outside, a thunderous grey sky obliterated the sun and in the distance I could hear the rumble of faraway thunder. It looked set to be a stormy day.

"Don't worry, I'm prepared for later – I've got some leggings and my trainers in my bag." Ellie was standing just outside my bedroom wearing loose pyjama-style trousers and delicate gold sandals. "But I have the feeling that even if the storm blows over, today won't be too calm or quiet for us."

"I think – I hope – you're right."

As Ellie and I dashed for the tramway, thunder rolled across the city in a series of loud cracks. We jumped on board just as the first heavy drops of rain began to fall. Twenty minutes later we arrived at the large palazzo where the Lei-Lei show was being held.

I'd never walked in a men's fashion show before and it felt weird to be surrounded by so many guy models.

And the amount of preening was incredible! I watched them practising their pouts in the mirror and sucking in their cheeks, to emphasize their cheekbones.

"Forget all their posing, what annoys me most about guy models," Ellie said as we walked in, "is that they all think that every female they encounter is dying to go out with them."

I could see what she meant. They really thought they were pretty hot stuff – but their attitude was a major turn-off. Not that they noticed.

I did keep an eye out for Alessandro – Ellie had mentioned he'd be in the show – but didn't spot him.

Ellie and I loaded up at the buffet table and then walked back to the seats that had been reserved for us at the backstage make-up area. As I passed the Lei-Lei mood board I noticed that in yet another uncanny coincidence – this time a fun one! – one of the major Lei-Lei runway trends for this season was for thick, black, geeky glasses – just like mine. In fact, the stylist thought I was wearing a pair of Lei-Leis and for a fleeting second I knew what it was like to feel trendy!

Ellie immediately got to work on her phone, checking emails and organizing her life for the next few weeks. She had some major bookings coming up and would have to fly between Europe and New York twice in the coming week.

I googled Cimitero Monumentale again and studied the images that popped up on screen. As I zoomed in and out the snippets of conversation that I'd heard in my dream began to replay through my mind…

I don't think she even owned a pair of sneakers…

I begged her to forget Falco and to let sleeping dogs lie.

I come to Milan twice a year, like clockwork…

On his deathbed Falco was racked with guilt over bad decisions he'd made – surely hiding the jewels was one of them…

She started talking to me about the jewel switch and how she had something important to do the following evening…

Big deal, Elisabetta went to the hospital every day when he was dying – so did I…

She told me that I had no idea what I was talking about and that everything was fine and going according to plan…

The stones on the most obvious parts of the dress are real, but the others are not…

She told me that Falco's ghost would finally be happy…

I could feel the strands of this story somehow pulling together at the back of my mind. I was trying to make sense of it all but something, some little detail I'd missed or had yet to find, was still eluding me.

A pang of fear gripped me as I sat in my chair. What if I'd got everything wrong? Time was ticking by and I only had until tomorrow – Saturday afternoon – to solve this case.

I needed to catch Elisabetta's killer.

You will, Axelle.

I took a deep breath and continued to look through the

cemetery images on my screen. It wasn't long, though, before my phone rang. It was my mum.

"Axelle, love! Great news! I'm flying to Milan tonight!"

Argh!!!

I nearly dropped my phone.

I felt my heart jump – and not in a good way. The last thing I needed was to have her breathing down my neck *tonight*!

I didn't know what to say. I sat, holding my phone, my mouth frozen into a grim line. Not that my silence mattered – my mum is a pro at filling in gaps.

"You know how I love a good surprise! I'm so excited – it's been ages since I've been to Milan. Anyway, the client I was going to meet later today has cancelled so I thought, great, I can fly out to see you tonight! This way we have the whole of tomorrow together now too. After all, this is the perfect opportunity for us to spend some quality time together before you leave for Tokyo on Monday."

Quality time! I nearly choked on the jam-filled pastry I was nibbling.

"Your father is home to look after Halley, so no worries there, and you and I can start early tomorrow on the shopping and culture. And be sure to tell Ellie and Sebastian that they can join us for everything, all right?"

Right, Mum, like trailing behind you is exactly what we want to do in our free time…

"Uh huh." I felt like a hare caught in the headlights

of an oncoming train. She wasn't just hijacking my weekend – she was now hijacking the last moments I had to solve this case, too! I couldn't let it happen.

"Um, but, Mum, there's no point in coming out today. Seriously. I'm busy the whole day with bookings and tonight Ellie and Sebastian and I have plans to meet up with a few new sus—" Jeez! I nearly said suspects! Argh! "Friends – new friends. And so we'll be busy. Very busy. It's men's fashion week so the city is buzzing…"

"Oh don't worry about me, Axelle. I'll be in late tonight – too late for dinner. I'll probably catch the last flight out. But don't change your plans on account of me – if I have the time I'd be delighted to meet your new friends."

Not if you knew that one of them trapped me underground…

"I can't wait, darling – we're going to have so much fun! I'll call you later to let you know when I land. And then first thing tomorrow morning we can start! The new autumn collections are probably in the stores! I've got to run now, though, Axelle. Bye, darling – or should I say *ciao!*"

"Sure, Mum. Great!" Grrr!

"From the little I overheard I think I can guess what happened," Ellie said with a giggle as I hung up.

"My mum is arriving tonight and she has no idea about what's going on – and somehow I have to keep it that way."

"Is she flying BA?"

I nodded. "She always does."

"Well if your mum is catching the last flight from London to Milan, it's at 8.25 p.m. which means she'll land at around 11.30 p.m. or so." One thing about models: they all know the routine fashion flights by heart. "In any case," Ellie continued, "she won't be in town until midnight. Can you wrap this case up by then?"

I nodded. "I'll have to."

"I'm sure you can. Besides, Sebastian and I are free to help you so..."

"So we'll do it." I smiled and Ellie and I high-fived.

"Ooh! Excited about the show, are we, girls?" cooed the hairstylist, Stefano, as his reflection suddenly appeared in the mirror in front of us. He was wearing what looked like a cowboy's holster – only instead of pistols it held hairbrushes.

He started fussing about with my hair while the make-up artist worked on Ellie. I, meanwhile, went back to looking at the images of the cemetery.

Stefano couldn't help noticing. "I did a shoot there once."

"What? At the Cimitero Monumentale? They allow that?"

"No. It is totally forbidden, but this was very early on in my career and it was for some test photos. We wanted to do a haunted story – all very Goth, you know. We had the most amazing long black coats that the stylist had managed to pull from a young designer. So we all dressed as if we were there for a funeral and the photographer hid his camera, of course. I even brought flowers – like a wreath you put on the graves, you know?"

I nodded.

"Anyway, once we found a good spot, the model quickly posed and then we took the shot."

"How many shots did you do?"

Stefano was teasing my hair at the back of my head so it stood straight up and I couldn't see his reflection any more. "We did a few. The model had to change behind the bushes. Once she even changed in one of the mausoleums of some rich banking family. That was a bit creepy!"

"I bet…"

"But the whole place is creepy. Have you been?"

"No. But I'm planning on going this afternoon."

Stefano nodded. "You should definitely see it – it's amazing. And it's so big you'll have the place to yourselves."

Perfect, I thought. "You weren't there for Falco Ventini's funeral, were you by any chance?"

"No. I wasn't important enough to be invited," he laughed. "But I went to the memorial service at the church of Santa Maria Grazia, that was open to the public. A lot of people went. But the funeral at the cemetery was by invitation only. The *crème de la crème* of Italian fashion was there, of course… Now if you could bend your head forward a little bit, like that, yes, perfect, I'm going to straighten this section at the back."

While Stefano concentrated on applying the tongs to my hair I suddenly wondered whether there were any photos of Falco's funeral online. I googled it but no images came up. Then I tried Instagram. I typed #ventinifuneral into the search box and to my surprise a number of pictures came up.

I scrolled through them, looking at each one carefully. Needless to say, I recognized quite a few of the mourners. Ugo was in many of the photos, as were Elisabetta, Francesca, Ginevra and Lavinia. Kristine, Coco and Alessandro were also in some of them. Then one photo caught my eye.

Hmm…it looked like another coincidence. *Or was it?*

Annoyingly it's impossible to zoom in on Instagram pictures so I quickly did a screenshot of the image that interested me and emailed it to myself. A minute later I had it on my tablet screen and zoomed in for a closer look. The quality of the image wasn't great, but it did help.

The picture had been taken by someone who'd been standing a little way back from the ceremony. The priest was speaking and Falco's family and friends were standing around what I presumed to be the Ventini family crypt.

The crypt appeared to be carved directly into a massive boulder. It looked like something out of a kid's illustrated Bible, designed to resemble a saint's or hermit's cave. The entrance was through an austere classical portico, with steps and columns; the rest of the crypt's exterior was composed of natural, unpolished boulder. What caught my eye, however, was a tiny sculpture on top of the crypt, just beyond the portico roof. The quality of the photo wasn't the best, but what I saw was a small figure, dressed in robes and on horseback. I felt the hairs stand up on my arms and neck.

"Axelle, please keep still," Stefano said through a mouthful of hairpins.

Annoyingly, when I zoomed in close the figure lost any kind of distinct shape, so I had no way of verifying whether it was a lady riding the horse. But it looked a lot like the image on the tarot card...the robes were very similar, and the horse was lifting one of its front legs. It couldn't be a coincidence that the statue was on top of the Ventini family crypt.

No way!

At that moment the make-up artist who'd been working on Ellie finished with her and left to touch up one of the guys. Stefano had also finished with me and moved on to Ellie. He turned the hairdryer on and without a word I passed my tablet over to Ellie.

She looked at it and then turned to me with wide eyes. "It's the figure on the card, isn't it?" She spoke loudly enough for me to hear her but with the din of the hairdryer in Stefano's ears I doubt he picked up anything we said.

"I think so, yes."

"Where is this?"

"You're never going to believe it…it's on Falco Ventini's family crypt at the cemetery."

"What! The one we're going to later?"

I nodded.

"You're amazing, Axelle. I don't know how you figure these things out." She high-fived me again.

"I don't know if it means that the gems are there…I'm only following my gut."

"Yeah, well I've never known your gut to fail you and it can't be a coincidence that that image is on Falco's family crypt."

I smiled as my grandfather's words came back to. "No, actually, I don't think it can…"

"Anyway, whether the gems are there or not I still have to figure out who poisoned Elisabetta. And I have to confront them by this evening."

Lei-Lei's "designer" was in fact a young duo. Pierro was Italian and Lena, American. Apart from their spare, edgy designs, and dislike of patterned fabrics, they were famous for their commitment to ethical fashion. #Fashionconscience was their mantra – and it was all over the place. As show time approached they came by to give us all a pep talk. They wanted us to project a certain attitude as we walked down the runway. We were to imagine ourselves as cool geeks with super style and a strong fashion conscience. Lei-Lei's collection was made up of minimalistic separates in tones of white, grey, black and a vivid midnight blue – and all were made from ethically-sourced materials and free of any animal products. So, no leather or fur – not even silk. "Remember that you guys are eco-warriors with clean consciences. At Lei-Lei we leave a super-low carbon footprint, we love this planet. And you are all a part of that. Be cool, be stylish – but have a fashion conscience. Feel it! Feel real! All right, let's go!"

Suddenly the music blared: it was show time. We'd each be going out twice. The crowd was an enthusiastic one, and the Lei-Lei front row was packed, as usual, with every celebrity vegetarian and vegan in existence. I finally saw Alessandro – he opened the show – and Ginevra too, in the front row, when I walked onto the runway (though somehow I doubted either of them was vegan). I didn't spot Sebastian, but guessed he was somewhere in the back.

For the runway floor Lei-Lei had commissioned a special rug. It was shaggy and resembled the green moss you find on the forest floor. Amazingly, from a distance it looked like the real thing – but it wasn't. Which, according to their show notes, was their point ("Plants feel pain, too!").

It was a wonderful surface to walk on and for once I felt that even if I did fall, I probably wouldn't break anything. The vibe was great and everyone was enthusiastic and happy. I stepped out, and, if I wasn't relaxed, at least I didn't feel as nervous as usual. Of course the fact that the guys were the main focus of the show helped, but the Lei-Lei shows were known for being fun too.

FASHION CONSCIENCE.

The words were lit up and beamed around the show space. They'd appear in one colour and on one wall, stay lit for a few moments, and then suddenly appear in a different colour and on another wall. It was pretty cool, actually. I wondered whether that sort of lighting set-up would work in my bedroom at home.

FASHION CONSCIENCE.

The words went round and round in my head. And then, out of the blue, my hospital dream came back to me – and I remembered the snippets of conversation that had been replaying through my mind earlier. But now they were starting to fit together.

FASHION CONSCIENCE.

A clean conscience.

Of course! In the end it's what everyone wants, right? But I'd been so intent on seeing only one thing that I'd made myself blind to other possibilities.

Lavinia, Tavi, Falco, Francesca, Ginevra, Elisabetta, Ugo, Alessandro and Kristine. Everything they'd said now held new meaning. And even if it still didn't point directly to the killer, it explained a lot…

As I stepped out on the runway, my legs moving to the beat of the music, some of the pieces of the puzzle clicked into place. Like shards of coloured glass, they shifted and moved slowly, finally revealing a pattern and overall design.

The show passed in a haze of thought and although I did my best, I felt as if I was moving on autopilot for most of it. "You guys did a killer job out there!" yelled the designers as we all swarmed backstage.

If only they knew.

I needed to connect the two strands of this case. There were the tarot cards and the gems, and then there was the killer. They all met up at some point, but where and how? And why?

For the stones, I felt certain that someone wanted them. People wanted the tarot cards, too. Because they led to the stones? But then why kill Elisabetta, the only person who understood the meaning of Falco's clues?

Who else knew for certain about the gems being switched? Were they the ones after the tarot cards?

Acording to Ugo and Tavi, Falco was secretive. Also, Ugo had said that the only person he could imagine Falco confessing the truth about the jewel switch to was Elisabetta. Based on that, it didn't seem far-fetched to think Falco wouldn't have told anyone but Elisabetta about the tarot cards either.

Anyway, Axelle, you have a motive, I said to myself. *And a plan. It's time to flush out the killer...*

As Ellie and I changed quickly, I made a quick call to

Ugo at work. I told him that I needed a piece of Falco's personal stationery and asked if he had any left.

"Falco's stationery?"

"Yes, Ugo. And it's urgent."

"Fine. I'll have a look, hold on."

He came back on the line after a moment. "Yes, we still have some. How much do you need?"

"One page of notepaper and an envelope, please. I'll come and fetch it now, if you can leave it at reception."

"Yes, okay."

"Oh, and one more thing – do you think you can sign it at the bottom? But not with your signature. I need you to sign as Falco…"

I wasn't totally comfortable with the idea of asking Ugo to forge Falco's signature but there was no other way. A killer was loose and I felt a fake Falco signature would up my chances of catching them.

"You mean, like, copy his signature?"

"Yes. Please. I know it's an unusual request, but this may be our only chance."

"Just his name?"

"Yes. I'm assuming you've got a reference for it – you know what his signature looked like?"

"Yes, of course," said Ugo, sounding a little bewildered.

"Well, make it a little sloppy, if you can."

"Okay." Ugo was obviously curious but too busy to ask me any more questions.

"And Ugo?"

"Yes?"

"Did Falco have a large hospital room?"

"Huh? His hospital room? Your questions always throw me. Um, yes, Falco had a large hospital room with its own private bathroom. Anything else?"

"No, not now, thanks. But I'll call you later – and hopefully with some good news."

"I can't wait."

"Me too."

I finished dressing and then Ellie and I headed for the door. We were just about to make it out through the exit when Alessandro showed up. "You, yet *again*?" he said. "I can't seem to avoid you."

"Are you trying to?"

Alessandro laughed off my comment, but I'd noticed a sinister flash in his eyes as I'd answered him. He stepped back and disappeared. I hooked my arm through Ellie's and we turned. But as we stepped away I caught Ginevra watching me, a smile playing at the corners of her mouth. I waved at her and continued on my way.

I sent Lucas a quick message as we rushed outside.

Sebastian was already there, waiting for us just down the street from the show exit. Ellie gave a quick wave and hello to the waiting paparazzi and fashion bloggers and then followed me as I made my way to him. I had to pick up Falco's stationery and then see Lucas but there wasn't space on the Vespa for three, so Ellie parted ways with us. "I'll do my appointments and you do yours, then why don't we meet at the cemetery?"

I nodded. "Fine. Can you be there at 4 p.m.?"

"You bet – and in trainers and leggings."

"Perfect."

Sebastian and I wove through the traffic smoothly and quickly. At the first light, I asked him, "And? What did you think of the show?"

"Well," he shouted above the din of the traffic, "clearly I have to work on my wardrobe – and my pout!"

When we arrived at Ventini, I jumped off the scooter, ran into the building and picked up the waiting envelope. Ugo had scrawled *Good luck* on a Post-it note. I smiled as I took it off. This afternoon I'd definitely need all the luck I could get.

Ten minutes later we turned onto the small street where Professor Greene's office was. Sebastian opted to wait outside on his scooter.

"I'm sure old Moony-Eyes would prefer to meet with you alone. Besides, I told Francesca I'd call her."

That awkward feeling immediately came between us again.

"Fine."

"See you in a few minutes, then."

Sebastian was already searching for her number so I went in alone. Lucas was waiting for me.

"So how can I help?" His eyes were the lightest green I'd ever seen – it was hard to ignore them, especially as he kept them focused on me. I took a deep breath and said, "Lucas, you told me that two people had *called* you asking about the three antique *tarocchi*…"

"Yes…"

"Well, I need you to call them back…"

I took the three cards out of my rucksack and slowly handed them over to Lucas. I had to give them to him. I didn't like doing it – especially when I knew I should really be handing them in to the police, but I didn't have a choice. Besides, if my plan worked then they'd be back in my hands again later tonight.

I explained to Lucas that I needed him to tell the anonymous callers that he had found the cards they were looking for. I asked him to call both of them in about one hour – I'd let him know when the time was right – and tell them that someone called Rinconi had just brought three antique *tarocchi* in to sell. If they wanted to buy the cards they were to come to the office within the hour because he already had another buyer lined up – a serious collector, who was leaving town in an hour and wanted to take the cards with him.

Of course that was all a lie – I only wanted the two callers to believe that they had an opportunity to buy the cards. Hearing this, I thought, would make the suspects move quickly – no doubt they'd want to get their hands on the cards as soon as possible. I also told Lucas that it was imperative that the two buyers didn't see each other. I asked him to schedule some time between the appointments.

"Fine, I can do that...but can you tell me why? Or are you going to be all mysterious again – not that I don't like it," he said, with an intense stare.

Did he ever stop flirting?

"I'll tell you – but later."

"I'll hold you to that, you know." He leaned in close to me and I swear he was about to touch my face with his hand.

"Fine," I said, pulling back sharply. "And another thing, Lucas..."

He smiled.

"When they come for the cards, you need to do something else...I need you to give something to one of them. But, first, would you mind helping me translate something into Italian?"

"Not at all." He motioned for me to sit down opposite him at the desk. Then he reached into a drawer and pulled out a piece of paper and a pen. I dictated my letter to him and together we tweaked it. Then I opened the envelope Ugo had given me, pulled out the sheet of Falco's personalized stationery and copied the letter we'd composed onto it...

Dear Elisabetta,

I cannot write well any more, so I'm asking one of the nurses to help me with this last note to you.

This is my final goodbye. I will have moved to another place by the time you read this.

You have been my true family – your friendship has meant more to me than you can ever know.

Remember the message in the cards, and use it to help yourself.

With all my love,

Falco

Ugo's forged signature looked perfect at the bottom of the sheet. Then, on the margin of the note I scribbled lightly, in pencil, the following words:

Cimitero Monumentale
Look under the statue on the Ventini crypt

I took the letter and folded it, wrinkled it up a bit and rubbed it quickly between my palms, trying to make it look less crisp and white. I put the letter in its envelope and then gave it to Lucas.

"So which one of the lucky callers gets this?" he asked.

I took a piece of notepaper from the top of the desk and wrote something down before pushing the slip of paper across the desk to him. "You are to 'sell' the cards to the person who fits this description. And you must give them the letter before they leave with the cards. It's important to tell them that when Signor Rinconi first came in with the cards he told you that the letter was attached to them. Act as if you are about to throw it away, but then ask if the new owner of the cards would like it. Say that it is from someone called Falco Ventini. Read the name – it's printed on the back of the envelope – when you do so. It is imperative that the 'buyer' reads the letter. Once they've done that they'll probably leave in a rush. Can you message me as soon as they've left here?"

I paused for a moment before continuing. "As for the person who doesn't fit the description I just gave you – can you tell them that the *tarocchi* collector you had lined up no longer wants to buy the cards. Therefore, Signor Rinconi is now free to sell the cards to any interested party. But tell the second caller that they must come back to your office tonight at nine to buy the cards. Is that all right with you?"

"You don't ask much," smiled Lucas, "but yes, I'll keep the office open – no problem."

"Tell them that tonight is their only chance to buy the cards because Signor Rinconi is scheduled to meet with an auction house tomorrow morning. Of course it's all a lie and the cards will be with the other person but…" I trailed off not wanting to say more.

"I'm curious, you know…" He smiled.

"You'll hear all later. And don't be surprised if I show up for the appointment at nine."

"I'll count on it."

I quickly said goodbye and left. Sebastian was waiting for me outside. After belting my trench coat, I slipped my helmet on, jumped onto the back of his scooter and we peeled away from the kerb.

I would give Lucas the signal to make the calls in about an hour – as soon as I was finished with my two go-sees. As we parked outside the building of the first, Sebastian asked, "Is there anything I should pick up that you think we might need later?" He nodded in the direction of some small shops lining the quiet street outside the photography studio I was heading for.

"Yes, ropes, please. Three of them."

"Planning on tying someone up?"

"Yes, you – if you don't stop with the corny questions."

"The final chase hasn't even started and already you're this punchy? It sounds like we're going to have some fun."

"Wait and see, Watson."

"I will, Holmes."

"Anything else?"

"Three whistles if they have them."

"I won't ask why."

"I wouldn't tell you anyway."

Sebastian laughed and headed off on his mission.

My next appointment was with Vittorio Ferrante, a

successful Milan-based photographer – which in the fashion world was bit of an oxymoron. Super-successful photographers are mainly based in New York and Paris, with a few in London – hardly any of the big ones are in Milan. While Vittorio carefully turned the pages of my portfolio, he asked me how I was enjoying his city.

"Well, it's much more exciting than I thought it would be," I answered honestly, if vaguely.

"I'm happy to hear that. I think it's a great city; most tourists head for Rome and Florence, but Milan has a lot of action, too."

I definitely agreed with that!

He asked me a few more questions about some of the work I'd done and then he took a couple of quick photos of me to show a client. "I'll be shooting their lookbook soon and I think you're the type they're looking for…"

He took a zed card from the pocket in my book and then I left.

My next go-see, at Italian *Elle*, also went quickly – although from the amount of times I checked my phone, anyone watching would have thought the time was crawling by. I couldn't help counting down the minutes until I could give Lucas the signal. I only hoped he'd remember everything I'd asked him to do.

Fortunately for me, the editor I was seeing was busy and had a no-nonsense approach to our appointment. There wasn't much chit-chat but she did ask me to quickly try on a couple of coats for a winter story she'd be shooting soon. She was pleased with how they fitted and called my agency to put me on option while I was still in her office. I could practically feel Tomasso's excitement vibrating through her phone.

Finally, my modelling tasks were over! Of course, no sooner had I burst out of the Italian *Elle* offices than Tomasso was trying to call me. But at this point there was no way I was going to let any more modelling stuff get in my way. The wheels of my plan were in motion and it was too late to stop them turning. I ignored his call. I'd call him back – later. Right now I had a killer to catch.

FRIDAY AFTERNOON

Killer Instincts

The Cimitero Monumentale – or Monumental Cemetery – was aptly named. I'd never seen anything like it. Even the online images hadn't prepared me for the reality. From its prominent position at the bottom of a wide boulevard, the Famedio – or Temple of Fame – the largest building in the cemetery, dominated the view. Many of Milan's richest families and most influential leaders in culture and politics rested here.

While Sebastian locked up his scooter, I looked at my phone. It was just past four o'clock. As I picked up my phone to call Lucas, Ellie drove up in a taxi.

I hoped Lucas would be able to get through to the suspects first time and sent up a silent prayer to the detective gods to help him. I knew, though, that once they heard it was Lucas calling about the cards, they'd want to meet him. And I was certain that the suspect who got the letter would head for the cemetery as soon as they'd read it. They were about to find the very prize they'd been searching for. I doubted they'd waste a second.

We had just under two hours until the cemetery closed – but I calculated it would be enough time. In any case, this was my one and only chance. By late tonight my mum would have me under her thumb.

"Come on," I said. "Let's get a map." We moved briskly in the direction of the sign marked "office".

We had the cemetery to ourselves. The friendly old man working the small office gave us each a map. I searched mine straight away, but didn't see any reference to the Ventini family tomb. So while Ellie and Sebastian started walking towards the Temple of Fame, I asked for directions.

"Bocconi?"

"No – Ventini. *Famiglia importante. Moda. Alta moda.*"

"Motta? Angelo Motta?" It was clear the official was hard of hearing – and probably didn't know where the Ventini family crypt was anyway. I looked at the time on my phone. We'd have to move quickly, but between the three of us, surely we'd find the crypt without too much difficulty.

I followed Ellie and Sebastian up the incredibly wide, formal stone staircase that led to the high, arched, central entrance of the Temple of Fame. The views from this height were spectacular, and the ceiling so ornately painted – but we weren't here to admire the scenery.

"So where to, Holmes? What are we looking for here?" asked Sebastian.

I took out my phone and pulled up the images of the cards. I'd quickly taken the photos this morning, when I'd had the idea of asking Lucas for his help.

"So, the grinning skeleton – death," I said as I held up my phone. "Like I said last night, has led us here. And this," I now pulled up the photo of the lady on horseback, "I think, represents a sculpture – most probably the one on the Ventini family crypt." I pulled up the screenshot image I'd grabbed and showed it to Sebastian.

He did a double take. "Good sleuthing, Holmes, you're definitely on to something. So now we just have to find the Ventini family crypt…"

"Exactly."

It was only after we'd walked through the cavernous central chamber of the Temple of Fame and stood on the outdoor terrace behind it that I realized how difficult this would be. Like a small forest, the heavily wooded cemetery spread far and wide beneath us and was crammed full of sculptures and crypts! I'd never seen anything like it. The three of us scanned the cemetery, hardly able to believe our eyes. Every square centimetre of the sprawling cemetery gardens was crammed with mausoleums adorned with statues of women, men, angels, horses, bulls, urns and columns, pyramids and obelisks, all carved in stone. Clearly, finding a particular family crypt here would take some time…

"I think I need help with this," I said as I reached for my phone and called Ugo. He wasn't answering – he was probably in a meeting. I sent him a message instead and hoped he'd get back to me quickly.

I put my phone away and opened my map. After studying it for a minute I divided up the work. Ellie would start along the western flank of the garden. Sebastian would cover the middle section and I'd start on the eastern flank and we'd each work methodically towards the very back of the cemetery. I sent them both the photo of the tarot card with the lady on horseback, along with the screenshot from Falco's funeral. After making sure our phones were on silent (we'd made sure they were all fully charged too), I took the bag of supplies from Sebastian and passed him and Ellie a length of rope each. "In case we need to tie anyone up." I took one for myself and handed out the whistles next.

"In case we need help?" Sebastian asked.

"Exactly, Watson."

Then we quickly walked down the stairs leading from the terrace to the cemetery gardens and split up to search.

The time flew by quickly. The vast cemetery was filled with a maze-like series of paths that took time to navigate. And just when I'd thought I'd seen every crypt and tombstone in a particular corner, something else, half hidden by a shrub, would catch my eye.

Huge topiary bushes and dark twisted pine trees added a sinister air to this place of death. I now understood, too, why Elisabetta had packed sneakers in her basket on Tuesday. If she'd been heading here that evening, she would have needed them in order to cope with the uneven ground – this was no place for heels.

I was about halfway through the area I was searching when my phone buzzed. It was Lucas.

"The caller I gave the letter to has just left – and as you predicted they seemed in a rush. I think they're on their way to the cemetery now."

I thanked him and rang off. The chase was on! I'd laid my trap and my number one suspect was on their way. Now I'd just have to find the Ventini crypt before they got to it. I sent Ellie and Sebastian messages telling them to stay alert. The suspect would be in the cemetery within the next quarter of an hour or so – and we couldn't let them escape. As I put my phone back into my pocket, the wind picked up and thunder cracked through the humid, grey air. A few heavy raindrops fell. Another storm was about to let loose.

Maddeningly, not one of us had yet found the Ventini crypt. I was just walking quietly towards yet another small family mausoleum when I saw a dark shadow flit through the juniper trees to my left. I quickly jumped behind the nearest shrub, waited until they passed me and then tried to follow them, but I lost them as quickly as I'd seen them.

A minute later I caught sight of them again. Yes, it was my suspect – despite the dark glasses and billowing coat, I recognized them easily – and they were heading towards the back of the cemetery.

I messaged Ellie and Sebastian, telling them our target had arrived and which direction they were taking.

The suspect moved quickly along the twisting paths with eagerness and confidence – and no idea they were being followed; they'd clearly bought the story I'd asked Lucas to tell. But the further they advanced the more cautious they became. I dropped further behind and was mindful of the twigs underfoot. But the suspect stopped twice and stood for a moment, as if they knew they were being followed. I made sure to stay far enough behind and as close to the bushes and monuments as possible, hoping they'd think any noise they heard was the wind rustling behind them.

Finally, towards the very back of the cemetery, the suspect slowed to a walk, stopped and turned, slowly sweeping their gaze from side to side. Sure that there was no one else around, they approached a crypt of some sort – I couldn't see it well from where I stood, it was half hidden by a large juniper bush. I watched as they pulled out one of Elisabetta's tarot cards and compared the image on the card to what I assumed was the sculpture on top of the crypt. So Falco's family crypt must be behind the large juniper bush?

As the suspect stood, holding the card in their hand, I kept in the shade of the bushes and got as close as I dared. What I saw was indeed the Ventini crypt – and it really did look like a hermit's cave. And there, atop the enormous granite boulder that formed the back of the Ventini family mausoleum, was a bronze statue of a lady dressed in robes and on horseback. And, as I had guessed, she looked exactly like the image of the lady on Elisabetta's *tarocchi*.

I sent Ellie and Sebastian a message directing them to an enormous juniper bush at the very back of the cemetery; I couldn't be more specific. Then I prepared myself for the move I'd have to make next. I crouched down on my hands and knees and crawled forward. The suspect was occupied with trying to reach the statue. It wasn't easy because it was set quite high up. I watched as they searched the side of the boulder with their fingertips, seeking out small edges just wide enough to hold the tips of their toes and fingers, and they carefully began scaling the boulder's craggy side.

I crawled forward so that I was now close to the crypt, but still under the bushes to the side of it. The suspect had climbed high enough and was now searching around the stone directly underneath the woman and her horse, probably looking for a hidden recess in the boulder. They didn't find one, but after further searching, it appeared there was a recess in the horse, underneath its saddle – and the lady was acting like a cover. The statue was not that small and it looked like solid bronze, but finally the suspect eased the lady and her horse apart.

I now got up onto my feet and, crouching low, I approached the crypt. I watched as the suspect reached into the recess of the statue, pulled out a bag and held it up to the light. Were the gems in there?

Sebastian and Ellie were still not with me but I couldn't wait any longer – not while the suspected killer was within my sight and I could catch them red-handed. Without further thought I ran out from the shadow of the bushes – I needed to build up as much momentum as possible. I sprinted, moving my arms and legs like pistons, then, without a sound, I lunged forward. I aimed for the suspect's legs, caught them, and yanked as hard as I could, hoping to pull them down. But their hands locked onto the small bronze horse, which was melded securely onto the rock.

Our struggle was on! With a hard backwards kick the suspect managed to loosen my grip on one leg and wasted no time in kicking at my head with the freed foot. Sneakers softened the impact, but still I felt a searing pain on the side of my head. Somehow I managed to hang on to the other leg with both arms but I could feel my hands slipping.

I glanced up to find Francesca staring at me, her face contorted with rage and desperation. Any trace of her flirtatious side was long gone; her eyes burned like a demon possessed. "You interfering brat!" she hissed. "The tunnel didn't finish you off, but I will!"

Despite my best efforts, my hold on her leg loosened and after another quick tussle I fell to the ground, landing badly on my ankle. I let out a cry of pain. I struggled to reach into my pocket and pull out my whistle. I blew harshly, letting its shrill shriek act as a scream. But in that short moment Francesca had twisted round and, like a werewolf crouched on a rock, ready to attack its prey, she looked set to spring. In one quick movement she threw herself down, screaming as she flew through the air. She landed on me with a loud thud.

She was larger than me and heavier, too – I stood no chance of displacing her. I fought back, though, trying my best to unseat her, but she was fast and any attempt to gouge her eyes or bite her was deflected. With one hand she was squeezing my throat while with her other she reached towards the steps leading to the Ventini crypt. Suddenly she smiled at me sweetly. Through my gasping and choking I saw her free hand grasp at the heavy glass and iron lid that covered an antique candleholder just beside her. The lid opened easily – in fact, as I was about to find out, it wasn't attached.

Francesca grabbed the weighty lid and held it above my face. Her smile vanished just as suddenly as it had appeared and, with a huge storm cloud behind her, she looked like vengeance and madness personified. "You never should have interfered! This is a family matter – do you understand! This is a *Ventini* matter. You and that nasty little snake

Elisabetta have nothing to do with my family! You're going to wish that you'd stayed underground where I left you!" I watched, helpless, as her face convulsed with hatred. "It's your own fault, you know. I *had* to lock you away. *You* were the one who insisted on following me over the Duomo rooftop. I could see you wouldn't let things go, so drastic measures were called for!" Then she laughed, tightened her grip on my throat and added, "This time I'm not going to let you go – alive!" Lightning cracked as she brought the lid down in one swift movement, aiming at my head. I tried my best to twist away from her falling arm. I managed to deflect the blow somewhat but it wasn't enough, and I felt a searing pain as it struck just above my right ear.

I saw Francesca raise her arm again, and this time I screamed, knowing that another blow was coming. But it never landed. Francesca was suddenly yanked backwards and the next thing I heard was a dull crash followed by a vigorous scuffle. I brought my hand to my head and rolled onto my side. From there I slowly managed to pull myself into an upright position.

Sebastian was sitting on Francesca, his hands encircling her wrists. Ellie meanwhile was making neat work of tying Francesca up with the rope. She was still fighting them – she was very strong, as I knew to my cost – and the struggle continued for another minute until finally, Ellie and Sebastian had her secure. While Ellie kept an eye on her, Sebastian called the police.

I watched as Francesca rolled onto her back and looked for me. Our eyes met, hers fierce and defiant. It was time to get some answers out of her. She started yelling as I tried to stand. She wriggled and screamed, her words coming out in a crazed jumble. She hollered about being Falco's true heir, how she should have inherited everything, and that Elisabetta was nothing but a gold-digging hanger-on, an interloper who didn't know her place. She was a Ventini, she screamed, and she had a right to be here – the jewels belonged to her (she seemed to have forgotten that they'd been stolen in the first place).

Clutching my head I walked towards her. As calmly as I could I asked, "Why? Why did you need to kill Elisabetta?"

"Because she was a nasty little worm who crawled into my uncle's heart when she had no right to be there. And she knew too much – stuff *I* should have known!"

"Like about the gems?"

"Yes! I'd heard the rumours of my uncle switching the stones; I knew he was trying to get some money together – and the jewels were as good as cash in the bank. And *I* should have inherited them! Yet he wanted to leave them to that ingratiating little maggot!"

I'd discovered enough to know that it wasn't quite like that. My grandmother's words came back to me – *clean conscience*. I thought about Tavi's twice-yearly visits to Milan, too. I'd put the pieces of the puzzle together and they told a very different story from the one Francesca believed. But I couldn't explain it all to her now. First I wanted to verify another of my theories…

"He'd already given me his precious collection of *tarocchi*, but I'd noticed there were three cards missing – the three most valuable cards in his – *my* – collection. I watched him give them to her on his deathbed and I was furious. He was so drugged at that point that he had no idea I was still in his hospital room – that I'd stayed on, hidden, after I'd said goodbye. I was certain that nasty little snake would come by – and she did! She was so boringly predictable. Every day at the same time – honestly, why wouldn't I take the chance to overhear them? Those cards he gave her were worth so much more than any of the *tarocchi* my uncle left to me – and not just because they were antique! No, these cards were much more special – these tarot cards led the way to the jewels."

"But you didn't hear *how* they led to the jewels, did you? That part was left unsaid…"

Francesca shook her head angrily. "No – no! It wasn't left unsaid. Uncle Falco *told* her! I couldn't hear because he was whispering, but I understood that the cards were the clues! It was all I needed to know."

"So you decided to get the cards, didn't you? In order to find the jewels?"

She wriggled in grotesque excitement as she ranted. "Yes, yes! I wanted the jewels – they were rightfully mine. But so were the cards. I had to get them back!"

"So you mugged Elisabetta and burgled her apartment to find them?"

"Yes – but the snake was careful – she'd hidden them somewhere safe."

"And that's why you planned to kill her, isn't it?"

"I was only taking back what was mine."

"You knew she had a brother – you'd probably overheard that, too, right? And you knew he was a serious drug user, you knew he'd sell whatever he had to feed his habit. And, most importantly, you knew that he was Elisabetta's only living relative, didn't you?"

Francesca nodded. "Yes, I knew all of that. We talked sometimes, you know – especially in the beginning. At the end she didn't seem to like me so much. But before she changed towards me I heard all about her boohoo family life."

"And you figured that if you killed her, her brother would inherit everything she had, and you'd approach him with a generous offer for the cards, assuming he didn't know their true worth."

"Yes, it was a good plan. And airtight – until you got in the way!"

"It was silly to poison her at Ugo's though, wasn't it, with so many witnesses around?" I taunted her.

"No one noticed. It was easy. I used the shawl I was wearing to protect my fingers, tore a leaf off the shrub, then ripped it into tiny bits and sprinkled it over the bruschetta. The stupid worm ate the piece I offered her."

Even if everything she said confirmed what I had suspected, I still felt shocked and horrified to hear how fervently she believed in her twisted truth. She was vicious and calculating, not to mention unhinged – she had killed someone in cold blood. Instinctively I moved away from her. I was tired, and talking to her wasn't exactly easy-going. But she couldn't seem to stop herself – she ranted on, now calling me a liar for masking the truth about my visits to Ugo. "A 'fashion project'? You liar – and you, too!" she spat at Sebastian. "You idiots never even realized I was onto you! You never even noticed me following you to Professor Greene's! I started out following Ugo, and then ended up following you."

So that's how she knew I had the cards. She was right, we should have spotted her. But I wouldn't give her the satisfaction of telling her that. I was suddenly curious, however, as to how she knew that the tarot cards had gone missing from the studio. How had she known that Elisabetta had taken them there on Tuesday morning?

She threw her head back and laughed when I asked. "It was a guess. I'd been following her a lot since my unsuccessful burglary and mugging, hoping to find the cards by chance, hoping she'd give me a clue as to where she kept them – and she did. The stupid little maggot finally did!" Francesca became very animated as she related her story. "Tuesday morning," she hissed, "outside her flat,

I watched her as she waited for her taxi, and saw how she pulled a grey envelope out from under her top and quickly put it into her basket. It was the same size as the cards and from the way she was glancing around, looking so nervous, I knew it must be something important and valuable. It had to be the cards! I followed her to the studio, so I knew she didn't stop off anywhere on the way there. Then, later that day, after she'd died..." Francesca stopped to smile. "I wondered what had become of them. Surely they were still in her basket? Of course, I flirted with the police officer who questioned me that afternoon. And the idiot conveniently left his file open on the table. I saw the list they had made of the contents of her basket – and there was no envelope listed! It gave me a real fright!"

"So you called Megastudio and asked them about it?"

"Of course," she spat. "I had to get those cards. But the studio knew nothing. Luck smiled on me later that day, though, when you two idiots suddenly showed up at Ugo's. After you started asking me so many questions about the party, I had the feeling you knew more – much more – than you were letting on. Anyway, like I said, you finally gave yourselves away by going to Professor Greene's."

The surprise of seeing Francesca, and witnessing her viciousness, had left Sebastian and Ellie speechless. Sebastian was staring at her in disbelief. She smiled back with mock flirtation, batting her eyelashes.

Suddenly something sparkly that I'd completely

forgotten about caught my eye. The gems! The bag of stones had landed under a small bush, when Francesca had leaped onto me from the boulder. I retrieved it now and as I lifted it, hundreds of loose gemstones rattled inside. Some were small, others large, and they were of every colour. And seen up close like this, even through the dirty plastic of their bag, they sparkled and danced in the light.

The police would be surprised, I thought – it wasn't every day a large bagful of gems was found in a cemetery. But before the police could respond to Sebastian's call, someone else arrived – the old man at the front office came running to us with security. He'd been making his final round of the cemetery, letting people know it was time to leave, when he'd heard my whistle. Then, a few seconds later, he'd seen Ellie and Sebastian running in this direction. He'd immediately called for help from his walkie-talkie.

I thanked him and together with the two guards we walked Francesca back to the Temple of Fame. I walked slowly, leaning on Sebastian.

"You're bleeding. You'll have to get your head checked, you know," he said. "And maybe your ankle, too."

"That's the least of my worries," I said. "What am I going to tell my mum? She'll be furious!"

"You can tell her an antique sculpture fell on you while you were getting your daily dose of Italian culture," Sebastian laughed.

"Actually, Watson, that's not a bad idea."

* * *

The police picked us all up from the cemetery entrance and drove us to the main station for questioning. I called Ugo from there and he came straight to the station. He spoke to the police and took full responsibility for having placed me in such a dangerous situation. Later on Lucas also came in for questioning. He'd had his appointment with the second anonymous caller at 9 p.m. Alessandro had shown up just as I'd expected, but because I hadn't made it, Lucas had let him go, saying he'd sold the cards to the collector anyway.

My guess was that Alessandro had become overly clingy and nosy about Elisabetta's whereabouts because he, too, was after the jewels. He would have been aware of the rumour and probably asked Elisabetta about it. She, in turn, may have let something slip about the tarot cards and jewels – and Alessandro, whose modelling career, and consequently his earnings, had taken a nosedive since he'd started trying to act, was desperate to take the jewels for himself. The police were out looking for him now. And although Lucas didn't say anything I could tell he was dying to hear the full story.

I was most thankful, however, for the fact that my mum was somewhere in the air and had her phone switched off. The last thing I needed was for her to hear about everything, now, from the police, and then let it stew for the next few hours while she travelled. Otherwise, by the time she arrived in Milan she'd be a ball of fire, waiting to burn me to a crisp. Instead, now, I could tell her when she arrived, and could hope that the timing would work in my favour. With some luck the late hour might blunt the force of the surprise.

I had to go over my story again and again. The police weren't exactly neglecting Elisabetta's case, but they'd pushed it to one side while they waited for conclusive test results. So I'd beaten them to the punch, so to speak. And while they didn't seem angry about that, they did need to verify my facts before everything went public.

Not that my name would be dragged into it all. I made sure of that. The last thing I needed was the added publicity of a high-profile fashion mystery.

"But you've done a wonderful thing," the police chief said. "Are you sure you don't want the recognition you deserve?" He peered down at me as I sat in his office, a doctor administering to the cut on my head. Happily, it didn't need even one stitch – although I'd probably be left with a small scar at my hairline.

I looked at the police chief as I swallowed the tablet the doctor handed me and shook my head. After setting the glass down I assured him that the last thing I wanted was to draw any attention to what I'd done. I didn't give him my real reason – the need to remain undercover. I simply told him I wasn't sure it would be good for my modelling career and that I wanted to finish my holiday here with my mother without being hassled by people who'd seen the story in the media. He bought my reasoning without any further explanation.

Francesca, meanwhile, was handcuffed and dragged away – and I do mean *dragged*. She put up a fight the whole way, screeching like a crazed spirit. Her greed and sense of entitlement knew no bounds.

Finally, the police finished questioning me (for the time being, anyway) and my colour returned – not to mention my appetite – but I still had a couple of hours before my mum landed. Ugo suggested that we all go back to his place. Maria could make us something to eat and he'd have his driver take Ellie and me back to our flat afterwards. He'd only heard snippets of my story and was eager to know everything, and, besides, my mind was still whirring. It would probably calm me to tell the full story. So together with Ellie and Sebastian I piled into Ugo's waiting car and we left.

"I never would have guessed it was Francesca," Ugo started as soon as he'd settled us in his comfortable sitting room. "And to think I've had her working so close to me all this time. How did you know?"

"I had no way of knowing for certain," I answered, "but in the end, everything pointed to her. The tricky thing about this case for me was that there seemed to be two separate strands, and for a long time I couldn't see how they were connected – and yet it was only by connecting them that I could make sense of everything that had happened. I made the biggest leap when I spoke with Tavi Holt. Only then did I have definite reason to think that Elisabetta knew something that was worth killing for – as Falco's best friend it was likely she knew about the gems and where he'd hidden them. Although if Falco hadn't fallen ill so quickly after switching the gems I don't know if Elisabetta ever would have found out about them. But because he went to the hospital without having sold the gems, and then stayed there until it was clear he'd never leave, it seemed logical to me that he'd have told his closest friend, Elisabetta, about the gems *while he was there*."

"Is that why you asked me about everyone's visiting times?" Ugo said.

I nodded. "Although when we spoke I hadn't yet made that connection. I was just curious to account for everyone in the days leading up to Ugo's death. But once it struck me that he would have wanted to clear his conscience before he died, I thought about those times again. Because Falco had no other option but to make his last wishes known from his hospital bed…"

"So?" Ellie asked.

"So I started to think that someone must have overheard him."

"That's why you asked me about the size of his hospital room!" Ugo added as the penny dropped.

I nodded. "I had to know that it was large enough for someone to easily hide in. And then I thought about the log-out times again. Ugo, can you hand me the logbooks, please?"

I set the open book down in the middle of the table. "Ugo, you told me that Elisabetta went to visit Falco at the hospital at 6 p.m. every day straight after she left Ventini – and the logbooks confirmed that."

"Okay…so?"

"And you also told me that, four days before Falco died, you were all told that he probably had only a few days left…"

"*Sì*. Correct."

"But up to that point there had been a chance that Falco might recover and leave the hospital, right?"

"Slim, but yes."

"So when he realized that he'd never leave the hospital, he had no option but to quickly tell Elisabetta about the gems, and how he had hidden them. Fine – right up to the end she left Ventini as usual at 6 p.m. But, interestingly, for those last four days, *Francesca*, who normally went to the hospital straight after work at 7 p.m., suddenly started leaving the office *before* Elisabetta. She told me at the cemetery that Falco had already given her his tarot collection and she'd noticed that those three antique tarot cards were missing and she saw those tarot cards as being rightfully hers. So she jumped to the conclusion, knowing that Falco had nothing else to give, because of his financial circumstances, that he was going to leave these three cards to Elisabetta as a parting gift.

"So, knowing that Elisabetta's visits were always at the same time, and, crucially, that Falco only had a few days to make his last wishes known, she simply left work *before* Elisabetta, hid in the hospital room, and overheard their last conversations. And, while she'd expected to hear him give her the three antique *tarocchi*, there was a twist to the gift that she hadn't expected: the cards also led to the hidden gems. From that moment on she was desperate to get her hands on them."

There was a collective sigh as we all leaned back in our chairs for a minute.

"Okay…" Sebastian said, "but what I still don't understand is why, if Elisabetta was hard up, she didn't go straight to the cemetery, find the gems and sell them? Why wait all this time? Falco died over seven months ago, after all."

"For a while that had me stumped too," I answered. "Like you say, she was hard up, and yet she knew where a fabulous cache of gems were hidden. And she also could have sold the *tarocchi* if she wanted to. So why wait?" I paused for a moment. "The thing is, she waited because Falco had asked her to…the decision had nothing to do with Elisabetta. It had to do with Falco…"

Ugo, Ellie and Sebastian looked at me, eyes wide. "Falco?"

"Like we said, it didn't make sense that Elisabetta waited – as long as I went with the assumption that *she* was supposed to benefit from the gems!" I stopped while Maria passed around small plates of pasta. "But what if Elisabetta had some other reason for wanting to find them? A reason that might make more sense within Elisabetta's time frame…?"

"So what was it?" Ugo's curiosity was palpable. I smiled as I watched him nearly jump out of his seat as he encouraged me to continue.

"Well, believe it or not, I only figured it all out as I was walking down the Lei-Lei runway this morning." *Who would have guessed*, I thought, *that modelling could be so inspiring?* "The words FASHION CONSCIENCE were lit up and beamed around the runway. And, funnily enough, in my dream last night my gran kept saying, as she lay on her deathbed, that she had no regrets and a clean conscience."

"So? I don't see the connection," said Ugo.

"So, what is it that most people want to do on their deathbed? They want to clear their conscience, right? They want to die knowing that any loose ends they've left behind them are tied up, and they also want to right whatever wrongs they've done. Keeping that in mind I started looking at the circumstances again and that's when it occurred to me that Falco must have been feeling horrible about what he'd done – especially once he realized he'd never be able to leave the hospital. Lavinia even told me she thought Falco had felt guilty at the end. So how could he clear his conscience and make right what he'd done to Tavi Holt while he was in the hospital and she was halfway across the world? He had no way – *or did he?*"

"Elisabetta," Sebastian said.

"Exactly. She was the perfect choice. She was his best friend and he knew he could rely on her utter discretion. He decided to tell her about the stones he'd switched and where he'd hidden them. Then he asked her to retrieve them and take them to Tavi *for him*. She wouldn't have to say anything – he'd write a letter to Tavi explaining everything himself. She only had to act as the messenger."

"But where's the letter now?" Sebastian asked.

"Probably somewhere in Elisabetta's flat. I'm sure the police will find it…"

"Okay, but, again, why the seven-month wait?" Ellie asked.

"Tavi answered that question for me herself. She told me that she came to Milan 'twice a year, like clockwork', to see the Ventini shows. I kept going over that in my mind until I realized that, of course, Elisabetta had to wait until Tavi returned."

"But why?" Ugo asked.

"Because," I explained, "if Elisabetta had fetched the stones straight after Falco had died, where would she have kept them? And what if someone had found them on her? She would have had a lot of explaining to do. I'm sure Falco told her to wait for Tavi. I can't imagine he would have wanted to expose Elisabetta to the huge risk that keeping those stones for all those months would have entailed."

"So that was the very important thing she had to do on Tuesday night – fetch the stones from the cemetery and take them to Tavi," said Sebastian.

"And that's also why she had a pair of sneakers with her in her basket on Tuesday – because of the cemetery," Ellie said.

"Exactly."

"Which reminds me," Sebastian said as he set his fork down, "how did Falco manage to get the bag of gems into the statue on top of his family crypt? He wasn't exactly in great shape after his last show…"

"True." I nodded. "But I think Falco probably went *before* the show – as soon as he'd switched the stones, in fact. He wasn't feeling well at that point, that's true, but he wasn't in as much pain as he'd be the week later. And it made sense for him to hide the gems at the cemetery straight away. The last thing he needed was for someone to find them at the Ventini offices or in his house."

We sat in silence for a few minutes, each of us lost in our thoughts – or maybe it was just that Maria's pasta was exceptionally good. Finally, though, Sebastian asked another question. "But why did Francesca *kill* Elisabetta? Why not just steal the cards from her – like she tried to do with you?"

"But she did try stealing them from Elisabetta, remember?"

"Ah yes, she was mugged in the spring!" Ugo said. "That must have been Francesca!"

"Exactly. And Elisabetta's apartment was broken into back in the spring, too – by Francesca. She admitted as much to me in the cemetery," I added. "The thing is, Francesca told herself that after two failed attempts at trying to get the cards from Elisabetta, she needed a more foolproof method. She probably overheard Falco saying something to Elisabetta about when to fetch the stones while she was hiding in his hospital room. Francecsa would have known she didn't have much time left to retrieve them – so by this point, in her unhinged mind, killing Elisabetta seemed like the easiest way to get the cards."

"Why was that?" Sebastian asked.

"She knew that Elisabetta had only one living relative – a drug-addict brother who would sell whatever he could to feed his habit. If Elisabetta died, he'd inherit, and if he inherited he would sell – and she could then pounce on the cards and either claim them as rightfully hers, or, she could buy them."

"That is evil!" Ellie said.

"It is. But, sure enough, as soon as she'd killed Elisabetta, she called up Professor Greene to say that she was looking for some antique *tarocchi*."

"By the way, we should get the test results back pretty soon about the poisoning," Ugo said. "They told me at the police station."

"It was the monkshood – she admitted it. I'm sorry about that, Ugo."

"I've already had the plant ripped out," Ugo said, his face sad.

I nodded. "It really was the perfect murder for her. She knew your apartment very well, she knew about the plant, she was a trusted member of your inner circle and she'd obviously planned it all out really carefully – enough, anyway, so that she felt ready to go through with it when the occasion presented itself. And don't forget: there was an added bonus for her if she did it at your place…"

Ugo looked puzzled.

"Suspicion would automatically fall on *you*. I don't think she's ever forgiven you for demoting her."

"That witch!"

Our conversation slowly came to an end and just as I was about to get up from Ugo's sofa, my mum called. She said she'd just landed and she'd be in town within thirty minutes. Then there was a long silence.

"Mum? Hello? Are you there?"

"Yes, Axelle, I am. And I think it's best to tell you now that I've had a call from the Milanese police chief."

Another silence.

"He's told me that you've been involved in the

apprehension of a suspect – a suspect involved in a high-profile murder."

Argh! The police had called my mum after all! I guess it was to be expected…but still, why did they have to tell her everything? "Well, um…yes, I was dragged into it without—"

Mum cut me off. "From what I understand, Axelle, it doesn't seem as if you were dragged into anything." Another silence. "Having said that, though, the police chief did speak very highly of you. He said you'd been a great help."

I let out a breath of relief.

"But we are going to have to talk about this. Your father and I expressly forbade you from getting mixed up in any kind of business like this."

"But, Mum—"

"Don't 'but Mum' me, Axelle. We will talk about this…"

I pursed my lips and then said, "I was only doing what any concerned citizen would have done in my place."

"Somehow, Axelle, I'm not sure I believe that."

I love my mum – don't get me wrong. But, honestly, did she always have to be such a killjoy?

At least she agreed that I should stay in the model flat again tonight. "It's too late for you to pack up and move to my hotel now anyway, Axelle. So why don't you and Ellie stay one last night together at the model flat and then you can join me tomorrow? I'll stop by quickly to check on you in thirty minutes."

By the time our conversation ended, it was time to leave.

Ugo asked his driver to take Ellie, Sebastian and me back to our respective flats. It had been a very long day, and finally knowing the stones were safely at the police station, and having talked everything through with the police and with Ugo, I was ready for bed.

My mum did stop by, but Ellie did a great job of distracting her and she seemed satisfied with how I looked – even if she wasn't satisfied with all of my answers. "I'll call you first thing tomorrow morning, Axelle, love, and we'll plan our day then. And I'll expect to hear everything, too."

SATURDAY

Sunset Sparkle

I woke up before Ellie. The flat was silent and for some minutes I enjoyed the fact that I didn't have to dash out of bed and face another day of combining modelling with detective work. It felt nice, actually, to just kind of do... nothing.

I was wondering when Mum would call when my phone rang. And because I was expecting it to be her, I didn't look at the number that lit up my screen.

But it turned out to be a policeman – who spoke excellent English.

For a moment I panicked thinking I'd said or done something wrong yesterday, that the stones were fake, or that Francesca was accusing me of assault. But the officer was surprisingly friendly. I listened as he told me that everything was fine, thanked me for my help with the investigation and said it was moving forward again. Apparently, Ugo had been at the station early that morning to answer a few more questions. I was just about to ask them why they were telling me all of this when the officer on the line finally came to his point.

Apparently they'd also asked Ugo if he could do one last thing for them, but when he'd heard what the task was, he'd suggested that I do it instead. So after bringing Ellie up-to-date on my morning plans I called my mum to tell her that I had to go to the police station one more time.

"Fine," she said. "But only because it's a request from the law. After that no more meddling, Axelle!"

I left the flat, and took the subway to the police station. The police chief in charge of the case was waiting for me and he handed me the gems straight away. They were still in the grimy bag. "As for the letter you suggested we search for, here it is," he said, passing it to me across his desk. "And you were right, it's addressed to Signora Tavi Holt."

I took the envelope and, sure enough, there it was, still sealed. And this time the handwriting was definitely Falco's.

"By rights the gems belong to Tavi Holt. We've checked this with the Ventini company, and Ugo Anbessa himself said that you should be the one to hand them back to her. So if you'd like to…"

I really wanted to know what the letter said – even if I already had a pretty good idea. And it would be fun to hand Tavi the stones back…I immediately agreed.

The police chief nodded. "Good, good. We have already called Signora Holt. She will be here shortly."

Sure enough, about ten minutes later Tavi arrived in a cloud of perfume and pastel-coloured clothes. And more than anything else, she seemed excited.

"This is such a surprise," she said. "I mean what could Falco possibly have for me? Of course we were friends, but, I mean, this is weird. It's like some kind of message from beyond the grave or something…"

Tavi rattled on while she made herself comfortable and I felt the stones move in the bag as I held it in my hand. Once she sat down I carefully handed them over along with the envelope from Falco. Her voice faded into silence as she saw what was in the bag.

"Are these gems?" she was lifting the bag high, turning it so the tiny stones caught the light.

I nodded.

"The gems from the dress?"

"Yes, I believe they are, but I'm sure if you read the letter Falco will tell you in his own words what this is all about."

Tavi carefully opened the envelope and pulled out the one-page letter. She read it slowly, out loud.

Dear Tavi,
I don't even know where to begin…of course I should start with a huge apology – and this I give you. I do hope you'll find it in your heart to forgive me for what I am about to tell you…

I am a dying man now, driven by the cries of my conscience to clean up my life as best as I can before I go. I have a confession to make and will come straight to the point, embarrassing though it is to admit...

I switched some of the gems of your dress. Yes, on the red one from my last collection. Before it was sent to you, I replaced some of the real gems with fake ones. I have no excuse for it. All I can say in my defence is that my business – my heart and soul, in essence – has been dancing on the precipice of failure. I thought that by switching the stones and selling them on I'd be able to pull myself, and those following me, out of the drastic decline we were facing. But in fact I am now facing my own decline. I cannot go without giving you back that which is rightfully yours.

I am sincerely sorry for all of this... I thank you so much for being such a wonderful client and friend and for your laughter and wit.

With love,

Falco

For a while Tavi sat rooted to the chair, rereading Falco's words until suddenly, with a shake of her fine head, she hooted with laughter. "Why of all the outrageous things! This," she said loudly as she shook the paper in her hand, "is typical Falco." I watched as she folded the letter in two and kissed it before sliding it into her handbag.

"Wait till I tell Rooster about this! What a story – even Rooster will forgive him. I think I'll ask Ugo if – does he know about all of this, by the way?"

"Yes, he does."

"Well I'll ask him if the atelier can replace the fake stones with these real ones…but, honestly, what a hoot! That Falco. Didn't I tell you he was like a character out of a fairy tale?"

I'd just said goodbye to Tavi when my phone rang. It was Tomasso. I hesitated between answering it and ignoring it…and finally, after reasoning that I'd given him enough of a runaround for one week (and I'd forgotten to call him back last night!), I took his call. *Just please, please,* I thought, *don't tell me I have a new casting or booking or something.* As it turned out, I could have kissed Tomasso!

"*Buongiorno*, Axelle!" He sounded chirpy and his Italian accent came through loud and strong as ever. "Listen, I am sorry to bother you, but I tried calling you last night."

"Sorry about that, Tomasso, I had so much to do," I said as I remembered peeling away on Sebastian's Vespa just as Tomasso's call had come in.

"Well, as you know, during the shows fashion never sleeps – even for the men's shows! Anyway, I remembered you told me your mother was coming to town…is she here?"

"Uh…yes. She arrived last night." What, I wondered, could he possibly want?

"Well, I have a couple of tickets to two of the men's shows – and one of them is for Gucci. I'd asked for them for myself, actually, but I have to chaperone one of our male models for some interviews, so I will have to miss the shows. But I thought maybe your mother would like to go?"

Was he joking! Does Prada start with a P? Does MAC make lip gloss?

And could the timing be any better for Sebastian and me? Not that he'd said anything, but I knew that the thought of us finally having the whole of Saturday free – and then having to spend it shopping with my mum – wasn't exactly Sebastian's idea of a great time.

It wasn't mine either, by the way. No offence to Mum – but Sebastian and I had a lot to sort out.

Basically, Tomasso's call was like a gift from the detective gods.

"She'd love the tickets!" I was practically yelling into the phone and eagerly agreed to collect them from Tomasso.

I called my mum immediately and told her the news. She was ecstatic. It seemed yesterday's exploits had already been forgotten.

Next I called Sebastian. He was just on his way to the cemetery to pick up his scooter and offered to collect me on his way back. He could then take me to the agency to fetch the tickets, and we'd drop them off at my mum's hotel.

By lunchtime Sebastian and I were on our own, my mum was planning what to wear for Gucci, and Ellie had promised to meet us at the flat later, to pack.

Sebastian and I didn't say a word as we walked back to his scooter from my mum's hotel, but from that moment on our day was magic. We went wherever our mood took us – no schedule, no plan, no chasing suspects.

We saw the amazing Castello Sforza, watched the street acts near La Scala Opera House, visited 10 Corso Como (yeah, it's a pretty cool store – okay, make that *very* cool), walked down Corso Garibaldi, and went back to explore the Navigli district – no underground swimming this time. From there we walked to the Columns of San Lorenzo, last seen as we'd been speeding past them in our attempt to follow Francesca.

"So, Holmes, where to now?" We were standing by Sebastian's scooter, each with a gelato in hand. The sun was slowly sinking and we still had about an hour to ourselves before my mum would insist on having dinner with us.

"Well, you still haven't seen the Duomo…" I said as I spooned the last scrapings of delicious pistachio ice cream into my mouth.

"I thought you might have had enough of it after this week…"

"It's beautiful, though, and I'd like to go back – with you."

We drove there in no time and parked. Our tickets were

still valid so we made our way directly to the queue for the lifts. We'd decided to start at the rooftop. In fact, I reckoned – forgetting all about the chase – the way I'd seen it the other day was actually a good way to visit the Duomo: start at the top, enjoy the view and see how the church is put together from the outside. Then go down the medieval stairs for some intense atmosphere before landing in the middle of the cathedral.

In the end, we lingered for a long time on the rooftop. And for once my fear of heights didn't rear its ugly head; it didn't stand a chance against Sebastian's warm, firm clasp of my hand. After winding our way to the highest point we found a quiet corner under the golden Madonna with a view over the Galleria Vittorio Emanuele II.

We sat quietly for a while, and as I gazed out over the terracotta-coloured buildings of Milan, images of Elisabetta flitted through my mind. And although I couldn't help but think of her with sadness, the feeling was now tinged with a sense of relief – and, yes, happiness even – that I'd finally managed to get justice for her. And as a bonus I'd also cleared Ugo's name and Falco's legacy. Justice felt good, I thought.

Sebastian finally spoke, and I turned to face him. "Listen, Axelle, I'm sorry about the start to our week. I shouldn't have used Francesca to wind you up." His blue eyes were watching me from beneath his tousled hair. "You were right to be upset. I'm sorry." He looked totally gorgeous sitting there with the whole of Milan spread out behind him, glittering in the sunshine. His sandy-brown hair was backlit by the soft, warm light and looking into his eyes, I could see he really was sorry.

I appreciated the apology…but I had one of my own to make, too.

"And I'm sorry, Sebastian."

"Sorry for what?" He looked at me, his eyes wide.

"For making you feel that maybe you don't always come first."

He was quiet for a moment but then asked, "So where do I rank?"

I was afraid he might ask this question. But I had to give him an honest answer. "I don't know. Sometimes you are first…"

"And sometimes I'm not…"

I nodded. "I wish I could be more clear about it. They always are in films, aren't they?"

Sebastian reached out and touched my hair, gently pushing the loose strands (yeah, there were lots) behind my ear. "Then maybe I should ask you another question…"

I waited.

"In your mind or heart is there anyone else that ever comes between me and your mysteries?"

I shook my head. "There's no room."

"So your mysteries are my only competition?"

"Yeah. Pretty much." I watched him.

He suddenly smiled. "Then I guess I'll try my best to live with that."

He leaned forward and we rubbed noses. Of course that only lasted about a moment before his lips found mine. Within seconds I'd forgotten everything else. My head was spinning as his hands ran down my sides and settled at my waist. He tasted amazing and we were completely lost in our own world when a loud cough interrupted us. It was one of the guides – an older man.

In heavily accented English he said, "Sorry, but we are on a church. A little respect, *per favore*."

We took the hint. Slowly we pulled apart but as I started to get up Sebastian stopped me. "Wait, I have something for you and I'd like to give it to you here."

I had no idea what he meant but his look was serious, and slightly unsure. I sat back down, thinking he was reaching into his pocket for the guidebook. Instead a tiny box with a pretty bow was sitting in his hand.

He looked slightly embarrassed as he held it out on his open palm. "This is for you. I saw it and thought of you."

Now it was my turn to open my eyes wide, because this was a proper gift. Like, carefully wrapped and everything.

I took it and gently undid the pretty ribbon and paper. Slowly and gently, I lifted the lid of the satin-covered box. What was inside took my breath away.

"I thought you deserved something, after, you know…"

I didn't give him a chance to say anything else though;

I threw my arms around him. "Thank you," I whispered in his ear. When I finally pulled back I handed him the box and without a word he took out the most delicate charm bracelet I'd ever seen. He slipped it onto my wrist and fastened the clasp.

Gently I fingered the minute charms dangling from the golden links: a tiny key, a golden heart and a teeny tiny Duomo. There was also a thin disc in gold. I looked closer at it and discovered that Sebastian had had it engraved with our initials and the dates of this week.

He smiled when he saw my look of surprise. "I figure we can add charms to it every time we solve a new case – in which case I probably should have found you a longer chain," he laughed. "Anyway, it suits you," he said. "I hope you like it…"

"I love it," I said. "Thank you." And I really meant it. I lifted my wrist to the light and watched as the tiny charms sparkled in the setting sun.

"Now why don't we get out of here, Holmes?" He reached down and offered me his outstretched hand. "We have to meet your mum in an hour and we still have a lot of kissing to catch up on."

"In that case, let's get going, Watson."

The End

HOW TO SPEAK SUPERMODEL

Axelle's guide to surviving in the world of fashion

If you want to blend in with the fashion set, it's worth learning the lingo. HERE'S A HANDY GUIDE:

* **BOOK:** This is another word for the all-important portfolio models have. A book or portfolio is used to show clients and designers both how a model looks in photos, and what kind of work they've done.

* **BOOKER:** A staff member at an agency whose job is to handle requests from clients and to represent and set up appointments for models.

* **CASTING DIRECTOR:** Hired by a designer to organize fashion-show castings. They meet hundreds of models, watch them walk and look at their portfolio, before narrowing the choice to those models that best fit the designer's vision.

* **FITTING:** A session that may take place before a fashion show or photo shoot where the clothes to be modelled are fitted onto the model.

* **GO-SEE:** An appointment for a model to see a photographer or a client. Unlike a casting, there is no specific brief.

* **HAUTE COUTURE:** Pronounced "oat-ko-chure" this phrase is French for "high-fashion". Couture is extremely high-end, tailor-made designer clothes that only a few dozen people in the world can afford.

* **LOCATION:** Any place, other than in a studio, where a shoot takes place.

* **LOOKBOOK:** A set of photos used by fashion designers to show their newest collections to clients. Usually bound like a small book.

* **MODEL FLAT:** A flat that a modelling agency owns and rents out to models who are either too young to rent an apartment on their own, or who are just starting out and have moved from another town or another country.

* **OPTIONS:** An option is put to a model by a client to see if he/she would be available for a shoot. Options are then either confirmed as a booking, or released.

* **STYLIST:** The person who chooses the clothes to be photographed for a magazine editorial or advertising campaign. They either work for a magazine or are freelance.

* **TEAR SHEETS:** These are photos which are literally torn from magazines, and which a model can use in her book. Tear sheets from magazines like *Vogue* and *Elle* are what every model hopes to have in her book.

* **ZED CARD:** This is basically a business card for models. A5 in size, zed cards normally show at least two photos, as well as basic info such as a model's hair colour, eye colour, height and agency contact details.

And if anyone's still suspicious that you don't belong, just throw in one of these handy phrases…

"Lace is so yesteryear!"

"I practise my pout every day."

"Spots aren't just for leopards, you know!"

"Yes, Jane Birkin is a handbag and a person…"

"Good news: black is the new black!"

"What! You take your heels off to sleep?"

"I always travel with a cashmere blanket."

"They're not spiders – they're my fake eyelashes!"

"I love to wear my overalls – to go dancing!"

NOW DON'T FORGET THE AIR-KISSES, DARLING! MWAH, MWAH!

Carina's favourite places to visit in the Italian city of style

"I love Milan! This discreet, elegant city has it all: monuments, opera, art, shopping and fashion - especially fashion. As one of the world's fashion capitals, Milan has more than its fair share of home-grown designers and trend-worthy style. So brush your hair (Milanese women have amazing hair), slip into your most glamorous jacket and get ready to explore this cosmopolitan city. Oh - and don't forget to treat yourself to some gelato! Ciao, bella!"

COVA AND MARCHESI: So you've spent all afternoon on Milan's most sophisticated shopping street, Via Monte Napoleone, and need a cup of tea and some melt-in-your mouth pastries? Look no further than legendary tea house Cova, or, further along the same street, the new outpost of Milan's other famous pastry maker (and sweetshop), Marchesi. Just don't blame me if you eat too much!

DUOMO: You can't go to Milan and not visit the Duomo! Smack in the middle of the old city, this awesome cathedral is one of the largest in the world and its rooftop view (go at sunset) is the most romantic in Milan. Before leaving, do as the models do at Milan Fashion Week and take a selfie on the square.

FONDAZIONE PRADA: Are you looking to get your fashion and culture fix all in one go? If so, make a trip to the Fondazione Prada, the new museum established by fashion designer Miuccia Prada (yes, her family created the famous brand). You'll find contemporary and classical art, super architecture, a great bookstore, and an oh-so-fashionable Prada cafe.

NAVIGLI: This neighbourhood shows Milan at its most laid-back and funky. Spend an afternoon strolling along its canals, and exploring the quirky shops and cheap-and-cheerful restaurants that line the quays. As you head back into the city centre, stop to admire the Columns of San Lorenzo, just north of Porta Ticinese.

CORSO COMO 10: Indulge your inner fashionista with a visit to this uber-stylish and edgy store. And although many of the sleek items on offer do cost an arm and a leg, not everything does – on my last trip there I bought a pair of Converse. From Corso Como walk down the Corso Garibaldi to the famous La Scala opera house.

GALLERIA VITTORIO EMANUELE II: This fabulous galleria is one of the world's oldest shopping malls and the perfect place to people-watch. You can also check out visiting celebrities and the crème de la crème of Milanese society at the Park Hyatt Hotel around the corner. Have a Shirley Temple under the soaring glass cupola of the lobby – and don't stare!

CIMITERIO MONUMENTALE: Don't let the idea of a bunch of creepy headstones scare you. As the burial place of choice for Milan's elite, this vast cemetery garden is packed with an extravagant assortment of crypts, statues and mausoleums. You've never seen a cemetery like this one.

PIZZA PAZZA: If you love pizza as much as I do, you'll love the classic tomato and mozzarella ones at this friendly, unpretentious pizzeria – preferably eaten at an outside table on a sunny day. Afterwards, walk across the Santo Stefano Square and check out the church of San Bernardino alle Ossa. The walls of the tiny chapel attached to this church are covered in skulls. Yeah, skulls!

BRAIDENSE NATIONAL LIBRARY: Want to feel like Belle in *Beauty and the Beast*? Then this ballroom-like library is the place you've been dreaming of! A grand staircase, enormous crystal chandeliers, and shelves and shelves bursting with rare antique books…you won't find a more magical place than this.

HAVE FUN!

ACKNOWLEDGEMENTS

THANK YOU:

To my agent, the lovely Jenny Savill, and the rest of the team at Andrew Nurnberg Associates.

To my brilliant editors, Sarah Stewart and Anne Finnis, and the rest of the eagle-eyed editing team at Usborne Publishing for your talent and time. Special sparkly thanks to Becky Walker.

David Brown and Alessandra Donato of D'Management Group in Milan, Italy. Thank you so much for sharing your advice, enthusiasm, and insider knowledge. You opened my eyes to everything Milan has to offer and showed me a very different city from the one I remember from my modelling days.

Simon Chambers, Sarah Doukas and the rest of the fabulous team at Storm Model Management in London, England. Time always flies in a flurry of excitement at your HQ. Thank you for all of your tips, pointers and generosity. Here's to more cupcake visits!

Priscilla – my research trip wouldn't have been the same without you. Nor my waistline – but that's another story! Thank you for everything.

Roberta, because you have the best address book in Milan and a fantastic sense for great locations – including creepy abandoned buildings. Thank you for showing me around, I enjoyed every minute in your company.